AMY'S REBELLION

GEMSTONE MASSACRE SERIES BOOK 1

JULIA GOLDHIRSH

To my amazing friends who support and accept me for who I am and gave me the courage to write gender fluid characters like me.

PROLOGUE - AMY'S DIARY

I was twelve years old the first time I killed a man. They called me the Amethyst Killer, but the Magic Council's leader, Opal, is the real killer. After the War of the Twin Swords, she tried to put me to death for killing a man during peace negotiations even though he attacked first. The only choice left for me was to run to the human world, but she followed me and took my friend, Night. Shortly after capturing or killing my friend, Opal destroyed our entire clan. But that wasn't enough for her. She won't stop until she gets what she wants, my death.

CHAPTER 1

*A*my stared up at the shining violet letters that read "The Gem of the Forest" above the front door of her shop. She sighed and stepped through the amethyst geode that doubled as the front door. The magic barrier that protected the place from malicious magic shimmered and parted to let her through. She flipped the sign hanging in the front window from open to closed. *Hopefully, no one tries to come in on my half day again. We close early. It's not a hard concept to grasp.*

The shelves near the glass display cases were strewn with a plethora of essential oils. As she skimmed the necklaces in the front window, someone whistled to get her attention, and lifted her head as Asher mouthed a "Thank you." while holding up the hand of their girlfriend.

A rose quartz choker clung to the girlfriend's neck and Amy mouthed back, "You're welcome" before slinking into the workshop portion of her store. Away from the gaze of snooping magic less humans.

She tucked her hair into a ponytail and was soldering some silver around one of her favorite gemstones, a black cat's eye, when the door chimed. "Was the closed sign not enough of a hint? Maybe I need to ward this place against humans as well." She muttered.

Amy looked at her enchanted Jasper and saw a pale, hunched over man with oily brown bangs covering his eyes. *Earl's wife must be at it again. Will he ever learn?* She shook her head and plastered on a smile before peeking out of her workshop.

"Hey, Earl. Is everything okay? I'm supposed to be closed at this hour."

Earl sniffled and wiped away tears. "I think she might be cheating on me... again."

Amy pressed her lips together. "All right. I'll take this one order just for you, but don't go telling anyone else about it. If the sapphire didn't work, you'll want a black cat's eye pendant this time. Just trust me on this."

His lower lip quivered. "Thank you. I'll do it. How much is it, and how soon can you get it to me?" He held out a few twenties.

She accepted his offer with a smile. "What you have there will cover it. I'll have it ready for you in a few days."

"Thank you." He shook her hand with sweaty palms and plopped the money onto the table before leaving through the front door.

Amy wiped sweat off on her black dress pants. "He'll never learn, will he?"

Once he'd left, she locked the door behind him and went back to her workshop. She held her hand steady as she fused the last bit of silver to the black cat's eye gem in a tight circle. It reminded her so much of Night. Amy licked her parched lips. *It should have been me that Opal killed that day, not you, Night. Opal wanted to kill me because I made the peace negotiations fail during the War of the Twin Swords. I'm the reason she burned our old clan to the ground, not you.*

The dark gem warmed Amy's hand, purple magic swirling around its surface as she recited the enchantment for wisdom. It wouldn't save his marriage, but it might give his wife some kindness and him some desperately needed happiness, and the willpower to move on from her. *If only moving on from losing her friend Night and her sister Chal were that simple.*

Amy gave a wan smile as she looped a silver chain around the finished pendant and crimped both ends before adding a clasp. When she held the necklace up to the light, a thin slit of white went down the center, resembling the slit pupils of a cat. "Take good care of him, Night." she whispered before putting the necklace in a white velvet box and closing it. She packaged the extra watch she'd thrown in as a gift in a black velvet box for him.

Amy pursed her lips as she put the box away. "I miss you more with each passing day, Night."

The whistled "coo" of the cuckoo clock made Amy jump. She turned to the light lavender walls. "It's 5:00 PM already? Maybe if I hurry, I can catch the tail end of the craft market." Amy shoved the finished jewelry into the safe deposit box, along with a wad of hundreds from the register, before setting the alarm and walking to her car.

Once Amy had parked, she slammed her door shut, paid for parking, and walked past "The Magic cookie" on Atlantic Avenue. She passed by an art gallery with a plethora of colorful Corgi sculptures and followed the crowd of people walking towards the trail of white tents. Amy turned down the next road into an alley brimming with huge lines of art booths. The festival was brimming with people.

It almost made her feel like she was back in the magic world... almost.

Artists creating cartoon portraits of passersby lined either side of the closed street, and one woman bent over a stack of tarot cards. A massive crystal quartz sphere decorated the center of her table.

A booth with vanilla bath bombs and lavender bath salts caught her eye, reminding her of the plant mages that had lived just east of the enchantress clan. As she approached the stall and inhaled the heady aromas of vanilla and lavender with a hint of lemon, she longed for her lavender pillow, the one enchanted to cure her insomnia. She'd had to leave it behind when she'd fled the magic world.

Amy held out a twenty. "I'll take the lemongrass and verbena bath bomb please." The woman smiled and leaned into Amy's ear. "Your bracelet really worked. My crush finally asked me on a date." She held out her silver and rose quartz bracelet and let out an ear-piercing squeal.

Amy grabbed at her wrist so she wouldn't slap her hand over her ears. "I'm glad to hear that. Thank you again for the bath bombs, Clair."

She waved. "No problem. Good to see you again, Amy." As Amy walked to the next booth, she caught sight of golden eyes, dark hair, and warm beige skin in her peripheral vision, *Night?* but when she turned back to look at the figure, they were gone.

Am I seeing ghosts of Night now? Amy shook off the thought. *Or maybe it was just another enchantment mage in hiding?*

Amy continued down the street of booths until a tent gleaming with sterling silver dragons caught her eye. She darted to the shop teeming with gemstones nesting in the claws of sterling silver dragons. Of course, it was Alex's booth. They always had the best craftsmanship she'd ever seen.

Amy ran her fingers along a rough Labradorite encased in a silver wire cage that resembled a flame. The cage hung from the claws of a pewter dragon.

She sucked in a breath as she picked up the necklace and nearly choked on the oppressively humid air. It made her long for the chill of Gemstone Forest, and the crisp air of the cliffs in the magic realm, but her home was only a smoldering pile of ash because of Opal.

"This one is beautiful, Alex. You've really outdone yourself this week."

Alex smiled and leaned against the table. "Thanks. They are rather…enchanting," he said with a wink.

Amy wrinkled her nose and nudged their shoulder. "Be careful saying things like that in the open, joke or not." *If Opal overhears jokes like that, she'll find me again, but I'm not moving. One of us will be dead and it won't be me. She has ruined enough of my life.*

Alex held up their hands. "Sorry. Sorry. It was in poor

taste, but if you're looking for some more jewelry, you should look at the new booth over there."

Amy followed where his finger pointed. Past the rows of dragon themed necklaces and cheap glass masquerading as gems was a booth with pewter and sterling necklaces. A yellow, orange amber gemstone glittered in the sunlight radiating ice blue magic.

"Thanks, I'll check it out." Amy shuffled over to the booth and picked up the pendant to check the tag, but there was no price listed. The chips and scratches on its surface showed its age. "Excuse me. How much is this?" Amy held up the pendant.

The old man's golden brown, weather-beaten face broke into a smile. "That pendant is special. You have good taste, dear. People here are only interested in flashy things, but this one had an inner beauty to it. Handle it with care. It has a bit of a temper."

She cocked her head to one side and said, just low enough for him to hear. "¿De dónde eres Enchantario?" But he just gave her a blank look. Her face fell into a frown. *I guess my gut instinct was wrong.*

After a long pause he whispered, "Soy de Avia."

Interesting, he's from Avia. That means he was a weather mage. Amy squinted at the pendant. *Then what is he doing with what looks like an ancient enchantress weapon?* Amy cocked her head to one side. "If you don't mind me asking, what's your name?"

He smiled. "I have many names, but let's just say that I'm a distant relative of yours and leave it at that."

Amy held the necklace up to the sunlight, and it shimmered like gold. "Was this one of Merlin's necklaces?"

He gripped his stomach and chuckled. "Don't let Freya hear you say that. Can you not tell it's hers by how the amber glitters?"

Amy shook her head. "We never learned about her in school. Is she a famous enchantress?"

8

The man snickered. "Not quite. Take care of the necklace."

"What about paying for it?"

The man pressed his lips together and the wrinkles on his forehead smoothed, making him look much younger. "Consider it a gift from a particularly generous family member."

"Okay. Well, thank you." She clutched the pendant to her chest as she walked away. When she looked back to wave goodbye to the man, he was gone, and the booth had vanished with him. *Maybe he controlled mist magic? Also, how am I related to a weather mage?*

He mentioned Freya too. How are we related?

A familiar sight made Amy's back straighten as a flash of yellow gold passed through her peripheral vision. *I wasn't imagining it. Someone is following me.*

Amy picked up her pace and put her hand to the Selenite around her neck to activate its cloaking magic.

She slid through back alleys and hid behind corners. Her home was near the plaza, but she took a roundabout way of getting to her front door. When she thought she'd lost the person following her, she slowed her pace but kept the cloaking magic up. She couldn't see the flash of gold and black in her vision anymore. Either she'd lost them, or they were excellent at being undetected.

She kept the main barriers up as she turned the key in the lock, only letting down the wards on the front door before slipping inside.

She heaved a sigh of relief when she slammed the front door shut behind her, but that sigh turned into a squeak when a voice said, "You didn't really think a barrier like that would keep me out, did you?"

She whirled around to see a figure. Sandy brown hair fell over eyes that were more hazel than yellow or gold. Her grip on her gem pouch tightened. "Are you here to kill me? If you are, then you'll have to fight me till my dying breath. I won't go to Opal willingly."

His lips turned up into a smile. "Who said I was working for Opal or that I wanted to kill you? Perhaps I'm just here to have a chat with an old friend."

Amy crossed her arms over her chest. "I've never met you before in my life."

He put his hands in his pockets. "You have, but I looked different back then."

Amy scanned over him, trying to figure out where she knew him from. Her eye caught on a silvery glint in his right hand.

She reached for a gemstone but was too slow. He threw the dart at her face. "Shit." Amy's limbs felt too heavy and slow. One hand reached for a gem, and she raised the other bracing for the dart. *Why did this have to be a physical fight? I could have handled a magical assault.*

But instead of feeling the prick of a dart, a bright light flashed behind her closed lids. Something clattered to the floor at her feet. Amy removed her hands from her face. On the floor, the dart glittered gold. The necklace glowed blue in her hand.

The intruder's lips curled back in a snarl. "Damn. I was too late."

He moved with the lithe grace of a cat and approached her, getting close enough for her to smell the scent of cinnamon wafting from him. It reminded her of someone, but she couldn't place the memory, and judging how the person following her had altered his appearance from when she'd caught him following her at the market, he had to be a shifter. *He acts so familiar with me, but I didn't know any shape shifters from our clan. It couldn't be him, could it? I need to ask Garnet later. If I make it out of this.*

The necklace crackled at his proximity, light spilling out from the amber at its center. He leapt back, flinching away from the light magic like a cat avoiding water. "I'll be back for you, don't worry."

He tossed a black gem to the floor at her feet. "Perhaps this will jog your memory. The name's Dusk. It was good seeing you again, Amy." His name sounded clunky on his tongue. His words lacked cadence in a way that felt familiar.

"How do I know you?"

"You knew me before you betrayed Opal and me, but I am not the same person I once was."

Before she could ask what he meant by that, his figure disappeared before her eyes. *If he's a shifter, how did he disappear like that? Weird.* Amy grabbed the stone he'd left from the floor and turned it over in her palm. A streak of light went through its middle, a black cat's eye gem.

The stone didn't glow with magic, so maybe he had them for show. She grabbed the stone and placed it next to her crystal quartz to pull any impurities from it. *It's just like Night's gem and their names sound similar, but Opal killed Night. And he mentioned betrayal. What did he mean by that? Maybe he just mistook me for someone else?*

She glanced down at the amethyst bracelet housing her familiar. *No. It can't be him. Naru said she was too late to save Night, and I doubt Opal would have kept him all this time. She's never been the merciful type.* Amy raked a hand through her hair. *He's dead, remember? Dead. You searched for him for years and every trail came back cold. Why don't you make yourself useful and look up why that necklace scared that assassin off so easily?* Amy clicked her computer's monitor on and pulled up an internet tab. *Maybe the humans have some information about Freya.*

She clicked on the first tab and skimmed the article. *She was vengeful and had a carriage pulled by cats. She sounds like my kind of woman.*

The amethyst bracelet on her arm glowed, and her familiar, Violet, must've heard her thoughts because she turned into her lynx form and curled up on the floor next to her. Amy stroked Violet's coarse, spiky, purple fur, and she purred contentedly.

"I heard you mention cats, and I wanted to come out to say hi, but there's no other cat here." Her silky voice curled around Amy's mind.

Amy continued searching through several more webpages and found a story about Brisingamen, Freya's necklace. It said that Freya was the goddess of sorcery, sex, lust, beauty, fertility, and death. *Wow, talk about multi-tasking. Wait, does that mean this was a sorceress's necklace?* She'd only ever heard of enchantresses using gemstones for their weapons. Well.... aside from the few crossover gems glass magicians used.

Amy gulped as she skimmed through a story about how Freya had lusted after the necklace so much that she'd given up her honor for it. *I'm glad I didn't have to pay such a hefty price.*

Amy yawned and looked down at the clock to see that it was almost 11pm. She yawned and closed the lid on the laptop. She bit her lip. "I should call Garnet for help, but if Opal knows where I am, I could put her in danger. Maybe if I do some jewelry making, I'll be calm enough to figure out some other way to fix this myself."

She pulled out some tumbled labradorite, some braided silver, crimp beads, and a clasp. Amy tried to steady her shaking hands by wire wrapping a Labradorite pendant for the storefront, but she jumped at each thump of branches against the window and the loud bang and hum of the air conditioner as it kicked on.

Amy took a deep breath. *Just focus on your work.* She held a bead up to her work lamp. The rough gemstone shone turquoise and green with streaks of gold. *Beautiful.* She drilled a hole through it so she wouldn't have to destroy the way the unpolished gem held the light. Amy beaded a thin wire with tiger's eye and obsidian for the labradorite necklace and put on a bevel and clasp. *Perfect.*

Her hands had stopped shaking and her breath had

evened out by the time she slid the labradorite pendant onto the silver wire. Amy's eyes felt like lead, but her heart raced in her chest. She glanced at her cellphone clock, and it was only midnight. *Maybe it's time to call Garnet. Hopefully, she's still awake.* She grabbed her cellphone in its clear case and punched in her sister's number.

After several rings, Garnet picked up. Her voice came in huffs. "You never call at this hour, are you okay?"

Either you were running a marathon, or I just interrupted something. The thought made Amy's face flush, and she cleared her throat. "About that. One of Opal's goons tried to attack me."

The phone's connection crackled, and Garnet shouted, "You're lucky I'm working close by this month. See, I told you settling down was a bad idea. I'll be right there. We'll get you moved out tonight."

"But I don't want to—" click. Amy sighed. *Well, at least she's on her way, but she won't be happy when I tell her I still don't want to move. If she's just visiting to help with the barrier, hopefully she'll be fine. She just can't stay or else...* Amy glanced back to the golden dart.

If it hadn't been for Freya's necklace, he would have captured or killed her. Amy reached a hand to the necklace, and it glowed as if acknowledging her thoughts.

Violet grumbled when Amy stopped petting her and got up from her work chair. *Let's go set up shop for tomorrow.*

The lynx's ear twitched. *You nearly died, and your response is to throw yourself into your work. How did I get stuck with the workaholic?*

Amy's shoulders tensed. *I know you're joking, but it still stings.*

Violet loped over to Amy and nuzzled her arm. *It's how you avoid your feelings. I much prefer scratching and biting the things that hurt me. We could scratch Opal's face.*

Amy gave a slight smile. *We will soon enough, but we need more time and power if we want to survive the encounter.*

Violet hung her head. *I've waited for seven years. I'm growing impatient.*

Amy reached down to scratch behind her ears. *As am I, but we need strength in numbers.* Amy pursed her lips. "And if we're going to the store, you'll need to change back. Can't risk any humans seeing you."

Violet bristled at the request, but she reformed herself into a bracelet in a swirl of purple energy. *I miss the open plains of the magic world.*

Amy shoved her hands in her sweatpants pockets. *I do too, but Opal's War took that away from us. No one can go back to that wasteland.*

Violet gave a low growl. *She deserves death. The forest is gone. The others are gone because of her.*

Amy wiped at tears forming in her eyes. *I know, and I miss my sister, Selenite, but if we try to fight Opal now, we'd join them in death.*

Violet's sullen tone echoed through their connection. *You promised you'd help me fight her.*

And I will. Maybe this amulet will be exactly what we need to turn the tables if it can turn darts to gold.

Violet trilled. *You make an excellent point, but how did he get through the barrier in the first place? I didn't sense him hitting the spell.*

Amy gulped. *I'm not sure. Maybe he was fast and slipped through behind me somehow.*

Or he really is Night. a voice in her head added, but she shoved it down. *Night wouldn't take Opal's side over mine.*

Amy scooped her gems in her hand and reinforced the protection magic at the front door before leaving the house. *Hopefully one of Garnet's homebrewed spells will be strong enough to keep him out next time.*

The evening had turned the air from scorching to tolerable.

The amethyst Geode at the shop entrance beckoned her, and she walked through the protective barrier. The human alarm system chirped, and she punched her code into the keypad to silence it.

Amy grabbed one of the mannequin heads in the shop window and draped the Labradorite necklace around its neck, admiring how it added a splash of color to the display. The gem had a certain wild nature to it. If you polished Labradorites, they lost their beauty, and it was like trying to tame a stallion when you wanted to use their magic.

It would be even more gorgeous when the sunlight hit the glass case in the morning. After surveying the store one more time, she reset the alarm and left.

Waiting at the entrance to her apartment was Garnet, dressed in black yoga pants and a loose T-shirt with no bra. Her normally smooth black hair was frizzy and tangled, sticking up at all ends. Sweat dripped down her dark beige skin. Her amethyst eyes were feverish. At times like this, Amy glanced at her own Iolite purple hair and amber eyes and wondered if they were really sisters.

Garnet paced back and forth, and Amy saw the small bite marks visible on her neck. "Playing with your vamp of the week again?" she asked.

Garnet covered the mark with a hand. "He's not my vamp of the week. I've been seeing him for months, and blood mages aren't vampires. That's a derogatory term. They're called Eztli got it? Eh-z-t-lee. He doesn't need my blood, and I don't need to be fed on."

Amy waved a hand and let her sister in. "Sure, that's what all the addicts say."

Garnet shoved Amy's arm. "You're pretty rude for someone who called me frantically at midnight because you need my help."

Amy shrugged. "You make a fair point, but that's also why you love me?"

She laughed. "Do I though?"

Amy gave her puppy dog eyes, and Garnet smiled. "Alright. I guess I love you, but Chalcedony is still my favorite."

Amy muttered. "Obviously you aren't her favorite because I know for a fact she prefers to go by Chal, just like I prefer being called Amy instead of Amethyst."

Garnet shrugged. "Whatever. Now do you want help with that barrier or not?"

Amy ran a hand along her face. "Yes, I want your help."

Garnet flung the door open and Amy had to hastily disarm the amethyst near the entrance so she wouldn't start stumbling around in a drunken haze. *Honestly, who waltzes into someone's house when they know it's warded? She's lucky my affinity isn't malachite.*

Amy shuddered as she thought back to Excalibur and the malachite embedded in its sheath. Those wards could fragment your sanity or curse you with worse luck than someone living through the Black Plague. She shook off the thought and lowered a glare at Garnet. "You're lucky I didn't have a more dangerous gem at my doorstep." Amy slammed the door shut so hard behind Garnet that it shook on its hinges.

Garnet shrugged. "If you'd had a more dangerous gem here, then I wouldn't have had to come out in the first place. Aren't you some kind of enchantress prodigy? Why didn't you just kill him while you had the chance?"

Amy pursed her lips. "You know exactly why I didn't kill him."

Garnet waved her off. "Ya ya. You lost control of your powers and killed someone in the middle of a war so now you hate fighting. So what? I killed a few dozen soldiers in that same war, and you don't see me whining about it."

Amy balled her fist at her side. "Well, I guess I'm just not like you, Garnet. Plus, it wasn't just one person. My actions resulted in the deaths of many. If I'd had better control over my powers, then the battle of Opal's Fall wouldn't have happened." Amy shivered despite the warm, humid air in her entryway.

Garnet stumbled over the purple rug in the living room,

and Amy clicked her tongue. "Are you blood drunk right now?"

Garnet's words slurred slightly. "No. I only let him have a little bit."

Amy let out a groan. "Let's just get this over with. Hopefully, you aren't so drunk that you forgot the words for the barrier spell?"

Garnet giggled. "Of course not." She pulled a piece of parchment from her purse and waved it at Amy. The stench of copper clung to it and crimson stains dotted the edges. "See, I've got it right here."

Amy sighed and curled her lip up in a smile. "Alright, then let's get to it. What do we need?"

Garnet squinted at the page, and Amy reached over to the table that held a spare set of Garnet's crimson reading glasses. "Thanks." Garnet took the glasses from Amy and skimmed the pages, her expression turning stern. "It looks like we're going to need at least one tiger's eye and a black tourmaline for each entrance."

Amy muttered a *damn* under her breath. Tourmaline enchantments weren't her strong suit since they weren't quartz or either of her gemstone's elements, water and wind. But the tiger's eye wouldn't be too bad since it was a quartz like Violet.

Amy held up a finger. "Wait one second while I make sure I have enough supplies for the spell." She walked through her lavender hallways and pushed open the door to her bedroom and office. She noted all the windows and doors as she walked over to her supply drawer. "A front door, five windows, and a sliding door for the back entrance. That would mean I'd need seven of each stone."

She crossed her fingers before rummaging through the gems. *Please let me have enough.* If she was even one gem short, she might have to leave herself vulnerable for the night. It was too big a risk, especially with Garnet here. One tiger's eye materialized, and when she kept pawing through, she found six others just like it, but there was only one black tourmaline. *You've got to be kidding me. I should have stocked up while I was at the festival today.*

Amy scooped up all the Tiger's eye and the lone Tourmaline and found Garnet already prepping the spell.

Garnet gave her pile of gems a once over and rolled her eyes. "For someone on the run from the most dangerous enchantress in the magic world, your gemstone supply is severely lacking." She flashed Amy a bright grin. "Lucky for you, I brought a few spares just in case." She reached a hand into her black clutch purse and scooped up a handful of tourmalines. "There. Now, we have enough."

The stones clacked against each other when she deposited them in Amy's hands, making her grit her teeth. "What do we need to do first?"

Garnet pulled a plastic bag full of pink salt from her massive purse. "We start by sprinkling this around all of the entrances?"

Amy squinted at the pouch. "Salt? Really?"

She nodded. "It might sound strange, but salt is a mineral, so it falls under multiple magical categories, including ours. We can enchant it."

Amy shook her head. "So, I can use spices for enchantments?"

Garnet laughed. "Not just any spices. It has to be rock salt that retains a crystal-like shape." She pulled a pocket-sized spell book from her purse and opened it to a page with a red sticky note in it. Right in the book it mentioned enchanting "rock salt." *Interesting.*

Amy put the gems on the floor and Garnet dumped salt into Amy's hand.

They scattered salt on each window ledge, door entrance, and the sliding glass door at the back of her tiny home. Once they finished, Garnet added. "Make sure you don't break the line of salt; it will weaken the enchantment. You're going to enchant it by saying "Shio o mamotte."

"What does it mean?" Amy hovered her hand over the pile of salt.

"It's essentially commanding the salt to protect you."

Amy nodded and said the words for each line of pink salt. The small crystals she enchanted glowed lavender, and Garnet's glowed a vivid crimson.

Garnet handed the tiger's eye to Amy next. "This spell will be similar. 'Toranome o mamotte.' For these, make sure you place them just next to the salt, but they can't touch because it might break their delicate crystals. I'll show you for this one, so watch me first." Garnet placed the stone down near the front door.

When she chanted the spell, "Toranome o mamotte." her hands glowed red. The magic transferred into the tiger's eye and jumped to the salt. The glow grew brighter and then fizzled out to a dim glow, but Amy could still feel the magic coming off it in waves.

Sweat beaded on Garnet's face, and she backed up so that she wouldn't disturb the spell before shaking out her hands. "That one made my hands go numb. Sorry, but you'll have to do the rest. I don't have much magic left."

Amy got up and grabbed a towel from the kitchen and handed it to Garnet, who dabbed sweat off her face before lying on her stomach on the floor. For the next few enchantments, Garnet gave instructions while Amy painstakingly placed the gems near the salt and repeated the spell to lock in the magic.

Her hands glowed purple as the gems leeched energy from her body. When her arms shook, and her breaths turned to gasps, she reached for the inhaler in her pocket, but Garnet smacked her hand away. "An inhaler won't help with magical exhaustion, don't be stupid."

Amy rolled her eyes. "Regardless of that I still need to keep breathing to do these enchantments."

Garnet waggled a finger at her. "You know exactly what you need to do if you want to breathe more easily."

Amy sighed. "You know I don't like asking Violet for favors, but if you insist on giving me no choice."

You don't need to be so hesitant to ask for help. Even if your clan didn't hold up their end of our pact by protecting the forest, I know you plan to bring down Opal.

Amy scrunched up her nose. *But it doesn't feel right draining your magic when I'm not fulfilling my end of the bargain.*

Violet purred, *You have no choice since you've exhausted your own magic. So let me do my job.* Power thrummed through Amy's body, making her limbs feel lighter. Amy flexed her fingers, and her magic turned from lavender to violet. When she finished the final word of the spell, The first layer of the barrier fanned out around her house, encasing it in thin web-like magic ready to singe any ill intent directed towards her and keep the person hunting her out like a bug zapper.

Garnet popped up from her spot on Amy's plush lavender rug. "Alright, now for the finishing touch, the black tourmaline. Be careful with these stones. They're potent if they aren't used correctly. Also, this part of the spell is experimental so don't hurt yourself."

Amy narrowed her eyes at Garnet. "I thought that the tourmaline was a necessary part of the spell?"

Garnet rubbed the back of her neck and turned her gaze to the ceiling. "I may have slightly lied about that one. It will make the enchantment stronger… but it's part of a different spell. A Latin based one."

Amy adjusted her amethyst bracelet. "I guess it's worth a try, but if your spell destroys my house, you're paying for it."

Her eyes lit up. "Great. You won't be disappointed. The enchantment will be. *servo mihi ex malum.* I've never tried to mix two spells from different enchantress regions and eras, so let's hope this works. I'll go first just in case the combination is unstable."

Garnet started with the enchantment for the bedroom window. She placed the black tourmaline next to the tiger's eye just close enough that they touched and chanted "servo mihi ex malum." The stones vibrated with energy. A spark zipped between the two stones with a loud pop and energy sizzled through the barrier.

Amy sucked in a breath. "Is that it?"

Garnet shrugged. "Unclear. We'll know more when the full barrier is in place."

Amy bit the inside of her cheek. "Thankfully nothing exploded...this time."

"Hey, my experiments don't always explode. Just 80% of the time."

Amy shook her head. "That's far too high a percentage and yet you can't help yourself."

Garnet gave Amy a black tourmaline with shaking hands. "Sorry, but you'll need to do the other six entrances."

"Fine," Amy said and shuffled over to the second opening, the sliding glass door. Her chest tightened as she gingerly placed the gem the way Garnet had, close enough to touch just near her sliding glass door, but when she repeated the chant, nothing happened.

She wasn't normally good with tourmaline, but she could at least do basic spells with it on a bad day. She turned to Garnet and cocked her head to one side. "Why isn't it working?"

Garnet shook her head. "You're saying it wrong. It's *ex*, not *ix*. Here let me show you." She snatched the stone from Amy's hand and started chanting.

"Wow, I must have been tired. My mistake." Amy shrugged. *That's one way to get you to do it yourself.*

"Wait, did you do that on purpose?"

Amy batted her eyelashes and placed a hand to her chest. "Me? I would never."

Garnet's trembling arms buckled beneath her and she collapsed to the rug on the living room floor. "I feel so useless. What's the point in knowing all these spells if I don't have the power to do even one by myself?"

Garnet covered her eyes with her arm, and Amy placed a hand on her shoulder. "Don't feel bad. I wasn't graced with much magic either. Most of it is Violet's power. Besides, if it weren't for your familiar's knowledge of the different enchantress languages, we wouldn't be able to set up this barrier at all."

Garnet grumbled. "I guess. Here. You'll need these to finish the other five entrances." Garnet held out the remaining black Tourmaline.

Amy shook her head. "Well, your knowledge came in handy. I couldn't have put together a barrier like this on my own."

Garnet placed a hand over her chest and drawled, "I mean I am the very best after all."

Garnet winced. "I mean we. Cardinal doesn't like to feel left out."

Amy snickered and grabbed the remaining gems from Garnet's open palm. She made quick work of the last few entrances, but as she enchanted the final tourmaline in her bedroom, a wave of magic knocked her back and a loud boom echoed through her home. The entire house went black.

CHAPTER 2

*T*he temperature in the apartment climbed, and Amy opened a window in her bedroom to see her entire block blacked out. *It fried the power in the entire neighborhood. Great.*

Amy lay down on the floor next to Garnet. "At least I didn't have to replace my sliding door like the last time you visited."

Garnet turned her head to meet Amy's gaze. "We can get Naru to help you repair the electricity tomorrow if it's not back up by then. Do you want to stay at my place for now?"

Amy held out a hand. "Let's try to keep Naru out of this. You know how she can get."

Garnet batted her eyelashes. "Are you concerned about her flirting with you or her getting captured?"

Amy flushed. "Both. She refuses to give up on us and has a tendency of running right into the fray when I get in trouble."

Garnet shrugged. "I mean personally it should be Naru's decision if she wants to take the risks that come with being with you, but I know that's not what you want to hear. Anyway, you didn't answer my question, are you coming over to my place?"

Amy rubbed at her sore arms. "Yes. I'll get up and pack

my things soon. I just need to lay here for a bit." The cold tile felt amazing on her sore muscles after using up so much magic.

It took fifteen minutes of lying on the tile floor until she regained enough energy to move again.

Garnet was the first to rise. She rolled herself into a crouch and stood up. "I know you're tired, but let's get going. It might be best for you to stay at my house tonight since the assassin knows where you live. He could try to come back tonight looking for you."

Amy nodded. "I guess you're right. Plus I don't want to be here in the morning without the AC." Amy rolled onto her side and pushed herself off the floor. She dragged her feet to her room to grab a large duffel bag. Amy shoved work supplies into it: some needle nose pliers, a crimper, some beads, earring hooks, some crystals and wire to wrap them. She glanced at the soldering iron on her work table but didn't move to grab it. *I'm not risking a massive bill after the last time I fell asleep working and set the motel carpet on fire. Then I'd be on the run from Opal and Garnet.*

She plopped the rest of her supplies into the side pocket of the bag and then threw in purple pajamas and an outfit for tomorrow.

After 20 minutes of loud tapping outside her bedroom, Garnet threw Amy's bedroom door open. "Are you ready yet?"

Amy gestured to the bag. "Yup. I just need to zip this up and then we can go."

Garnet raised an eyebrow. "Well, I'm sure you're a responsible adult but just in case. Did you pack a hairbrush, toothbrush, and toothpaste?"

Amy gave a sheepish grin and Garnet ran a hand over her face. "I figured as much. Let me guess you forgot deodorant too? I swear you'd lose your head if it weren't attached."

Amy threw her hands up in surrender. "Well sorry that I

can't do anything right. Maybe I should take advice from little miss walk of shame?"

Amy knew she'd hit a sore spot when Garnet threw the deodorant at her head. Amy held a hand out to snatch it from the air, but it whacked her in the forehead. "Ow that actually hurt." she rubbed at the tender skin.

Garnet peeked her head out of the bathroom doorway. "So did your thoughtless comment. Now let's get going. You might want to bring some of the meager food you have left in your mini fridge-freezer, so it doesn't spoil. That is if you have anything in there worth salvaging."

She knows me too well. Amy pursed her lips as she thought of the water bottle and various condiments that littered her fridge. "I think I have one frozen meal left in there and an apple. The sauces should keep even with the power out. Oh, and I have a bag of cheese."

Garnet smirked. "Are you sure you weren't born part mouse shifter at birth?"

Amy made squeaking noises and they both dissolved into fits of giggles before gathering up the rest of Amy's things. They threw the perishables into an old thermos bag and left the house for the night.

Garnet's familiar glowed a dark crimson at her neck and she placed a hand over the pendant. "No, we aren't going to stop for French fries on the way home." She remarked and the light in her necklace died.

"I'm surprised Cardinal has such a craving for junk food considering you won't touch a French fry with a ten foot pole unless it's a homemade baked organic sweet potato fry."

Garnet sighed. "I know it drives me up the wall and there's no logical way to explain it to my coworkers."

I shrugged. "Just tell them you're having cravings because it's your time of the month. That always worked for me."

Garnet cocked her head to one side. "You know that idea isn't half bad. I might try that next time."

On the way to Garnet's motel, Amy jumped at any loud noise, her head swiveling towards idle conversations. She clutched the amber pendant around her neck but unlike her familiar bracelet, this gem didn't howl in pain or talk back when she bit it or dug her nails into it.

Amy jumped at a loud bang only to see a car putting along and realized it was the ancient vehicle backfiring. She shook Garnet's shoulder. "Are we there yet?"

Garnet looked back to Amy. "We'll be there soon. Settle down before you give yourself a heart attack."

Amy placed her hands on her hips. "You'd be on edge too if Opal's assassin was chasing you."

Garnet pushed a stray strand of hair behind her ear and picked up the pace. "Well, the faster you walk, the faster we'll get there. Hurry up or you'll have to sleep on the street like you did when you first ran away to this world."

Amy shuddered and raced after her. "That's not funny! Don't even joke about that."

Garnet stuck her tongue out at Amy. "Well, it got you to move didn't it."

"I can't believe you're the older sister." Amy raced after her and grabbed her arm.

She laughed and shook Amy off. "But in all seriousness, we're here." Garnet nodded her head towards the "Motel" sign. The "M" light was out, making it read as "Otel."

Amy shook her head. "You couldn't have found a nicer place to stay?"

She sighed. "You might be a successful jeweler, but I'm still working for the Renaissance Festival. They don't exactly pay well."

Amy wrinkled her nose thinking back to when they'd spent their nights lying curled up on the dusty floors of their tents even when it poured rain and they woke covered with red bumps from mosquito bites. "Fair point. Let's go in I guess."

They both clomped up the creaky metal stairs and Garnet pushed open the scratched up wooden door to her room.

Garnet tried to force the swollen wood shut, but had to deadbolt the door to get it shut. Amy scoffed, "And this is safer than my apartment, how?"

Her sister waved it off. "The door doesn't close correctly, but at least Opal's little helper won't know where you are."

Amy crossed her arms over her chest. "I guess, but there are human threats too. This isn't exactly top notch security."

"Noted, but we also can magic our way out of most human problems." Garnet plopped down on the bed closest to the door.

Amy sneezed, and it kicked up a cloud of dust. Her gaze lingered on a ruby colored stain on the carpet and traveled over to Garnet's discarded clothing littering the floor and the wet towel draped over a chair.

Amy screeched when a cockroach scuttled over her shoe. "You didn't warn me about roaches. You know I hate roaches!" She jumped up onto the bed gripping the frame with white knuckles. *How does she live like this?*

Garnet's gaze scanned the room and when the roach got close, she stomped on the insect. Amy shuddered at the wet squish.

Garnet covered a smile with her hand. "You've been living in Florida for a year. These things are everywhere, so I thought you'd be used to them by now. Have you gone soft that quickly?"

Amy tucked her shoulders back. "You overestimate me. I was just never good at camping and rough motels to begin with."

Garnet slid off her black boots. "Well, I'm going to wash this off. You can go ahead and put your bag anywhere."

Amy plopped her bag down on the small office chair in the corner. Its legs wobbled under the weight but didn't collapse.

She stripped the filthy looking bed covers off and threw them on top of the dresser.

She dumped out the jewelry making supplies from her overnight bag and as the shower turned on and a black crop top, jeans, and black boots got tossed out of the bathroom door.

Garnet squeaked and poked her head out of the door. "Hey, can you pass me one of my boots? I found that other roach's buddy."

Amy slid out of bed and handed her the boot through the bathroom door before slamming the door shut so it wouldn't escape.

"Thanks." Garnet called back and yelled. "Die evil creature!" through the thin bathroom walls.

Amy covered her mouth to stifle a laugh that shook her shoulders, but her smile faded as she thought back on the necklace and her doubts about them being sisters.

Every time she'd asked their mother, Sardonyx, about it she'd always smile and say, "You're special, but you're my child just like Garnet, Chalcedony, and Selenite." before running off to another clan for supplies or heading to the human world to get human world technology for their import business.

Amy crawled back into bed and grabbed her phone to look up a video tutorial on how to make a butterfly wire cage, but when she went to connect to the internet, a home page asking for a password popped up.

Amy ran a hand along the nightstand, rifled through the drawers of the work desk, and scoured the countertop near the beaten-up box of a television but didn't find anything with the password. "Ugh. Where did she put it?" Amy gave several loud raps on the door until the water shut off, and Garnet thumped to the door.

Her dripping wet head poked out. "Is there something I can help you with? I was kind of in the middle of something."

"Hey where's the wifi password? I need it for work."

Garnet flicked wet hair out of her face. "The password is just my name and the hotel room number 325. If you forget, the password is in my bag by the bed. Now let me finish my shower in peace."

She slammed the door shut so quickly that Amy jumped back to avoid getting smacked in the nose.

A loud bang that sounded like a gunshot cut through the honks and hums of the nearby highway. It could have been another car backfiring or fireworks, but it sounded a little too close for comfort. Amy fastened the chain to the door and then put the wobbly chair with her suitcase in front of it for good measure.

A man shouted, "I'm gonna kill you when I get my hands on you," and Amy peeked out the window to see a stumbling drunk man with a woman holding a half empty liquor bottle.

"You're cut off." the woman said with a hand on her hip and left the man behind in the hallway.

When the shouting faded, she sat back down on her bed and pulled up a video called "How to wire wrap a butterfly." Her worries from the possible gunshot and screaming man were long forgotten as she used her pliers to curl the wire for the first antennae and then folded the silver wire into the corner of the first wing. She smiled at how the blue, gold, and green Labradorite with its crisscrossing black lines on its surface made her pendant look like a real butterfly.

Just as she twisted the last piece of wire onto the gem, a cloud of steam came from the bathroom and Garnet emerged with an off-white towel around her waist and another in her hair. Amy suppressed a gag at the yellow tinge and frayed edges on the towels.

If she couldn't keep Dusk at bay, she'd have to go back to being on the run. She wasn't about to let that happen.

"Garnet. Do you like your job and the constant moving?" Amy cocked her head to one side.

Garnet laughed until she saw the look on Amy's face. "Oh. You're serious. No, I hate it, but it was the job that was safest for you and the only portable job I was qualified for. Now that I've been doing it so long it just feels like leaving it would be like leaving behind a part of myself. You know? Anyway, we should probably set up a barrier for tonight just in case your secret admirer finds us here."

Amy laughed. "Interesting way to refer to Opal's assistant."

Garnet shrugged. "Listen if they're hot enough I say go for it. It's better than the zero love life that you've had."

Amy crossed her arms over her chest. "My sex life or lack thereof is none of your business."

Garnet sighed and rifled through her purse until she found an Amethyst and a Garnet. "These should do for tonight and they'll expend the least energy since they're our familiar's gems."

She grabbed Amy's hand and they chanted together. "Piedras de fuego y aire protéjannos de los que nos quieren hacer daño. Quemen a los intrusos con corazones llenos de odio." The two stones glowed as they cast the spell.

Once the gems were bloated with magic, Garnet placed one by the room's lone window and one by the front door. "That should do for now. Now, let's go to sleep. Put away your jewelry stuff."

"It's not just stuff. It's my job." Amy said and scooped up her equipment.

Garnet waved her off. "Ya ya whatever. Let's go to bed." She shut off the light by the front door and flipped the switch for the lamp near the bedside table. Garnet was snoring after just a few minutes, but Amy lay awake thinking of Dusk and the clue he'd left her until the night turned to a grey dawn.

CHAPTER 3

*L*ight spilled through the dirt smeared windows. Amy groaned and rubbed at the grit in her eyes. She took in the drawn curtains and the coppery stains on the tattered carpet. Two more roaches lay dead, snared by haphazard roach traps placed near the nightstand and entrance door.

Amy gulped when she didn't see or hear Garnet, but her bags were still here. Amy peeked her head into the bathroom. "Garnet? Hello?" But the bathroom was empty. Amy's mouth went dry and her hand shook when she checked the enchantments. The magic had been undone. The metal chain on the door was intact but unlatched. No one had broken in, so where was she? *Shit. Shit. Shit. What if she's in trouble? What am I supposed to do?*

Amy looked over at her phone and saw a message from an unknown sender. Her blood froze as she hit play on the voicemail and a scratchy voice answered. "We have your sister. If you want her, you'll need to turn yourself in."

Amy dropped the phone to the floor like it had bitten her. *Why would they take her but not me? How did they find us?*

Muffled giggling came from the other side of the door and

Amy peered through the window and caught a glimpse of a tawny arm and strands of Naru's dark black hair. Amy suppressed a groan. *You weren't supposed to bring her here, Garnet. It's too dangerous.* Amy cracked open the door to see Naru and Garnet crouched by the window. Amy placed a hand on her hip. "Is this your idea of a joke? I thought Garnet was actually in trouble."

Naru grinned up at her. "Your sister called me and told me you needed some additional protection. Sorry about the prank. It was her idea. I didn't think you'd actually believe that Garnet captured herself. That was her voice on the phone." Naru pointed a thumb at Garnet.

Amy glared daggers at Garnet. "You have a sick and twisted sense of humor."

Garnet got up from her spot on the floor and gave a dramatic bow. "Why thank you. I take pride in my work." Amy scowled at her, and she rubbed her hand on the back of her neck. "Okay. Okay. It was in poor taste, but I brought your friend. Cough. Cough. And love interest."

Amy let out an exasperated sigh. "Yes, after I told you not to because it's too dangerous. How did you know she would come?"

Garnet elbowed Amy, "You know exactly why she didn't hesitate to come here."

Naru flushed. "It wasn't just that. I'm also here on assignment." She tapped her pointer fingers together. "It-It's good to see you, Amy. You're still cute as ever even if you have a bad case of bed head."

Naru looked Amy up and down in a way that made Amy's cheeks heat. Amy smoothed out her hair, running her fingers through the violet strands.

"Maybe I should leave you lovebirds alone to make googly eyes at each other," said Garnet.

"We're not love birds!" Amy shouted.

Naru just twirled a strand of hair around her finger. "But we almost were. Remember that...photo shoot we had."

Amy gulped and her fingers went to her lips remembering the softness of Naru's mouth on hers. "Can we not talk about that now?"

Garnet batted her eyelashes. "I remember *those* photos. And yet you still deny your feelings for her. How cold."

"I-I" Amy's mouth went dry and she licked her lips. "It didn't mean anything."

Garnet's stomach growled. "Sure, it didn't. Let's get breakfast and then we can check out." Garnet clicked her phone on and her mouth opened in an O. "On second thought, you might want to leave now. Your store opens in 30 minutes, doesn't it?"

Amy held out her hand for Garnet's phone and checked the time. It was 9:30 a.m. The store was supposed to open at 10:00 a.m. "Shit, you're right. I'll catch up with you later."

Amy ran off and Naru followed after her. "I'm coming with you," she said.

Amy didn't slow her pace. "Okay, but you're helping me set up shop and you're going to have to move faster." Amy reached back and grabbed Naru's hand, pulling her along.

She was halfway to the shop when she looked down and realized she'd left all of her equipment behind and still sported fuzzy pants with cats all over them. "We'll need to make a quick stop."

Naru placed a hand on her hips. "I don't know, I'm rather enjoying the view." Amy pulled up her already sweat soaked white tank top.

Amy huffed. "That'll happen over my dead body."

"Or under my living one." Naru smirked.

Amy sputtered, staring open mouthed at Naru.

Naru clapped a hand to Amy's shoulder. "I know; I'm fine, but stop gawking before my fine behind makes you late for work." She strode ahead of Amy making sure to exaggerate the sway of her hips as she walked.

Amy focused on keeping her eyes straight ahead as they headed back to her place so she could change and grab some much needed supplies for work. She sent a text to Garnet saying. "Hey. Make sure to bring those supplies by later."

Garnet sent back "K." and nothing else. Amy squinted at the phone. Garnet usually sent paragraphs instead of messages. Amy used to jokingly tell her she'd be better off sending me emails. Amy shook her head. *You're overreacting. She's probably just lazy texting because she's eating. I can text her again once I get to the shop.*

Amy held up a hand to stop Naru when they reached the entrance to her apartment. "Make sure you don't touch the salt when you come into the house."

Naru rubbed her forehead. "And why do you have salt in your doorway?"

Amy's expression lit up. "It's part of an enchantment to protect the house. Garnet taught me about it. Apparently, it's because the salt has a larger crystalline shape, it can be enchanted like other gemstones and…"

Naru smiled and held up her hands, stopping Amy. "I love that you're excited about the new spell, but I have to stop you there or we'll be late. Hm, I guess that means there is some truth to those things you see about salt in all those TV shows."

Amy cocked her head to one side. "What do you mean?"

"Oh ya that's right you aren't from 'this world.' In fantasy shows, it keeps away evil stuff like demons."

Amy ran a hand through her hair. "I guess it's kind of like that. This type of salt is like a crystal so we can enchant them for protection, but they break easily. If you touch any of it, the enchantment gets weaker and could shatter."

Naru pulled up the long pant's legs on her jeans and tucked them into her shoes. "I guess I'd better be careful then. You go first."

Amy crept over the threshold, eyeing the line of salt to make sure she didn't disturb a single crystal and then held out her hand to help Naru over the boundary.

Naru blushed when she took Amy's hand. Amy relished the scent of spring rain that always clung to Naru's hair as she helped her into her home. *I wish you knew how much I wanted to kiss you right now, but you'd just end up another target for Opal.*

When Amy made no effort to move, Naru glanced down at her phone and her face fell into a frown. "You have maybe two minutes to get changed. Go." She shooed Amy into her room. "You're already late to open up your own store. It's ten on the dot."

"Alright, alright, I'm going." Amy stepped into her room and clicked the lock shut behind her. She stripped off her pajama bottoms and tank top and switched into a silky lilac blouse, black slacks and her favorite black flats.

After giving herself a quick once over and yanking a brush through the knots in her hair, Amy lifted her chin and flung open the bedroom door with a flourish. "Presenting. The idiot who's late to open her own store."

Naru winked. "Well, at least if you're a mess you're a hot one. Let's go." A blush rose all the way to Amy's scalp as Naru grabbed her by the hand and yanked her out of the house.

Thoughts of the barrier and not setting her alarm flitted through her mind, but those thoughts were quashed when the store came into view along with a customer with curly hair that bordered on fire engine red. The woman tapped her foot as she waited outside of the shop door. As she glanced down at her watch, she said, "Where is she? I'm going to be late for work."

When the woman saw Amy, she waved frantically. She rushed up to Amy and grabbed her hand. "Oh, thank goodness you're here. I was starting to wonder if you'd gotten sick or something. I was hoping to pick up that....piece of jewelry we'd talked about yesterday. The rose quartz pendant for my girlfriend."

Amy's eyes lit up as her name popped into her mind. *Arlia. The one that wanted a charm to attract love...well more like sex.* She nodded. "Of course, Arlia. I'll just turn off the alarm. Sorry for the wait. I was running a little late this morning."

Her gaze went to the disheveled Naru beside her. "I can see why." Naru stifled a laugh as the women kept gushing. "Plus, you seem to always have just the right gemstones for me. It's like you have the magic touch."

Amy rubbed at her neck. "It's nothing like that. Just call it a strong intuition for other people's lives."

Naru suppressed a snicker and Amy elbowed her.

Arlia gave a knowing smile and flipped her hair over her shoulder. "Well, my girlfriend and I love your work," she said with a strong emphasis on *love*.

Amy gave her a strained smile. "Thank you. That's so kind of you to say." *At least she didn't start talking about the rumors of magic gemstone jewelry, so I suppose that's a plus.*

Amy walked over to the counter and picked up a necklace that emitted a bright pink glow, urging her to touch it, to harness its magic. Amy's fingers twitched as she lifted the tumbled rose quartz necklace with the heart design wire wrapped over the front of the stone. The silver chain glittered in the sunlight and Arlia gasped. "You've really outdone your-self this time Amy. It looks beautiful. My girlfriend will love it."

Amy blushed. "Thank you. Tell her I said hi. I hope she enjoys her anniversary gift."

Arlia smiled and reached into her wallet to pull out two twenties. "I'll let you know what she says and how the date goes. Goddess bless." Arlia reached over the counter and pulled Amy into a hug. Amy stiffened in her grip, but allowed Arlia's arms to wrap around her. Hard to explain that your culture wasn't the hugging type when they didn't know it existed.

Arlia turned on her heel and headed to the exit. Before she walked out, she said, "I'm sure I'll be back again in a few weeks. Merry Part and Merry Meet Again."

Amy laughed and said in an octave higher than her normal voice. "Same to you, Arlia. Enjoy the rest of your day."

The door jingled closed behind her and Amy slumped down to the floor in front of her desk.

Naru gave her a knowing smile. "She's gone. You can turn your customer service voice off now."

Amy rolled her eyes. "It's not that I hate her, but I really don't like when she hugs me. I think she hugs everyone. The first time she greeted me by kissing me on the cheek" Amy shuddered. "That's too much physical affection. Major overload."

Naru whistled as she took in the store. "You could just say you're from somewhere that's not big on hugging if you want her to back off."

Amy shook her head. "It's fine, I can handle it. She's gotten better about it actually."

Naru held up her hands. "Alright." She skimmed the rows of essential oils and neat lines of gemstones organized by type with her fingers. "I haven't been here since you bought this place. Your setup is surprisingly organized. Is there anything I can do to help?"

Amy gestured to the display of essential oils and the mismatched piles of tumbled gems in the corner. "You can help me re-organize these gems by type. Some customers put them back wrong and I was in a rush to leave yesterday. Quartz should go together and beryl at the bottom. Don't let the lodestones anywhere near any electronics since they're magnetic, and stay far away from opals. They're bad luck unless you were born in October. And can you fix the oil displays that my customers made a mess of?"

Naru scratched at her head. "I think I got most of that. The beryl's are mostly milky apart from the cat's eye which has that big slit that looks like a cat's pupil. The lodestones are those dull grey looking ones that kind of look like normal rocks, right?"

Amy's lip curled up in a half smile. "You remember."

Naru reached out to pick up one of the tumbled Amethysts, and her hands brushed Amy's. "Of course I do. I love when you talk about your gems. I know you love them almost as much as I love you."

Amy's heart fluttered in her chest. Her palm glowed purple, and she jerked her hand back. "Sorry. Sometimes my magic still has a mind of its own."

Naru cocked her head to one side. "I'm surprised that's still happening to you. Didn't you take classes to hone your specialization in the magic world and do training with Iris?"

The corner of Amy's mouth tilted up in a grin, and she tucked a strand of hair behind her ear "You remember that? Yes, I took some classes in the magic world, but I had about maybe one year of specialization classes out of the four to five years we'd normally receive because I fled two years after my Choosing. And it wasn't too long after that before, you know, she blew up our entire clan in a massive hate driven explosion, so there aren't many enchantment mages left from my clan and many of those left would turn me into Opal."

Naru gritted her teeth. "Oh, but didn't they train you to control your magic before the specialization classes?"

Amy stared down at the mismatched gems. "The teachers tried, but according to them most of my outbursts didn't look like Enchantress magic. They look like some other sort of magic...maybe telekinesis, but they weren't sure."

Naru propped her elbows on the glass table, and Amy had

to put a hand out to keep gems from toppling to the floor. "What about Iris?"

Amy bit her lip. "Iris tries to help, but they can only do so much as a shifter."

Naru pursed her lips together. "Telekinesis. Interesting, so you might be from dual clans like Night and I."

Amy frowned at the mention of Night.

Naru touched her shoulder. "Sorry, that was insensitive. I know losing him was difficult for you."

Amy pulled away from her. "It's okay. I just wish I knew what happened to him and if he was alive. I mean...I was the first person he told about being part shifter, about not wanting to be called Cat anymore. He was one of my only friends aside from you. And then just like that Opal took him from me."

Naru placed a hand on Amy's shoulder. "I know I can't imagine what it was like growing up in that other world, but I'm glad you found me otherwise I wouldn't have known how to control my elemental magic. Mother was determined to hide that from me even though our clan has been here since the Malachite Massacre in Merlin's era."

Amy rubbed her neck. "Most elementals consider it a source of shame that they got forced off their land by a single invading soldier, so I can understand why to an extent, but she should have at least told you that you had magic."

Naru bit her lip. "It's probably a good thing I met you that day. Otherwise, I would have gotten in far more trouble than I already had."

Amy rubbed her eyes. "I'm glad I met you too. If I'd lost both of you that day, I'm not sure what I would have done. I just wish you'd been able to save Night before Opal had gotten to him."

Naru frowned. "Amy..." Her gaze flickered to the ground. "I need to tell you something about that day, but promise you won't get mad."

Amy placed a hand on Naru's shoulder. "I trust that you wouldn't even do anything to hurt someone. At least not on purpose."

Naru shook her head. "It's about Night, Amy. I had a chance to save him."

Amy's mouth dropped. She leaned in so suddenly that she knocked into a vial of lavender oil, and it crashed to the tile floor and shattered upon impact.

She reached down to pick up shards of glass from the floor, but Naru stopped her. "Don't. You'll hurt yourself. I'll get it." She grabbed a dustpan and broom from behind the counter and moved Amy aside so she could scoop up the glass, but Amy didn't care about that right now.

Amy wanted to know what Naru had been about to disclose. "Naru, what do you mean you had a chance to save him? I thought Opal had already gotten him. You were too late to help him, right?"

Naru couldn't meet Amy's eyes. She intently stared at the shards of glass on the floor. "Promise you won't hate me if I tell you what happened."

Amy hesitated, her gaze taking in the tight set of Naru's jaw. She longed to run her fingers along Naru's cheek and to say that she could never hate her, but not until she knew why Naru rarely came around after Night's disappearance. *Not if he's gone because of you.* "I promise." Amy said.

Her familiar's voice purred, *liar.*

Naru bit her lip. "All those years ago when I said I didn't have a chance to save Night...I was lying. The truth is...I saw Opal heading to your hotel room when I went to get my phone from the lobby. I might have been able to sneak him out before she got to him, but I didn't even try to warn or rescue him." Her whole body shook. "I ran away. Like a coward. He might be dead because of me." Naru's voice caught on the last word and tears spilled from her face onto the floor. Electricity crackled around her, and Amy took several steps back.

Guilt struck Amy like an arrow to the heart. *If I hadn't run with my sister, maybe Night and Naru wouldn't have had to face Opal alone with no warning.*

She wanted to blame Naru, but given the choice, she probably would've run too. Opal was a force of nature that you didn't want to trifle with. Her home and her youngest sister, Selene had been lost forever in the battle of Opal's Fall when Opal single handedly destroyed the entire sorceress clan and the Enchantress clan in her rage over Joan's death and Amy's escape.

Amy rubbed at the forming tears with the heel of her hand. "I don't blame you Naru. Opal is the problem. Is there anything she won't take from me? I was a child. I didn't mean to kill that man. She was the one that let a kid battle in a war." Her lip trembled.

Naru blinked. "Wait. Back up. You killed a man?"

Amy's voice cracked when she spoke. "Yes, but it wasn't my fault. It happened when I was enlisted to fight in the 'War of the Twin Swords.' During Opal and Joan's negotiations with the sorceress army, their general tried to kill us, and I lost control of my magic." Crying turned into choking sobs.

Naru sat down beside Amy and rubbed her back. "Hey. Hey deep breaths. We don't want a customer coming in and seeing you like this." Naru reached into her jean pocket and grabbed a packet of tissues. "Here, blow your nose, you look like a mess."

Amy grabbed a tissue from Naru and blew her nose. Her sobs turned to hiccups as the bell jingled and a customer came in. Amy wiped tears from her eyes and tried to chirp out "Welcome to the store." But her voice cracked.

Naru shook her head. "I'll take care of the customer. Go wash your face with some cold water and take some time to calm down."

Amy nodded. "We'll talk about Night later. I need to know more about what happened."

Naru gave her hand a slight squeeze. "We will. Later, I promise."

The man tripped over the threshold as he walked into the shop. He had dark brown hair that stuck up in all directions. "Hi Amy." He called out as he approached the counter with clunky movements, but Amy kept walking without responding.

Naru jumped in for her. "Hi. I'm Amy's shop assistant, Naru. She's not feeling well, so I'm helping out today. How can I help you?"

The man picked at his nails. There was a slight tremor in his hand. He mulled over his words. "I put in a custom order a few days ago. It's a lapis lazuli embedded watch."

Naru nodded and walked over to the display case. "Can you point it out for me?" The man leaned over the glass until he came across a watch with checkered silver on the band and a gem polished smooth, marbled with small dots of blue and gold. The gem sat in the center of the watch's clock face.

Naru glanced at the price tag and rang it up for him. "That'll be $150 dollars." The man nodded and handed over a credit card. He took the watch from Naru's outstretched palm and fumbled with the clasp.

"Here let me help you with that." Naru grabbed the watch and clasped it on his wrist.

When the latch clicked, He smacked his hand into his palm. "That's right I put my flute in that clothing organizer." He flexed his hands and wiggled his fingers "Perhaps it will be easier to play now. Tell Amy I said thank you, and have a good rest of your day. I've got to go." The man rushed out of the store with graceful movements and the bells jingled as the door swung shut behind him.

Amy came out of the washroom in the back of the store. Her eyes were still slightly red rimmed and her face damp with water.

"Were you able to find his watch?" Amy asked.

"Ya. He pointed it out to me. What does that gem do by the way?"

Amy shrugged. "It depends on how you use it, but it's good for mind altering spells and protection from mind readers."

She leaned in closer so that her hair brushed Amy's face. "What was his enchantment for?"

Amy waved her hands. "That's an interesting story. He has a condition that makes it difficult to play the flute, so it's enchanted to help with the tremors and damage to his coordination."

Naru gave her puppy dog eyes. "Your enchantments are so impressive. Can you give me an enchantment to help me in the love department? I'm starting to think I'm unlikable or something."

Amy wrinkled her nose. "Maybe I should give you an enchantment to help you become less oblivious, then you'd have better luck."

Naru giggled. "Look who's talking about being oblivious. I mean how many ways do I need to spell it out for you? Must I pin you to the bed?"

Heat flooded Amy's cheeks, and she crossed her arms over her chest. "I'm not oblivious. Did you ever think there's a reason your over the top advances aren't working?"

Naru tucked a strand of hair behind her ear. "Because you're hoping I'll do something particularly bold like pushing you up against the wall?"

Naru smirked and Amy shifted under her gaze, heat settling low in her stomach. "Don't use that against me. I told you that in confidence!"

Naru tucked a strand of hair behind her ear and snuck out from behind the counter. "I'd be more than happy to fulfill that wish if you gave me a chance."

"You know why I won't."

Naru crossed her arms over her chest. "Yes, but it's a stupid reason because I'm going to put myself in danger for you either way, and I can handle myself."

The bells on the door clinked, and another customer walked in, interrupting their conversation. Naru glanced at the door and then back to her. "Did you ever hear back from Garnet aside from the k message?"

Amy shook her head. "No, I'm starting to get worried."

"In that case, I'll go check on her. I'll text you later to let you know what happened. Good luck with work!"

"You're leaving me all alone?" Amy pouted.

Naru smirked. "Somehow I think you'll be fine."

"Traitor." Amy muttered, but as the customer approached she plastered on a smile. Her mind kept going back to the abrupt "K" Garnet had sent last. *What if Opal's goon got her? No, Amy, you're probably overthinking it. Garnet kept us safe for this long, she wouldn't get captured now.*

Amy's fake smile turned genuine when the customer's auburn hair turned to a rainbow hue, and a small fang peeked out of their mouth.

"I wasn't expecting you today, Iris. Our next training session wasn't supposed to be until tomorrow."

Iris slid onto the table. Their legs dangled off the side of the glass counter. "I decided to visit early. The place I was staying at is being demolished today." They glanced around the shop. "Are there any humans here?"

Amy shook her head. "Not right now, but the shop is open until 5 today."

Iris smiled. Their hand touched the cat's eye pendant Amy had given Iris to keep their shifting from being visible to normal humans. "Good because I can't keep myself from shifting for much longer." They jumped over the counter and ducked out of sight.

Amy grimaced at the sound of bones breaking and reforming. Hair sprouted from skin and Iris let out a howl of pain. After a few too long moments of glancing at the door and hoping no one came in, they had reformed into a creature with long ears and pale fur, a fennec fox. Their snowy white fur had little rainbow patches behind the ears. Amy still found it a bit ironic that her mentor lacked magic control because Iris has been captured and experimented on by some overly nosy humans.

"I think I like you better this way." Amy laughed and reached out to scratch Iris's ears, but they bit Amy's hand. "Ow that actually hurt. Rude."

Amy could swear Iris glowered at her, but she couldn't communicate with her shifter mentor when they were like this. Amy grabbed a steel bowl and went to the sink to fill it with water. "When you change back, I need your help with something. I need to find a way to stop Opal."

Iris's ear perked up at that.

IF IRIS COULD TALK RIGHT NOW, they'd probably lecture Amy about not jumping into the enemy's den, but that would be hypocritical considering that's how Iris had gotten captured by those scientists in the first place.

After escaping, they'd run and ended up at Amy's doorstep one day still in animal form. Amy helped Iris find places to stay hidden from the scientists and kept them fed. In exchange Iris helped Amy learn magic control. When she pushed Iris about how and why Iris had sought her out, Iris had always given vague Amy vague lines like "a little bird told me."

Iris had no magic control of their own because of the experiments, but they'd been taught all the strategies for magic control since they'd been old enough to walk since shifter powers developed early in life.While the emotions that governed their powers were different, the importance of harnessing and controlling emotions for magic was similar for all magic clans.

Since Garnet had no clue how to teach magic control, and Amy was on the run from any Opal or Magic Council loyalists, this was her best and only choice.

Thankfully, no customers came when Iris transformed back into human form a few moments later. "Look away." Iris chastised, and Amy flushed and threw a shirt and pants at Iris.

After a few moments, she heard the slipping of fabric as Iris redressed. They let out a huff. "You can turn around now."

Their hair stuck out at odd angles and their mascara had gotten smudged.

Amy shook her head. "I don't know why you bother with makeup and hair anymore."

Iris narrowed their eyes at Amy and finger combed their hair. "Because I like to waste several hours of effort for nothing? I don't know. Anyway, you had something juicy for me. Why do you want to take out Opal, aside from the usual reasons? You know it's a suicide mission, right? Especially because she has the power of both of Merlin's twin swords ever since the Twin Swords, Excalibur and Clarent, fused together. Do you really think you can beat the Dragon of destruction and Tiger of Triumph?"

Amy threw up her hands. "I know, but she found me and sent an assassin after me. What am I supposed to do, run for the rest of my life? I'm tired of it."

Iris placed a hand on Amy's shoulder. "Well, get used to it unless you're tired of living. Running is your best shot unless you're going to lead an army to her." Iris looked Amy up and down, appraising her. "And you never struck me as the leading type."

Amy grabbed a stool she kept behind the counter and sat down. "I know, but I can't do this anymore. It's bad enough living with the guilt of what happened to that soldier, but she's blaming me for Joan's death too. I was a kid, and I feel bad enough about what happened. What can't she just move on?"

Iris's gaze softened. "Those swords corrupt feelings that are already there. What you did would've been enough to break her heart. Unintentional or not. And that isn't something she will just move on from."

Amy muttered. "As if she ever had a heart."

Iris's lips curved up into a half smile. "You say that now, but I know deep down you don't believe that...not completely. Some part of you still hopes you can help her just like your customers and like Night." She pointed a finger at Amy's chest. "I can see it clear as day here."

"You're wrong, and don't mention Night. I just found out some disturbing information about his disappearance." She frowned.

"Alright, suit yourself, but I'm going to get some food." Iris got up and walked to the mini fridge.

"Iris, don't you dare steal my lunch again!" Amy shouted as she ran after them. Too late. Iris had her peanut butter sandwich in their mouth.

Iris shrugged. "What? Shifting makes me hungry."

Amy gritted her teeth. "Well then you're buying me lunch since you just ate mine."

Iris inhaled the rest of the sandwich and licked their lips. "Fine. I'll be back with your lunch in an hour. Enjoy work." They smiled and sauntered out the door just as another customer walked through the entrance.

Today is going to be a long day. Amy thought and shouted "Welcome to the store!"

CHAPTER 4

*a*my's stomach grumbled, and she looked down at her watch. It was 3:00pm. *It's been almost two hours and Iris still isn't back with my food. What gives?* Just as the thought crossed her mind, A little raccoon with rainbow ears scurried towards the shop with a wrapped-up sandwich in its mouth. *You've got to be kidding me.*

Sure enough it was none other than Iris scratching at the door. She opened the door and Iris scurried in. They dropped the sandwich into Amy's outstretched palm.

Amy scratched at her head, "Hopefully, no one saw you transform. I really don't want to siphon any memories today."

Iris shook their head.

"Good." Amy scooped Iris up and brought them back behind the counter. "You're lucky I keep extra clothing for you in case something like this happens."

At that point Iris transformed. *Their transformation was on purpose?*

When Iris turned back into their human form, they were shaking from head to toe, and the color had gone from their face. "You may have to fight after all."

Amy ran over to the door and changed the sign from open

to closed. She could deal with any grief from customers later. Amy shook Iris's shoulders. "What do you mean I might have to fight? What happened?"

Iris rubbed their arms as if trying to keep the cold off of their skin. "When I went to get your food, I ran into Opal. She was dragging Garnet's limp body away through a back alley near the sandwich shop. I turned into something inconspicuous so I could get away."

"No. No. No. I'll call Naru, maybe she knows what happened. I just need to find my phone. Where is it?" Iris locked the door as Amy pawed around her desk drawers and peeked under the counter.

Iris squinted at the chair and pointed at the cushion. "Uh Amy. You were sitting on it again."

"Oh, thank goodness. You're a lifesaver." With shaking hands, Amy unlocked the phone to see Naru had sent several panicked texts and she had a voicemail from an unknown number. "Iris, can you play the voicemail, please?"

Iris held out their hand for the phone. "Sure. Give it to me." They placed the phone on speaker and Opal's voice crackled on the line. "I have your sister. I'll make you a deal. Your life for hers."

Amy's voice shook. "I'll kill her for this. Let's leave for the magic world now."

AFTER AMY and Iris had turned off the lights and drawn the curtains, Iris pelted Amy with questions. "What's your plan? How are we going to gather an army?"

Amy kicked the stool over. "I don't know. Okay. Maybe we can find some magic users with a tracking spell? I can probably enchant a gemstone to track Garnet, but we'll be of no use without help. Opal is too powerful."

Iris ran their fingers along the buttons of their shirt. "Well,

I can introduce you to the clan of shifters that I came from, but the closest portal to my clan is in Israel. Can you book a same day flight?"

"If there are any flights left, it'll cost a fortune that I don't have." Amy pulled out her phone and scrolled through ticket prices. "Are you paying for your ticket?"

Iris patted Amy on the shoulder. "That's cute. You think I can afford a last second flight to Israel?"

Amy's voice dripped with sarcasm. "And I'm just oozing money. You could at least chip in."

Iris sighed "Fine. I'll transfer you some money. What's your Paybuddy?"

"My username on there is Thepurplewitch."

Iris reached a hand into their pants pocket and gave Amy a sheepish smile. "Uhhh, I think I lost my phone when I shifted to escape Opal. Can I pay you later?" They pouted. "Please."

Amy rolled her eyes. "You owe me big time for this." She clicked the book flight button and took out her credit card. "If I don't get that money by the end of the month, I'm hunting you down for it later." She narrowed her eyes at Iris.

Iris chuckled. "Please, I'd love to see you try. I can fight circles around you."

"Fair. The tickets are booked. We leave at 10:00 PM tonight. I'll give Naru a call. She was going to see Garnet before Opal took her, maybe she saw something we didn't."

"Good idea."

Amy punched in Naru's contact details and tapped her foot while the phone rang, but it went to voicemail.

When Amy texted Naru, she punched away at the keyboard so loudly that Iris shouted. "What did the phone ever do to you?"

Amy glared at Iris but stopped mashing the keys. *Hey. I wanted to make sure you're okay. Iris just saw Opal dragging Garnet away.*

The checks turned blue, indicating Naru had read the message, but she wasn't typing. *Did she give up my sister's location to Opal? If she says she didn't, can I trust her? Has she been captured too?*

Rock music blared from Amy's phone, and she checked the caller ID. It read Naru.

When she clicked the answer call button, Naru screamed, and Amy pulled the phone away from her ear. "What do you mean Opal came after her? How did she know where she was? Shit. It could've been me. I visited her for lunchtime. She was fine less than an hour ago. I left when work called me for another travel writing project. I've been out with my camera taking pictures for the article. I was just about to call you to let you know she was okay when I saw your text."

Amy let out a long sigh. *At least she's safe, and she didn't sound guilty.* "I would ask if you'd come with us to Israel to gather the shifters, but I guess you'll be busy with work. I'll let you know when we touch down safely."

Amy could hear crackling on the phone. When Naru spoke, her voice was uncharacteristically high. "You're going to the magic world without me?" She huffed. "Fine, I'll try to find any other elementals in the area after I've finished my assignment, but next time you have to take me with you. Promise?"

Amy bit her lip. "You've got yourself a deal. I don't know what I'd do if I lost you too, so just be careful. Okay?"

Naru snorted. "Don't get sentimental on me now. You can flirt with me when we both make it out of this alive."

"Deal." Amy ended the call. She wasn't sure what kind of troops they could rally, but maybe this little rebellion could spark a war. One big enough to take Opal and her Council down for good.

Opal and The Magic Council had killed Amy's younger sister and separated her from the rest of her clan, and they would have hell to pay.

AMY LED Iris back to her house so Amy could pack for Israel. *I guess I'll have to close the store for the time being.* She texted her human emergency contact for the store. *Hey Tiff. Can you take over the store for a few days? I'm going to be out of town.*

The three dots appeared as she typed.

Uh sure. It's a little short notice. Is everything okay?

Amy turned to Iris. "What do I say?"

"Just tell her it's a family medical emergency. Usually they don't ask too many questions once they know that."

Amy typed up her response and showed it to Iris. "Does this sound believable? That my mother got injured hiking on her trip to Israel and ended up in the hospital?"

"Ya, I'd buy it. Go ahead and click send."

Amy sent the message and waited. Tiff's reply came quickly. *I'm so sorry to hear that. I'll take care of the store. Just leave the key in the usual spot for me.*

Thank you. I will. Amy typed back and checked the time. It read 5:00pm which meant they only had five more hours until their flight.

Amy frowned. "Maybe you should get ready at our usual training spot? I'll be fine here."

An ear poked out of Iris's hair. "Are you sure that's a good idea? What if the assassin comes back?"

Amy balled her hands into fists, her nails digging into her palm. "I'll make him regret that he was ever assigned me as a target."

Iris's lip curled up in a smile. "I like this side of you. Okay. I'll be just down the road. If you need me, send me a text message or just scream really loudly. I'll probably hear it."

Amy wanted to laugh, but she knew Iris was only half joking. As Iris was walking away, she caught a glimmer of silver on the rug and picked it up. "You dropped your necklace. You'll need it so others don't see you shift."

Iris grabbed the necklace and headed to the door. Before they stepped over the salt at the entrance, they turned back to Amy. "Just make sure you don't get killed or I'll have to bring you back to life just to kill you again for scaring me like that."

Amy giggled. "All right. All right. Now go. You need to be ready or we'll both be late."

Iris waved as they walked to the front door of Amy's home. "You're worrying for nothing. You always get there too early." After the door shut behind them, the apartment became deathly silent.

As Amy folded her clothes into her suitcase, floorboards creaked and she turned towards the sound but didn't see anything. *Strange.*

As Amy shoved the last of her belongings into her over-filled suitcase, the hairs on the back of her neck rose, but she still couldn't see anyone. *What is going on?*

Amy reached out towards the source of the noise, and her fingers brushed flesh.

A crushing grip wrapped around her neck, and her black spots danced in the edges of her vision, but she still couldn't see anyone. She lashed out with her arms and her nails dug into skin. *A cloaking spell? But my assassin was a shifter, wasn't he?*

She dug her nails into the hand on her neck and pulled at the grip on her throat, but it didn't loosen. *How do I aim at what I can't see?* She dead weighted, hoping to loosen the grip, but he held firm. Her knees hit the floor. Black hair and golden eyes shimmered into view before her.

Amy gasped out. "Iris."

"I was rather hoping my name would be the last one on your lips, old friend, but no matter." He said as the illusion dissipated.

The gleam of a silver pocket watch with a black cat's eye in its center was the last thing she saw before her vision blurred and went black.

CHAPTER 5

$\mathcal{I}$ris's ear perked up when Amy's voice whispered their name. Iris slammed their half-filled pack shut and ran to Amy's apartment. Their feet pounding the pavement in time with their erratic heartbeats.

Iris's heart dropped into her stomach when they saw the front door ajar. Magic didn't push at Iris's skin when they entered the home. The salt line that had sealed the entrance was broken, and blood smeared the white tiled floor. Amy's phone lay discarded in the center of the living room.

Iris picked the phone up with shaking hands. *Did the assassin get her? Is she still alive?* They thought. Iris pulled up Naru's contact information and waited while the phone rang.

After three rings, Naru answered. "Amy. I thought you were going to go rally the shifters?"

Iris's voice shook when they spoke. "They got Amy."

Naru's words came out choked. "But how. Her house was encircled in barrier magic."

Iris scraped the toe of their shoe against the tile floor. "When I came in, something had cracked the tourmalines. I'm not sure if that's how the assassin got in or if they know enchanting magic. Either way, we should be cautious. It seems like Opal has powerful allies. I'll rally as many shifters as I can in the magic realm. I would suggest you find as many elementals to help as possible. We'll need them."

Naru's voice crackled on the other line. "I'll do my best. Let me know if you find out any information on Amy's whereabouts."

"I will." Iris clicked the end call button and pulled up the tickets. Now, they were glad that Amy had never been one to bother with putting passwords on her phone. *She's such an old young person.* Iris thought, staring at her brick-like excuse for a smartphone.

Iris opened up Amy's email and glanced down at the tickets. *The flight leaves in five hours, so I have to leave now if I want to make it in time and I don't have a driver's license. Great.* Iris opened up Karz and booked a ride.

They paced back and forth outside of Amy's door. *What am I going to do when I get to my old clan? Will they even listen to me after I disappeared for years? I haven't gone back there since the...experiments happened.*

Iris bit their lip and touched the amulet Amy had made them. The cat's eye gem around their neck could hide their transformations so long as no one touched them or talked to them while transformed. Iris clutched the pendant on their neck. They had to do this for the rest of the magic world. If they didn't fight back, Opal would destroy the Earth just like she'd destroyed the Enchantress and Sorceress clans.

Iris shuddered thinking back to the large dome of silver and gold magic blanketing their land. The screams that echoed throughout the land and Opal's hollow grey eyes emerging from the carnage with a smirk that haunted Iris's nightmares. *We need to stop her.* Iris thought to themself.

Iris reached up to adjust their hair and felt fur underneath their fingers. Their ears twitched when they touched one. Judging by the shape, it was rabbit ears, and Iris groaned.

Iris breathed deeply like they'd been taught when they

were young and still learning to control their shifting. After a couple of minutes, the ears retracted, and Iris's shoulders moved away from their ears.

When a honk sounded in front of Iris, they took a quick picture of the side of the car and the license plate before climbing into the passenger side door. *Hopefully he doesn't find out what I am.* The gem necklace wasn't one hundred percent foolproof. If he had magic blood in his veins, he had a chance of being able to see through the illusion.

When he turned back to look at Iris, his mouth was moving, but Iris zoned out. He frowned and waved a hand in front of Iris's face. Iris shook their head. "Sorry, I didn't get that. Can you say it again?"

He rolled his eyes. "Where are you heading?"

"Oh, sorry. I'm going to Fort Lauderdale airport."

He smiled, revealing a lone dimple. "Got it. We should be there in about thirty minutes. When is your flight?"

Iris glanced down at Amy's phone. "It's in about four hours or so. No rush." He gave Iris a thumbs up before turning back around.

On the way to the airport, Iris's thoughts kept drifting to Amy. *Will we make it in time, or will Opal kill her right away? But if her plan was to just kill her, why would Opal kidnap her?*

Iris ruffled their hair, and Amy's phone lit up with Naru's name. "Let me know how negotiations go once you touch down in the magic world."

Iris typed. *Will do.*

Her response came back immediately. *Where is the magic portal in Israel? I went there for a photography job in Israel before, but I never noticed it.*

Iris shook their head. There was still so much Naru had left to learn, but at least she wasn't on Opal's side. Her command of air and fire magic was amazing. Not many had managed to combine both elements to create lightning with no training. *Getting to the portal without humans noticing is tricky. It's nestled in the center of a huge prayer site and tourist attraction, The wailing wall.*

Got it. I never knew there were portals hidden in plain sight like that. Naru typed.

Iris scrunched their nose. *The beacons of magic needed for the portals have an interesting way of capturing human creativity.* Iris punched in, *They are able to remain there because only those with magic can see them. If anyone without magic tries to pass through the portal, they'll forget what they were doing.*

Actually, that makes a lot of sense. Maybe that's why the Bermuda triangle became famous. Naru replied.

That's a different story for a different day. Iris sent back and shoved the phone into their pocket.

As the airport came into view, Iris's muscles tensed. Crowds of people with suitcases swarmed the airport. Iris gripped the straps of their day bag tighter, and when their ride finally pulled up at the terminal, they added a tip using Amy's card. "Thanks." Iris said and flung the door open.

Iris kept their head down as they entered the airport. They covered their ears as the car drove away and gritted their teeth at the sound of thousands of people dragging their feet against the ground. The scrape of wheels on cement was like nails on a chalkboard. A fang poked out of Iris's mouth, and they were glad to be wearing Amy's pendant as a reminder that Amy was alive and that even if Iris changed in front of all these people no normal humans would notice.

Iris bit their lip and winced when they drew blood. They headed into the airport with their small overnight bag and placed their bandanna over their head in case their ears shifted. Even with the enchantment, they still had to worry about partially human mages with magic sight.

One ear was trying to poke through Iris's skull, causing a migraine. They rubbed at the top of their head and adjusted the bandanna as they trudged over to the check in machine to print their tickets.

Images of Amy chained up or being engulfed in silver and gold magic skittered through Iris's mind. They shivered as their ticket printed and snatched their ticket and bag tag for their lone carry on before rushing over to security with their forged human world passport.

Iris glanced down at the ID admiring the perfectly copied watermark. *What kind of friends in high places does Garnet have? If we survive this, I'll have to ask her about it.*

When Iris got over to the security, they had to slip off their bandana and pin back their ears. Thankfully, the illusion necklace was silver, so it didn't set off the alarm.

A tail pushed against the back of their pants as they stepped into the scanner. They froze when a man looked directly at them and cocked his head to the side. He didn't say anything and didn't approach. He just stared at her with his mouth agape. The amulet glowed in response like it recognized his presence. *Could he have magic?*

When he blushed, his mussed brown hair fell over his eyes, his violet eyes. The same eyes that were common in one clan, the Enchantress clan. He kept glancing over at Iris and rubbing at his ochre arms like he was trying to keep the chill off his skin in the warm airport.

Iris ripped their gaze from him and placed their arms above their head while the scanner ran over their body. The seconds ticked by too slowly as the TSA agent eyed their rainbow hair and golden-brown skin, but he cleared Iris. Iris grabbed their day bag and shoes from security, and their gaze flickered back to where the man had stood, but he wasn't there. Iris's stomach dropped. *He might have made a good ally.*

Iris felt a hand on their shoulder and whirled around to see the violet eyed man from before. "Hi. I saw you acting strange during the security check, and I had to ask." His gaze darted around, and he lowered his voice. "Are you a Sila? I saw animal ears poking out from under your bandana."

Iris blinked at him.

I guess that's what they call us here. It's just like the name used in the magic world. Iris nodded. "Yes, I am but they call us shifters here. How did you know what I was?"

He shrugged. "I was just guessing. I've always been able to see colors surrounding people, but when I try to explain it to anyone here...well let's just say I was told anything from 'you have synesthesia' to 'you belong in an asylum.'"

Iris wrinkled their nose. "You'll be pleased to know that you aren't out of your mind. You're just a...unique situation that this world isn't prepared to handle."

Iris held out their hand which was starting to sprout fur. "I'll give you my contact information in case you decide you'd like to help us. We could use someone like you. What's your name?"

He pushed back the hair from his face. "It's Ro'im, but you can call me Ro. Are you sure I'd be helpful?"

Iris nodded. "Yes. You have a rare gift of being able to see through illusion magic. Only a few clans have that ability and out of those clans only a handful of people in the entire clan can do what you just did. That would make you either an enchantment mage or a magic creature like me."

Iris's gaze was drawn to Ro'im's vivid violet eyes once more. "You have the same eyes as an enchantment mage. Do you feel a pull to any gemstones?"

He placed a hand to his eye. "No. Just the colors."

Iris glanced up at the schedule board. Their flight was scheduled to board in an hour. Iris grabbed his hand. "Let's walk and talk. If I don't hurry, I'll be late for my plane, and I still need to go through immigration. You aren't heading to Israel by chance, are you?"

He nodded. "That's where I'm from. Why?"

Iris pursed their lips. "How do you feel about visiting the magic world?"

His eyes widened. "There's a magic world?"

A fang poked out in Iris's smile, and their feet began to

shift. "Yes." Iris shoved their bag at him. "I'm going to need you to hold this for a bit. My body is refusing to stay in this form."

He took the bag and glanced away when Iris slipped their shirt over their head. "What are you doing? Won't someone see?"

"No, they won't, and I don't want my clothes to get destroyed. I was given the pendant I'm wearing by another Enchantment mage. It has illusion magic. Only you can see what I'm really doing." Fur itched at Iris's skin and the ground rose up to meet them. Iris sighed when whiskers sprouted on their face and their teeth lengthened. *At least this animal is small.* They glanced down to make sure the pendant had stayed in place. The mage gaped at Iris as they hopped over to customs.

"Not to be rude, but don't shifters usually turn into wolves or something?"

Iris's whiskers twitched as they looked up at Ro'im, their head cocked to one side. *I can't answer you.*

He smacked a hand into his palm. "That's right you can't tell me right now. I'll have to ask you when you change back."

Iris's ears fell back in what they hoped resembled annoyance, but Ro'im laughed in response. "I'll help you get through customs, but in exchange I want you to tell me everything. Ok?"

Iris nodded and his purple eyes glowed with excitement. He practically skipped over to the line with Iris's passport in hand. Even though Iris had a fake U.S. passport, and Ro'im had a real Israeli one, he somehow convinced the person working at the desk that Iris wasn't able to speak right now because they had laryngitis, and that he had to help Iris through the line.

Iris's body stubbornly refused to change back, and they were starting to wonder what they'd do if they changed into something odd when they had to go see the other shifters. Iris wasn't sure if they were ready for Luna and the rest of their clan to see what had become of their ex leader.

Once Iris and Ro'im got to the waiting area, Ro looked at Iris and then glanced down at his ticket. "My flight is going to Israel, but it looks like we're on different planes. I can at least stay with you until you...change back." He said with a smile.

Iris hopped along beside him until they made it to the gate. Iris had to stand by the chairs since sitting down would give them away. He kept glancing over at Iris. "I know you can't talk, but don't you have another way to communicate when you're like that?"

Iris shook their head. *Not unless you suddenly become a shifter or develop telepathy.*

His leg bobbed up and down while he sat in the chair. "The suspense is killing me. I want to know about this magic world."

As if he'd willed it into being, Iris's bones began to crack. Iris had to bite down on their tongue to keep from crying out in pain as limbs rearranged themselves and fur shortened, revealing skin.

Iris crossed their hands over their chest, knowing damn well it did next to nothing to cover their chest. Iris held out their hand. "Mind handing me my clothes?" Iris shoved his shoulder, and he moved a hand away from his eyes.

He made the mistake of looking down and his face flushed. "Sorry. I was trying not to look." He said.

"Don't worry about it." They grabbed the clothing and walked towards the bathroom. "I'll be right back." Iris shifted uncomfortably when people made eye contact with them. Iris was glad the people here couldn't see what they really looked like right now because it would be quite the spectacle.

The line for the bathroom stalls went to the door, and Iris tapped their foot impatiently. A faint groan escaped their lips and three women turned and stared at them. Iris ground their teeth together, stifling any more verbal complaints.

One woman with sleek black hair tapped Iris on the shoulder and flashed a timid smile. "Don't worry about them. I like your rainbow hair by the way. What's your name?" Iris sucked in a breath at the woman's touch, glad they weren't shifted right now.

Iris smiled back at her. "I'm Iris. What about you?"

She flushed. "My name is Chihiro, like the girl from that movie."

Iris raised an eyebrow. "What movie?"

She laughed. "Never mind. I don't mean to be so forward, but do you live around here?"

When Iris flashed her an easy smile, Chihiro's ears turned pink. "I'm a bit of a wanderer. I don't tend to stay in one place all that long. Why?"

Chihiro batted her eyelashes, and Iris already had an idea of where this was going. "Can I get your number?"

Iris sighed. "Unfortunately, I don't have a phone on me, but you're welcome to write yours down for me." Iris smiled and held out her hand.

Chihiro grabbed a pen and scrap paper from her bag and scribbled down her number before placing it in Iris's open palm.

"I'll call you." Iris said with a smile as a door to the restroom opened, and Iris slipped into the stall.

Iris leaned against the closed door and crumpled the paper before tossing it into the bin. "Better luck next time, Chihiro." Iris mumbled and slipped on their pants and shirt, gathering their thoughts so they could figure out what they'd say to Ro'im. Iris felt like they knew him somehow, but they couldn't place why.

When Iris left the bathroom and headed over to the gate, he still stood there with Iris's bag. His eyes lit up and he bounced on the balls of his feet as Iris approached. Ro closed the gap between them with two long strides. "Can you tell me about the magic world now?"

Iris clapped a hand over his mouth. "Please say that a little louder. I don't think the people on the other side of the airport heard you."

His gaze fell to the floor, and he lowered his voice. "Sorry. I was just excited. Please tell me more about the magic world and the enchantment mages."

Iris gestured to one of the chairs near the gate. "Your kind of mage uses gems to channel magic. Enchantment mages with higher magic potential have familiars that they get on their eighteenth birthday. If you never had a Choosing, there's a chance a familiar is still waiting in Gemstone Forest to bond with you." *If that familiar wasn't killed in the war*, Iris thought.

His eyes widened. "A familiar? Really?"

Iris nodded. "Normally, you would go into Gemstone Forest for a Choosing and a familiar would pick you but..." Iris's voice trailed off, and they focused their gaze on the wall.

He shook her shoulder. "But what?"

Iris couldn't meet his gaze. "But you were born here, so you weren't able to complete your Choosing."

He narrowed his eyes at Iris. "That's not the only reason. What aren't you telling me?"

Iris's gaze unfocused, and Ro'im's voice faded. Iris rubbed at their eyes as gold and silver swarmed the land in a thick smoke. Their skin burned as they pushed towards Gemstone Forest. The scenery felt fuzzy as they walked. Silver and gold magic drew closer, fragmenting the familiar's crystal bodies. Iris gasped for air as the magic choked them, draining the life from their skin and the air from their lungs, but they couldn't leave. Iris had to save their comrade, the shifter with enchantment magic.

Iris felt a phantom touch on their shoulder. The image of black hair and golden eyes before them shook. A pocket watch with a black gem at its center dangled from the mage's pants. Iris froze when they saw Opal beside him. Traitor. Iris reached out for the shifter, but their vision blurred.

A faint voice whispered "Iris. Iris. Snap out of it."

The shaking jostled Iris, and the images blurred around them. The howling screaming of the dying and the burn of silver and gold magic was replaced by a steady grip and burning violet gaze. Iris's throat felt raw and people all over the airport stared at them. *This is real. You aren't in the war anymore, Iris.*

Iris gulped air, but their hands shook as they sat down in the chair. "Sorry. When I talk about the past, sometimes my mind gets trapped in memories of the war." Iris gripped the arm of the chair. "Gemstone Forest was destroyed by a leader who let a need for vengeance overrule compassion and common sense."

Ro placed a hand on Iris's shoulder. "I'm sorry to hear that."

Iris licked their parched lips. "Be glad you weren't there when it happened. People and familiars were screaming and running with their faces half burned off. You would never know it was done by one angry enchantment mage."

He shivered. "That sounds like a nuclear bomb. How did you survive?"

Iris glanced at the boarding gate and then back to him. "Shifters heal quicker than most clans but walking through there was still painful. The ravaged land drains your life force."

His face went white. "Who would do something like that?"

Iris sighed. "An enchantress with a vendetta and far too much power. She got control of a powerful enchanted sword after watching her lover killed before her eyes. I can't entirely say I blame her for seeking vengeance, but her actions were unforgivable."

"I see." He said and ran his fingers through his hair.

"Final boarding call for the 9:30 PM flight to Israel," droned over the loudspeaker.

Ro's head popped up. "That's my flight. I'm sorry but I have to go. Let me give you my messenger username and you can contact me when you touch down." He grabbed Iris's phone, downloaded the app, and added his name in before shoving it into their hands.

"I'm sorry about what happened, and I hope you succeed in overthrowing her." He said before turning to run towards the exit gate as they announced the final boarding call over the loudspeakers.

Iris's stomach turned at the thought of overly salted airplane food. They glanced at the clock. There was still another thirty minutes before their flight started boarding, so they slipped into the line for the closest cafe. They sipped a coffee that smelled of vanilla and hazelnut and nibbled on a blueberry scone. They glanced at the gate every couple of minutes to make sure the plane didn't leave without them.

Iris's limbs felt weak and their nerves frazzled as they made their way to the boarding area. They waltzed to the back of the line and checked Amy's phone to see a message from Naru.

Ren has some ideas to get us some allies, but it's dangerous. If you see a Florida woman headline with my face, you'll know what happened.

The message chilled the blood in Iris's veins. This rebellion seemed like more and more of a suicide mission by the second. Iris only hoped that they'd be able to gather enough allies to succeed. They clicked the phone shut as they found their seat and slid their bag into the overhead compartment.

Iris gulped down water and a couple sleeping pills as the flight attendant went through the safety instructions. As the plane reached its full altitude, Iris shut their eyes and drifted off to sleep.

CHAPTER 6

*A*my opened her eyes, but all she saw was black. Fabric scratched against her eyelashes. *A blindfold?* Amy tried to reach for her face, but metal dug into her wrist. Amy's magic pressed against her skin like a soda that had been shaken and left unopened. She wriggled in the chair and metal pressed against her torso. The lack of the weight on her hip told her she'd been stripped of her gemstone pouch.

A familiar laugh echoed through the room and sent a chill down her spine. "I'm glad Dusk brought you in alive. I want to see your face when I kill your sister."

Amy bit her lip hard enough to draw blood, and sweat dripped down the back of her neck.

Opal removed the blindfold. Silver hair shone in the fluorescent lights and slate gray eyes bore into Amy's gold ones.

That stare made Amy's blood boil with an anger she hadn't felt since she'd been drafted for the war. Her lips curled up into a snarl. "You should have killed me when you had the chance. If you've laid a finger on my sister, I'll make you pay." Amy hocked up her saliva and spat in Opal's face. *Why did I do that? Am I stupid?* Amy felt like a helpless twelve-year-old all

68

over again lashing out with her tongue since she couldn't lash out with fists.

Opal's smile disappeared. Stars danced in her vision, and her cheek burned. Opal cupped the tender skin on Amy's face in a rough grip, forcing their gazes to meet. "If you insult me like that again, I'll run you through with my sword."

Amy struggled against the chains, and glanced down to see a trail of blood. The lead chains had small spikes that dug into her skin. Amy smirked. "I guess I hit a sore spot. Are you mad that I dared spit on our great and powerful Council leader?"

Opal's face flushed, and she squeezed Amy's chin. "Because of you, someone I cared for is dead. You put our entire nation in jeopardy because of your reckless behavior. If you hadn't fought in that battle, Joan might still be alive. I did what I had to do." Her voice shook.

Amy bared her teeth. "I was twelve and didn't know better. You were our leader. Instead of choosing what was best for your people, you chose what you thought was best for yourself. You killed the Magic Council that was supposed to balance the power and reformed it to feed your need for more power and your even more massive ego." she said, her voice rising to a yell.

Opal sucked in a breath. "You're wrong. That Magic Council was corrupt, and the power balance skewed with the headquarters in Sorceress territory. I rebuilt the Council with members of merit. I moved the new Council's base somewhere neutral. I took out the Sorceresses and their corrupt Council members, so they'd stop trying to seize our clan and kill off leaders like Joan. I even contracted myself to this monster of a dragon familiar to gain enough power to keep the Magic Council from seizing Excalibur." She said brandishing the fused Clarent and Excalibur which glowed gold and silver.

Amy rolled her eyes. "You got the most powerful sword in the land and a dragon familiar to do your bidding. I don't see how I'm meant to feel sorry for you. You killed my sister, but you don't see me going on a revenge driven rampage."

Opal swung the sword at Amy's leg and pain lanced through her. Amy bit down on her tongue. *I won't give you the satisfaction of seeing me cry.* She looked down to see blood drip from the wound. Opal slashed at Amy's left hand with a smile. "You talk too much, maybe I should aim for your tongue next."

The sword glowed and Amy clenched her teeth together and turned her gaze downward.

Opal's forehead scrunched up, and she stopped her sword mid swing. "Why not?" Opal said to the air. She placed a hand on her hip. "Fine." Opal grabbed a cloth from her gem bag and wiped the sword clean before sheathing it once more. "My familiar Clarent makes an excellent point. I still have something I need from you before I can...dispose of you. Why were you able to kill that soldier in the war? What you did wasn't just enchantress magic. What are you?"

Amy raised an eyebrow. "I don't know, but if you figure it out, tell me." Then a thought crossed her mind, and she looked down to see that the amber necklace was gone.

Opal's lip curved up in a smile as she pulled the pendant from the pocket of her black pants. "Were you looking for this? Dusk told me you used it to stop him the first time. Now tell me what you are, or I'll kill Garnet."

Amy's face went paper white, but she forced a laugh. "You act as if you weren't planning on doing it anyway. If you want me to tell you anything you need to free my sister first."

Opal's hand clenched around the pendant, and Amy gulped. The sound of Opal's laugh grated on Amy's nerves. "That's cute. You think you're in a position to make demands. I'm curious about your lineage, but not that curious. Even if you're dead, I'm sure I could torture the answers out of your sister, or I guess she's your half-sister. She was too ordinary to be your full relative. Although she put up a decent fight when I went to capture her. We had to rough her up a bit."

Amy's nose wrinkled, and her gaze snapped up to meet Opal's. "If she dies, I will hunt you to the ends of the Earth. I don't care if you have the strongest weapon Merlin ever created. I will kill you."

Opal clucked her tongue. "We both know if you were able to do that you would have done it a long time ago. Instead, you ran and hid like the coward you are."

Amy scanned the room for anything she could use to escape. Her gemstone pouch and familiar bracelet lay on the opposite side of the room. The fluorescent light glinted off the amethyst bracelet, but it was out of reach. *If I can escape from these chains, maybe.*

Opal's gaze followed hers, and she walked over to the bag and the bracelet and scooped them up off of the floor. "Don't get any ideas. I'll ensure that these are locked away safe and sound when I leave. Dusk will be here soon to search you for any potential weapons."

She stroked Amy's cheek, and Amy bit her hand. The scent of copper and sugar filled her mouth, and she spit it on the floor. *Why does her blood taste like malachite poisoning?* Amy squinted at Opal's now exposed arm. malachite green veins encircled her forearm and crept along Opal's sword hand, pulsing under her skin. Her nail beds were radioactive green.

Opal forced her sleeve back down. "You saw, didn't you?" She grabbed a fistful of Amy's hair and yanked her head up. Her normally grey eyes were threaded through with silver and gold. "Try that again if you want to see what Clarent's wrath looks like."

Opal's gaze froze Amy as surely as facing down a dragon's maw.

"That's what I thought." She said and released Amy's hair.

Tears welled in Amy's eyes when a hair pin stabbed her scalp.

Opal smirked at Amy before sweeping her hair back, turning on her heel, and striding out of the room with the Twin Swords at her hip and Amy's gemstones in her hand.

The moment the door clicked shut beside her, Amy bucked desperately at the restraints, trying to find some way to allow a hand or finger to slip free, but all she succeeded in doing was making the chains bite viciously into her ankles and wrists. Each movement made her chest and lungs seize up, but she still craned her neck, searching for anything that might help her escape.

The malachite poisoning on her arm is severe, but how did she get it? Maybe Merlin's seal on Excalibur's sheath broke when Opal fused the two swords. It would explain why the poison was coming from the sword. I have to tell the others, but I can't do that here.

Amy thought back to the War of the Twin Swords and one detail stuck in her mind. When she'd been distressed, she'd thrown a man back into a tree...without touching him. If she had telekinetic magic, it wasn't affected by iron or lead. She had a chance to escape. It was a long shot, but it was worth a try.

She closed her eyes and thought about her village in a smoldering ruin because of Opal's need for revenge. Anger boiled up within her, but she shoved it down, focusing on one thing...her golden hair clip.

She pictured the clip slipping free from her hair and picking the lock. It tugged at her scalp painfully, and she cracked open an eye to see it floating before her. "Yes." escaped her lips just before the pin clattered to the ground.

Amy's ears strained listening for footsteps. When the room remained silent, she tried again. This time, she kept her eyes open when she focused on the pin. It rose slowly but steadily this time, floating closer to the lock. *If I can unlock the chains on my wrist maybe I can get out of here.*

The pin scraped metal but didn't make it into the lock. It fell from the air and into her lap. Her breathing came in gasps after just two attempts. *How am I supposed to escape using magic I didn't even know I had?* It was like she'd been handed a spoon and asked to dig a lake. Her face dripped with sweat, and her eyes drooped. Amy leaned back into the chair and her vision blurred and faded to black.

~

WHEN A DARK CHUCKLE echoed through the room, Amy bolted upright causing her muscles to seize up. Her nose itched, and her legs tingled with pins and needles when she tried to move them.

Dusk approached her, his golden eyes tracked her movements. His walk was lithe and graceful as a cat's, but something clattered at his side. It sounded like gemstones, but that didn't make sense. *Why would a shifter carry a gem pouch? Unless he really is Night.*

She trained her gaze in the direction the sound had come from, but she couldn't see anything. She desperately wished for a green and purple fluorite gem to dissolve whatever illusion was hiding the source of the noise.

He caught her staring at his waist, "I can't tell if you're admiring me or looking for a way to kill me." The cadence of his voice was rough and slightly off beat, familiar. She couldn't place where, but his words haunted her mind.

Amy leered at Opal. "Why don't you come closer and find out?"

"Because I'm not a fool. I've fought alongside you once before. Don't you remember me, old friend?"

Amy narrowed her eyes. "Did you fight in the War of the Twin Swords? Did you once go by a different name? I thought I heard gemstones on your belt, but what use would an assassin have for a noisy weapon like gemstones?"

Dusk clutched something at his side. "You got all that from a sound? I don't think I gave you enough credit." A shiver went down her spine when he ran a taloned finger along her chest. "I've gone by several names and several faces."

Her back stiffened. "You had a pocket watch with a cat's eye. I saw it when you captured me, and you keep calling me old friend. Who are you really?"

His hand grabbed the fabric of her shirt, pulling her into the metal chains. "If you don't know by now, you're either in denial or you forgot about me. It's a shame. I could have helped you if you hadn't abandoned me."

Abandoned him. I'd never abandon a friend. This doesn't sound like Night, but I have to ask.

He flashed her a feral smile. "We were allies once, but I was a fool to think you could be trusted."

Amy's skin stung from the chains, but she kept her eyes on him. "Are you part enchantment mage? Did you used to go by Night?"

Peals of laughter echoed off the metal walls of the room. "I was wondering when you'd remember. Perhaps your memory has begun to fail you and at such a young age. What a shame."

He looked so different, but she should have recognized him sooner.

Tears pricked her eyes, and her voice came out a whisper. "Night? You're okay."

Dusk's lips curled up into a snarl. "I'm thriving no thanks to you. And I'm not Night anymore. That name died along with our friendship when you handed me over to Opal. Lucky for you she decided to take me in instead of kill me, but perhaps that's because she doesn't know who or what I am."

Amy's nails dug into her palm. "I'm so sorry Ni-I mean Dusk. Garnet didn't give me a choice that day. She knocked me out, and by the time I regained consciousness we were several states away."

His talons lengthened, and he pressed one into her leg. "You expect me to believe that? Just after you'd been 'kidnapped' Naru left the room. The next thing I knew Opal was barging in looking for you and your sister. She'd told me your sister offered me up in exchange for her own safe passage."

Amy shook her head. "That doesn't make sense then why would Opal capture Garnet now if she'd bargained for her safety? Why would Garnet do something like that?"

Dusk shrugged. "Maybe you can ask her from the grave. Opal is planning to execute her as soon as she gets the okay from the Council. Her crime was severe enough where The Magic Council got the jurisdiction to hold the sentencing for her crimes without a trial."

Amy's shoulders tensed. "What crime?"

He pressed a finger to her chest. "You're looking at the charges. Aiding and abetting a fugitive and a murderer."

Amy's skin flushed, and the hair pin stirred against her leg. "After the war, I stood before Opal and the Council in the courtroom. I told them Joan's death wasn't my fault and that man I killed in battle was an enemy. But the Council feared Opal and refused to oppose her. She's a sadistic dictator who bullied our courts into disregarding the evidence. She charged me as an adult. I may have gone to my Choosing and yes, I was a legal adult according to the Enchantress clan laws, but I was 12 years old. I may have consented to fight in the battle, but Opal was the one who enlisted me in the first place. The blame for Joan's death should rest solely on her shoulders, not mine."

Amy's voice froze in her throat when Dusk's grip on her leg tightened. "She's not some heartless dictator. You're wrong about her, and you'll regret choosing the losing side in the upcoming war. That I promise you." The pouch clacked, and a black glow flickered in her vision, the cat's eye pocket watch briefly came into view.

If this is Night, how can he hear me? He'd always signed and read lips, but I wasn't looking at him the whole time I was speaking. Amy searched for any sign of a hearing aid but found none.

75

She suspected his magic could hide a hearing device if he'd hidden the pocket watch. Amy focused her gaze on the hair pin in her lap. If she could disrupt the functions of whatever he was using to hear her, perhaps that would be enough of a distraction for her to escape. But first she needed to get out of these chains. She needed to buy time.

When she wriggled against the shackles again, he smiled. "You're not getting out of those. They were designed to dampen enchantment magic."

Amy bit her tongue and wiggled her legs. "It's not that. I just need to use the bathroom."

Dusk clicked his tongue. "Well, I guess you'll have to piss yourself. I'll leave before this place reeks of vinegar and despair. See you." He wrinkled his nose and released his hand from her leg before turning his back to her and heading for the exit door. As he left the room, his illusion flickered, and she caught the outline of a brown device cradling his ear.

When the door slammed shut behind him, she got back to work with the golden pin.

CHAPTER 7

*T*he portal pulsed a vivid violet as Iris approached it alone. Their gaze searched the mob of tourists, making sure none of their eyes were on Iris before they stepped a foot into the inky chasm. Iris's legs wobbled when they appeared in the tunnel, and they raised an ear to the sky listening for the scrabbling of claws or an inhuman howl.

They used the barren tree branches to hold themselves up, their eyes skimming for the glimmer of teeth so as not to be caught by a ravenous portal creature. They clomped towards the shimmering black hole marking the other side.

The portal's exit was only a few dozen yards away when a mix between a howl and a human scream echoed through the clearing, sending a shiver down Iris's spine. They quickened their pace, but every step was like trying to walk along a trampoline while several people bounced on it. The ground beneath Iris vibrated with every step, the tenuous magical connection between worlds frayed, threatening to snap.

Out of the corner of their eye, Iris caught a glimpse of matted fur and twisted horns. The creature's hooves pawed at the ground and the fetid stench of rotting flesh hit Iris's nose.

A snarl erupted beside them. Iris broke into a run. When they glimpsed the creature's claws lifting off the ground and hurtling towards them, Iris dove for the black circle writhing just a few feet ahead.

Iris's arms scraped dirt and they bit their tongue to keep from crying out when their chin scraped the ground. Their hands went over their head expecting to be torn apart, but when the world around them was silent. They peeked through their fingers.

There were mounds of sand as far as the eye could see. A pool of water sparkled in the distance, and if they didn't know better, they'd think it was a mirage. The sun painted the sky flamingo pinks and monarch butterfly oranges as it set over the horizon.

When Iris pushed up off the sand, the wind whipped past them, sending a shiver through their body, and they shrugged the backpack off their shoulders.

Claw marks ran along the pack's fabric and a shirt spilled out of the opening. Iris gulped. *That could have easily been me. Maybe I should have brought Ro'im to make myself less of an easy target.*

Most of the clothing in the pack was shredded or torn including the lone sweater that they'd packed. Iris sighed. Ears pressed against their skull, feeling like a hammer to their head, but instead of fighting the change, Iris slid off their clothing and tossed it into the destroyed bag.

The change ran through them like a shot of adrenaline. Their pulse quickened, and a howl tore from their throat as fur slid from skin and Iris lowered to the ground.

Their surroundings were painted in shades of red and blue. The sand along their feet was a blue tinged white. Iris's snout wrinkled at the lingering scent of rotting flesh from the Soul hound's saliva as they picked up the destroyed bag.

Iris ran to their old clan, feet flying along the sand, kicking it up in all directions. The sun had almost set when Iris reached the metal arch with intertwined wolves marking the clan's entrance. Iris was home.

A familiar voice shouted "Iris! Is that really you?"

Iris's ears swiveled at the sound of their name, and they turned to see long black hair change to fur as Luna leapt into the air, landing paws first into Iris's side and toppling them to the ground. Luna's snout nuzzled against Iris's fur. *I thought I smelled you, but I had to see it with my own eyes. When you didn't come back from the human world, I'd feared the worst.* Luna smacked Iris's muzzle with a paw. *Why didn't you come back sooner? I thought you were dead. I never thought you'd abandon your own clan. We were supposed to lead together you, me, and...Kito.*

I'm sorry Luna. I... Iris couldn't finish the thought because Luna sniffed Iris and a growl escaped her throat.

Luna pinned Iris down with a paw. *Why do I smell an enchantress on you? You aren't working for Opal, are you?*

Iris shook their head. *No, it's nothing like that. I've been training the enchantress that Opal wishes to kill, but that's a long story. Perhaps we should shift back first?*

When Iris lifted their head, they'd caught the attention of a handful of wolf shifters, the golden gaze of an eagle shifter with his wings spread, and a lynx shifter with her muscles coiled and fangs bared.

Luna's gaze met Iris's and then her fur rippled, and bones cracked. Iris turned away when she transformed. *I think I've spent too long in the human world. Why am I embarrassed to see my own girlfriend naked?*

Luna nudged Iris. "Come on. There's no need to be shy all of a sudden."

Iris huffed but raised their head. *Please let the transformation work.* Iris focused on calming their emotions. At first nothing happened, but when they closed their eyes fur shortened, smoothing into skin. A hawk shifter kept flicking his gaze between Iris and Luna with his feathers ruffled.

Iris crossed her arms over her bare breasts and Luna

raised an eyebrow. "I know you've been gone awhile, but I've never known you to be the modest type," she said. Her lips curled up in a grin.

Iris's face flushed. "A lot has changed since then, love."

Luna turned to face the group and put an arm around Iris's shoulder. "This is Iris." Luna turned to look at them. "Is it they or she right now?"

Iris gave a small smile. "They."

Luna cleared her throat. "For the new members here, they were a former co-leader of this clan and one of my partners. Iris aided us in obtaining a truce with the Kitsune clan several generations ago. Regardless of what you may think about their prolonged absence from this clan, if you harm them, you will face severe punishment, understand?"

Iris felt a glare on them that raised the hairs on their arms and legs. Luna called out, "Ze'ev. Don't you dare."

A sandy colored wolf stalked towards Iris with hackles raised and fangs bared. Luna barreled after him, picking him up by the scruff of his neck. He turned and attempted to snap at her, and she smacked him on the nose. "You know better. Go back to your tent until you can learn to be polite to our guest."

A girl with auburn hair that matched the wolf's fur bared her teeth and spat. "They're no guest former leader or not. They're an intruder, and they reek of enchantress magic. That thing around their neck holds one of their illusions. If they're an ally, what are they hiding?"

Iris's hands reached to the necklace Amy had given them. "I'd completely forgotten about this. I wore it on the plane in case…"

Iris placed a hand over their mouth. Luna nudged Iris's shoulder. "In case what?" Luna whispered.

Iris threw a glare at the twin wolf, Ayla. "Thanks a lot."

"It's your fault for not being entirely honest," she sneered.

Luna ran a hand through her hair. "Iris what aren't you telling me?"

Iris rolled their shoulder, "I'll tell you about it, but I'd like to speak with you alone."

Luna nodded. "You're all dismissed. Please continue about your day. I will speak to our guest, in private."

Gradually everyone left the clearing, and Luna pushed Iris towards their old home. She shoved open the door and led Iris into the cobbled stone walls of the home they'd once shared with Luna and Kito. Despite the evening's chill outside, the inside of Luna's home warmed Iris's skin the moment they stepped through the door.

Luna gestured to a brown fabric sofa in the small living room. Iris plopped into the chair while Luna perched on one of its arms. "Tell me everything, but let's start with why you didn't contact me. I thought you were dead. I mourned your loss."

Iris pursed their lips. "I didn't want you to see me after what the humans did to me."

She placed a hand over Iris's. "Iris, I missed you. You'll always have a place here." Luna placed a hand on her chest. "No matter what the humans did. I'm sorry you didn't feel safe enough to come back here." Tears gleamed in her eyes, and Iris wiped them away with a thumb, but one of Iris's nails lengthened into a claw, and they jerked away. A small scratch marred Luna's cheek. "I'm sorry. I didn't mean to. Are you okay?"

Luna placed a hand to the already healing scratch on her face. Her eyes flickered to Iris's hidden hand. Her head cocked to one side. "I'll be fine, but why did you just lose control of your shifting?"

Iris sighed. "The experiments. Some scientists captured me when I was in animal form, probably thinking I was a regular wolf, and when I transformed in their lab...they ran experiments on me. It changed my shifting, made it unstable. It's like when we were kids only worse. That's why I have the necklace."

"I'm sorry. I had no idea. Maybe a healer can help you?" She took Iris's hand, the one with a lone claw protruding from the skin and threaded their fingers together.

"Unfortunately, I don't think what they did is reversible," Iris's lips turned down into a frown.

She squeezed Iris's hand. "We can at least try. If need be, I will track down the humans that did this and make sure they fix this. If they can't, they'll pay with their lives. What they did was beyond evil."

Iris brushed hair from Luna's face. "Right now, we have bigger problems to deal with. We need to save Amy and her sister from Opal before it's too late."

Luna's gaze darkened, and her back stiffened. "If that's the case, you should consider her lost. Even with an army, we hardly stand a chance at defeating her. Look what she did to Gemstone Forest and the sorceress clan."

Iris lifted her chin, so their gazes met. "I have never known you to back down from a fight."

Her eyes filled with tears. "A lot has happened in your absence. Opal's assassin. He killed Kito. I couldn't stop him."

Iris placed a hand over their mouth. "How? When?"

Luna's voice cracked. "The bastard killed Kito by cutting off his tails one by one. It happened a few months after you went missing."

Luna held up her arm to reveal a long, thin, pink scar. "When I heard the shrieking, I went over to his home."

Luna's voice sounded hollow, and Iris gave her leg a light squeeze. "It's okay. You don't have to talk about it if it's too painful."

She gulped. "No. You need to hear this in case you ever see him. He's a shifter. A hawk shifter. When I tried to stop him, he lunged at me with talons and it caught me by surprise. He'd clawed into my arm, and I'd flinched away. I tried to jump on top of Kito, but there was some sort of magic barrier up. I should have screamed and called for backup, or done something but instead I clawed at the barrier while he got torn up. I ran for help when he begged me to stop fighting, but by then it was too late. I can't let that happen to anyone else," Luna said the last words so quietly that Iris barely heard them. She leaned against Iris's shoulder.

Iris pushed back Luna's bangs and kissed her forehead. "It won't happen again. We'll stick together so it can't happen again."

Luna shivered. "A few hours before you came here, he paid us a visit."

Iris bit her lip. "I didn't expect Opal to get someone here so quickly. What did he say?"

Luna covered her face with her hand. "Opal has a teleportation mage on her side. He warned us that you would come. He said if we joined you in the fight, our clan would meet the same fate as Gemstone Forest, and he offered sanctuary to any shifter that brings Opal your head."

A shiver went down Iris's spine. *That explains the angry stares and why that younger shifter tried to attack me.* Iris pulled Luna into a hug. "I will not force your people to fight, but we need aid and most of the enchantresses will not turn on their leader. Amy's own people abandoned her when Opal went on her rampage, and she has few allies. Regardless of your decision, I will go and save her. I can't stay here knowing Opal is hurting her." Iris placed their hand over their heart.

Luna gave a weak smile. "Risking your life for others. Why does that not surprise me? I can't let you have all the fun. I'm coming with you."

"Are you sure?"

Luna pressed her lips to Iris's collarbone. "For you, I

would travel to hell itself and even you wouldn't be able to stop me." Then Luna's head cocked to one side, and she picked up Iris's bag. "Your pack is glowing. Is it meant to do that?"

Iris cocked their head to one side and reached into the bag. A stone glowed golden brown. Iris's eyes widened. "That's right. Amy gave me this so she could communicate with me. Maybe she's sending a message." Iris pulled the stone out and placed their hand on it. The message "Opal's weakness. Malachite curse," appeared in the air.

"What is a Malachite curse?" Luna asked.

Iris stared down at the stone. "I think Amy told me about this when I was working with malachite at her shop. Those gems absorb toxins like radiation and the poisonous residue from some spells. It can be enchanted so that if it breaks all toxins held within it seep into you, slowly killing you."

Luna rose from her chair and straightened her back, lifting her chin high. "This is good. We have a weakness we can exploit. That means we have a chance. I will speak to the others, but even with this knowledge I don't expect many to join. Few are willing to face such a powerful threat."

Iris nodded. "I understand. Thank you for helping me even if I did abandon the pack."

Luna cupped Iris's cheek. "I knew you'd never leave unless it was to protect someone. It's okay to take actions to protect yourself and your heart. Now, come with me. We'll greet them together." Luna reached out her hand and Iris took it, following Luna into the courtyard.

Luna strode as lightly as an air elemental with a gust of wind beneath her feet. She put her hands to her mouth and gave three long, sharp whistles. Wolf, lynx, fox, coyote, eagle, and even a rabbit and ox shifter appeared in the clearing.

The prey animal shifters hung towards the back in human form, but their scent was unmistakable. The rabbit shifter smelled of clover and wildflowers. He was short with messy platinum blonde hair and hid behind an ox shifter with a massive chest and broad shoulders with swirling tattoos adorning his warm brown skin. His black hair was pulled back in a ponytail.

Luna cleared her throat, drawing everyone's attention. "You may have noticed that we have a visitor here," she said, gesturing to Iris. "I know we thought them dead, but they're back to request our aid in saving Amy, Opal's most hated enemy. Amy has been captured by Opal, and Iris plans to rescue her."

"Why should we help them? They abandoned their position as leader when they abandoned us." Ayla snapped.

Luna looked directly in Ayla's eyes, making her squirm. "Because Iris is still your leader just as I am whether you'd like to acknowledge that or not. And we've received word about a weakness that we can use to take her down. While I will not force you to join this fight, I will accompany Iris in this battle with or without you. Regardless of what that hawk shifter told you, you aren't safe if you choose Opal's side. Attack my guest, and I will consider it treason, and we all know the punishment for treason," Luna said with a low warning growl.

Low murmurs hummed through the crowd, and Iris's gaze skimmed over dozens of scowling faces. Ayla glanced at her brother Ze'ev, the same brother that had attacked Iris earlier, and they both stepped forward. "We will join you! Where Luna goes, we go." Ayla said with her chin jutted up.

At that, Luna held up a hand. "Your brother almost hurt Iris earlier and you're both still too young to join a battle. You're still learning to control your shifting."

The girl's eyes darkened, and she shouted. "Our parents died because of Opal. I'm sorry for our actions earlier, but Iris abandoned the pack. How were we supposed to react?"

Ayla's grip on her brother's hand tightened, and Ze'ev

mumbled. "I'm sorry for earlier as well. I let my anger control me. Coming back after almost five years like nothing had happened." He stared down at his palms. "Did we mean nothing to you?" His gaze searched Iris's.

"It's not about that. I had to help a friend who was being hurt by Opal too. I guess you can say she's like an adopted pack member to me now, but it doesn't mean I forgot about you."

The young shifter squared his shoulders. "I think I understand." Determination glinted in his eyes when he looked up at Luna. "Can we join you, please?"

Iris's gaze darted to Luna, gauging her response. She placed a hand on Ze'ev's shoulder. "You can join us, but I'm keeping you away from the front lines. If it gets too dangerous, you'll be ordered to run. Understand?"

The twin shifters saluted her. "Yes ma'am." and then moved to stand beside Luna.

"Anyone else?" Luna asked.

The remaining shifters whispered amongst themselves, but no one else stepped forward. Iris's heart dropped into their stomach. *This isn't nearly enough.*

Iris was ready to sink into the floor when a man with a shock of hair the color of desert sand and a strong vanilla scent like a cactus flower lingering on his skin stepped forward. *That can't be him, can it?* His broad shoulders and cold scowl caused the rest of the shifters to move aside as he cut through the crowd, and when she passed him, she caught fox tails peeking out from the waistband of his pants. A fox demon, a Kitsune, and Kito's brother at that. *He's much bigger than the pint-sized hyperactive teen I remember.*

Eiji stood beside Luna and placed a hand on her shoulder. "I'll join you. I have an ally in the west. If we can convince them, we'll have a better chance at surviving this fight."

When his hair fell over his face, and he smiled at the

crowd of shifters, he looked so much like Kito that it tugged at Iris's heartstrings. It must have created the same reaction in Luna because her voice caught when she said, "Are you sure, Eiji?"

He nodded. "Like you said. Regardless of what side we pick, we aren't safe here. Especially if you won't be here to lead and protect the clan."

Luna's gaze dropped to the floor. "I'm sorry I couldn't protect your brother."

Eiji squeezed her shoulder. "It's not your fault. You did everything you could. No one expected one of our own to betray us like that," His gaze flicked to Iris when he spoke.

Guilt pricked Iris at the double meaning behind his words and glance. *As if I don't feel bad enough about not coming back. I can't take the disappointed look from you too.* Iris shied away from Eiji's as he spoke to the rest of the clan. "If you refuse to fight, you shouldn't dare call yourself a shifter or a member of this clan. Unless you want shifters to be known as cowards."

That drew a few hateful stares from the crowd. The oxen shifter pushed through the crowd, towing a rabbit shifter along even as he dug in his heels, protesting each step. Iris raised an eyebrow at the rabbit, but he crossed his arms over his chest. "If he's fighting, I'm fighting. He won't give me a choice."

Luna cocked her head to one side. "Are you sure you want to do this? You are both prey shifters."

The oxen shifter bit his lip. "You shouldn't have said that."

The rabbit shifter narrowed his eyes and pointed a finger at Luna. "First of all, we have names. I'm Shophan and this is Abir. Second of all, do you think we can't be useful just because our animals are the kind that normally get hunted? Well newsflash for you, there's a reason we're able to survive. I'm fast and good at hiding and he's stronger than most of you. You'll need 'prey shifters' like us if you're going to get through this mission without dying."

His nostrils flared and Abir pulled Shophan into an awkward side hug. "Sorry. He really doesn't like being called a prey shifter, but I'm joining you and he goes anywhere I do." Shophan flushed when Abir patted him on the head.

Iris looked over to Eiji, "So who is this ally to the west?"

Eiji pointed in the direction of the forest that led to the glass mages, and Iris cocked their head to one side. "The glass mages? Why would they help us? They're complete recluses."

Eiji blushed. "Because I may have created an 'alliance' with their leader. His name is Enzo."

Luna blinked. "By alliance. Do you mean you...?" She gestured at the air, "Use your Kitsune wiles on him."

Fox ears popped up from his head, and his face flushed fuchsia. "Maybe a few times, but that's not important. What's important is they might be willing to help us. You're welcome."

Iris coughed to cover a laugh, and Eiji shoved Iris's arm. "This isn't funny."

"Little Eiji is growing up." Iris said and batted their eyelashes.

He crossed his arms over his chest and stomped in the direction of the forest. "Follow me and stay close, Iris." Eiji led their small group west towards the misty forest that led to the glass mages.

The transition from the desert to the forest drenched Iris's body in sweat and caused their clothing to cling like a second skin. Birds with the heads of women swooped overhead, and they all placed earplugs in so as not to be tempted by their song.

A hooved creature with a woman's face and snow white wings swept through the treetops and landed on a tree branch just above Iris's head. The branch strained under its weight, and the creature opened its mouth and let out a loud caw, but when Iris didn't react it flew off. Fairies the size of thumbnails buzzed around like mosquitoes, but none of them dared swat the pesky creatures for fear of angering the dryads that lurked in the depths of the forest.

The mist in the air grew thicker as they pushed onward, sending a shiver down Iris's spine. Hopefully, that didn't mean they were getting closer to the Druids. Iris had no desire to walk into this thick magic mist especially considering the Druids usually weren't far behind when it appeared, and Iris wasn't thrilled with the idea of coming into contact with those religious zealots. Especially seeing as how they could be more than a little temperamental.

Iris reached out and grabbed onto Luna's sleeve as they continued through the mist. One of the Sirin flew overhead singing their enticing melody. Luna turned back to Iris and smiled. Luna's thoughts whispered in Iris's mind. *It's just a little further. On the way back, we can ask them if they have a safer path home.*

Iris gave a weak smile and tightened their grip on Luna's sleeve, but said nothing. They pushed further through the forest, and when Luna moved aside a branch, it snapped back hitting Iris in the forehead. A scowling face appeared on the tree, and Iris mumbled. "Sorry." and patted the branch before continuing on.

When a rushing waterfall with a massive pool of midnight blue water came into view, their group paused to fill up their canteens. Everyone removed their ear plugs now that the Sirin, or owl women, had moved on to another part of the forest.

As Iris dipped their canteen in the water, their skin itched. Iris glimpsed silver scales lining the top half of their left arm and the side of their neck. But looking down at the endless depths of the water set Iris on edge. *Thanks, body. There are probably mermaids in this water especially considering it's a dark pool in a magic forest. My choices are possible death by mermaid or death from lack of oxygen. That's great.*

Iris glared at the water. They dipped a toe into the cool

placid pond. Luna grabbed their arm "What are you doing? That's dangerous."

Iris held up the arm with the scales. "I don't have a choice."

Iris jumped into the water's depths and heard several shouts of "What the hell are they doing?" and "Do they want to die?"

Scales grew along their skin, spreading to their whole body. Lungs became gills, and they went from struggling for air to breathing freely.

Iris froze when shimmering indigo and silver scales glided through the water just under Iris's newly formed tail. Their gaze drifted up to the dorsal fin that glowed in the water like phosphorescent moss. It jutted up from between pale shoulder blades. A curtain of silky black hair and raspberry red lips would have lured Iris in like a moth to a flame if it weren't for the sharp rows of shark-like teeth screaming at Iris to stay away.

The mermaid swam towards Iris, her long fangs bared in a spine-chilling grin, and she stroked Iris's scales with a long, curved fingernail. Iris shuddered and propelled themself back with their silver fins.

"Interesting. It looks like you know what I am. Does that mean you're a shifter?" Iris tried to push themself back, but the mermaid gripped Iris with her black nails. "It seems you are. I've heard their flesh makes a delicious meal, is that true?"

Iris opened their mouth and dug their lower fang like teeth into the mermaid's hand. She snarled and released her grip on Iris. Iris spun around and swam up towards the surface, hoping their body would change if they left the water.

Two mermaids swam up from the depths to join the first. "Get them before they get away," the first mermaid shouted.

Iris reached out with their mind, *Everyone. Red alert. There are mermaids in the water.*

A splash rippled the surface of the water, and a mermaid with a violet tail bolted towards the disturbance. She wrapped her arms around a small shifter with light brown hair, Shophan, and dragged him into the water. Iris dove for him, looking back and forth between the mermaid closing in on her and the one leading the small shifter to a death by drowning. *Come on body. Change. Become something more useful than a regular fish.*

Iris imagined pink flippers and a long snout. Instead of gills, they pictured lungs and a blowhole. At first nothing happened, but then their tail elongated, and their scales shed, turning into a leathery hide. They risked a glimpse to the side and saw pink. *Yes.* They thought and raced towards the mermaid letting out a loud screech.

"Where the hell did an Encantado come from?" The mermaid grumbled and dropped the shifter, swimming away. Iris grabbed the shifter by his shirt collar using their small razor sharp teeth and propelled themself up out of the water. When Iris's head broke the surface, they let go of him and sucked in a breath before diving back down.

Several of the others' thoughts reached Iris's mind. *What is an Encantado doing all the way out here?*

I thought Iris was a wolf shifter, how did they change into a dolphin?

Who is that? I don't remember bringing a dolphin shifter with us.

Iris tried to will themself back into human form, but their flesh felt stiff and unchanging. The mermaids circled, but didn't approach Iris. Iris swam towards one of the mermaids and butted into her with their snout and then bared the tiny razor-sharp teeth that lined their mouth.

The first mermaid skittered backwards, and the rest followed suit. Once they were out of view, Iris's body shifted, and they swam full force towards the water's surface as fins contorted changing to legs mid stroke. Their lungs shrank, burning with a desperation for air.

Iris burst to the surface with one hand and one fin. They

tread water until their tail fin turned to legs, so they could pull themself onto dry land. A shivering Shophan clutched onto Abir muttering, "I knew coming on this mission was a bad idea." as the other shifters stared on at Iris.

Shophan glared down at a couple of those gawking at Iris and reached out to help Iris up despite the teeth marks on his hand and the blood still dripping down from his skin. "Thank you for helping me. I didn't hear your warning in time."

As Iris pushed themself off the floor with Shophan's help, their chest rattled. They sucked in air, and their legs shook. Damp rainbow hair clung to their face.

Eiji whispered. "Are you okay, Iris?" He reached out a hand for Iris whose eyes widened as his hand inched closer.

Luna stood in front of Iris and held up a hand. "They'll be fine. Just give them some time."

Iris shook as they risked a glance up at their comrades. Some of the shifters' jaws dropped and others cocked their head to one side in confusion.

Ze'ev, the wolf shifter twin, broke the silence. "Is anyone going to explain why what we thought was a wolf shifter just changed into a pink dolphin?"

Iris tried to laugh, but it turned into a cough. Luna answered instead. "Iris was experimented on by humans. It's a long story."

Shophan tightened his grip on Abir's arm at the mention of experiments, and Iris turned away to avoid their gazes, trying not to focus on how naked they were sitting before everyone.

Eiji cleared his throat and Iris felt fabric brush the side of their chest as he shoved a shirt and pants at them. "You might not care if we see you naked, but the glass mages have a different idea of modesty. Get dressed."

Iris used their hands to wipe away any excess moisture the best they could before slipping the clothing back on to their damp body. The fabric clung to Iris's skin, and they picked at it as they made their way along the forest trail toward the city.

By the time the trees began to thin out, the searing heat had dried Iris's wet clothes and been replaced with sweat brought on by the humidity and unrelenting sun.

After what felt like hours of walking, the rainbow sheen of the glass dome criss-crossing over the city came into view as the mist cleared.

Modern day skyscrapers of silver and glass spiraled upwards as if trying to touch the heavens. Massive silver windows adorned the sides of buildings and beautiful glass lamps filled with fire magic dotted the side streets. *How are there elemental mages here? I thought they were all in the human world.* Iris thought as they entered the town.

There was no one stationed at the entrance to the town, but Iris supposed that made sense considering all sides of the town were surrounded by a forest teeming with aggressive, territorial magical creatures, an ocean, and the ravaged wastelands of bygone elemental and shifter clans.

Far off in the distance on the eastern horizon, waves of silver and gold magic undulated in the skyline over the sea. Its tendrils decorated the sky like haphazard paint streaks. It was the lingering reminder of why Clarent and Excalibur had been separated in the first place. Their magic was too powerful.

One step into the silver and gold magic residue would sear skin and steal your life from you minute by minute. A shudder ran down Iris's spine as they stared at the magic, but the sound of "Hey there, my little fox." turned Iris's head.

A mage with curly red hair and bright blue eyes ran right past Luna and into Eiji's arms. Eiji returned the man's embrace and pulled him in for a kiss on the lips.

Eiji pulled back from the kiss with a wide grin on his face. "Do you have a sixth sense for Kitsune or something like that, Enzo?"

This is the glass mage's leader? Iris raised an eyebrow as they appraised him. *He looks like he's maybe twenty, and he's a good six inches shorter than me and I'm not that tall.*

Eiji caught Iris staring and said, "Don't let his height fool you. He's almost as old as I am, and you know how slow Kitsune age."

Enzo got up onto tiptoes to plant a kiss on Eiji's cheek. Then, he hooked an arm around Eiji's neck and turned to face Iris. "He's right, you know. It's one of the glass mage's many secrets, but I have so much more to show you. Follow me."

Enzo let go of Eiji's neck and led him along by the arm. They all followed behind Eiji and Enzo, and Iris noted that Ze'ev and Ayla stayed glued to Luna's side. Iris couldn't say they blamed the twins. This place was completely different from what they were told.

Iris pointed to the lamps dotting the streets. "Do you have elemental mages here too? Those look like their handiwork, but I thought they all fled to the human world."

Enzo grinned at the street lights. "You have a good eye. We purposefully spread that narrative, so their enemies wouldn't continue to hunt them down. During their mass migration to the human world, we offered sanctuary to displaced mages in the destroyed clans adjacent to use. We love having water and fire elementals since they're quite compatible with our magic. That's actually how we were able to craft our most powerful spells. The alliance was a certain Kitsune's idea," He said and elbowed Eiji.

Eiji pursed his lips, "He gives me too much credit. They were already allies of the glass mage clan. I just suggested offering them sanctuary. Having them in the human world was a disservice to the glass elementals and the plant mages."

Enzo smiled. "He's too modest. If it weren't for him, we would've been overrun by the enchantresses and sorceresses ages ago, but they've mostly left us alone since they don't believe we're a threat. I'm glad because otherwise we would be

94

part of the rubble," he said and jerked his chin towards the ocean.

As they walked through town, Iris's thoughts drifted to Amy and the message she'd sent with the calligraphy stone. Iris bit their lip. There was no way to send Amy a message back or offer a thank you. *Please don't do anything too reckless. Survive until we get there.*

CHAPTER 8

*A*my fiddled with the hair pin. With each passing minute its movements became less erratic. This time the lock clicked before the pin fell from the air and into her lap. She hissed out a breath. *So close and yet so far away,* she thought. Her breaths came in gasps, and she tugged against the chains. If Naru and Iris were to have any chance at rescuing her, she had to get them that information on Opal's weakness.

Amy made the clip rise once again despite the ache that pounded at her temples and spread through her body. She felt around the inside of the lock to undo the pins, and this time she heard two short clicks before the chains on her arms loosened, sliding down onto the floor with a clatter. A sharp pain niggled at her skull, and she rubbed at her temples in an effort to dull the pain.

Amy winced when she moved her hands and looked down to see that her wrists were red and raw with tiny puncture wounds marking her skin in a bracelet-like circle. She leaned back into the chair, eyes closed. *But how am I supposed to get out of here if I can barely control my enchantment magic?*

She jerked upright when metal clinked on the other side

of the door and arranged the cuffs so they looked like they were still on her wrists. The door creaked open to reveal black hair and citrine yellow eyes. Dusk carried a metal bucket at his side.

Amy clenched her jaw. "What are you doing here?"

He held up the bucket. "You said earlier you needed to use the restroom, so I brought one."

Amy wrinkled her nose. "You can't be serious?"

He placed it on the floor in front of her. "Dead serious. If you need it, you'll use it while I'm here. I'm the only one aside from Opal with the keys."

Amy shifted her legs in the chair. "I'd rather piss myself."

He shrugged. "Suit yourself. Opal's not stupid enough to let you out of these chains, and I warned her that you can be more dangerous than you appear."

Amy let out a shaky breath. "What did Opal do to you? The person I knew would never act like this."

He flinched. "The person who made me this way wasn't her. It was you and the backstabbers you've aligned yourself with."

Amy tilted her head down to the chains on her wrist. She forced tears into her eyes and then glanced up at him. She forced a quiver into her voice. "I don't know what Opal told you, but I never would have left you behind. You were my best friend and it made my heart so happy when you told me about being a..." He glanced up at the camera and then back at her and shook his head.

She couldn't see the camera, so it must have been behind her, facing the door no doubt. When she didn't finish her sentence, his gaze softened. He pointed a finger to his ears and eyes and said. "I won't show you any sympathy. You know how Opal and the Council feel about half breeds like you."

Amy's mouth opened in an "O." and then her grin widened. She leaned forward and beckoned Dusk closer so that he could see her lips. "Fine. I'll keep my mouth shut for a price. Like perhaps a trip to a real bathroom?" She said just above a whisper.

Then, she said loud enough for the microphones to hear. "I'm not using that wretched thing."

He raised his voice. "You aren't allowed out of this room or those chains for any reason. It's the bucket or nothing at all."

She pleaded. "You can keep the shackles on my arms and legs. Just remove the ones keeping me to the chair, so I can use the bathroom. I still can't use gem magic with the shackles on my wrists."

He crossed his arms over his chest, but caught a glimpse of a cat's eye gem as it materialized in his palm. Magic flowed through it, and he held it up to the camera. He yelled. "I'm not an imbecile. You're using the bucket. I'll unshackle you from the chair, and you'll have two minutes. If you try anything, I'll make you regret it."

With shaking hands, he undid the chains around her waist. She adjusted the shackles on her arms so the closed part faced up when she stood. He pulled her along by her elbow. She tried to peek over his shoulder as he typed the code to get out, but only caught the first two digits 1 and 0 before he shoved her back.

Well, so much for getting the code that way, Amy thought.

He covered the keypad as he typed the remaining numbers and the door opened.

Amy gulped as they exited the room and walked down the hallway to the bathroom. Her legs wobbled as she walked, and he stopped in front of a plain door. "You have one minute to use the bathroom, so make it quick. If we're gone too long, the spell I used will dissipate and we'll both be in trouble."

Amy opened the door and slammed it shut behind her. Once she'd clicked the lock shut, she slid her hands from the shackles.

With a shaky breath, Amy started working on the metal

that bound her legs. Now that she could use her hands, she made quick work of the locks on her ankles, but a knock on the door interrupted her.

"Are you almost done?"

Amy flushed the toilet and turned on the water. "Almost."

Amy forced the chains loosely back on her ankles, shut off the water, and shuffled out of the doorway.

Dusk circled her, scrutinizing her from head to toe. "Hold up your hands."

She rolled her eyes. "Do you really think I found gemstones in the bathroom or something?"

"I'm not taking any chances. Hands up."

Amy only lifted her arms up halfway, moving her limbs slowly so the chains wouldn't fall from her wrists.

"Is your flexibility so lacking that you can't hold your hands all the way up?"

Amy wrinkled her nose. "I haven't been able to bathe since you've kidnapped me, and that room you put me in is stifling. I'd prefer to spare you from the smell."

He shook his head. "Fine. I'll pat you down as is." He ran his hands along her hair, neck, and chest. When his hand inched closer to her cuffs, she held her breath.

His yellow eyes flickered with amusement. "You're looking rather tense. What are you hiding from me?"

She gave a dry laugh. "Maybe I'm hiding my undying affection for you. You were just fondling my chest a moment ago." *Amy bit her lip. Why did I say that? What is wrong with me?*

His face flushed, and he pulled his hands away from her cuffs. "That wasn't what I meant." He reached down for his pocket watch and glanced at the time.

"I don't know what you're planning, but it won't work. This place is a fortress and a maze. You won't escape."

Amy shrugged. "I never said anything about escaping."

"Then what do you want?"

She walked towards the cell. "Tick tock. The two minutes

are almost up. If you want to know, we'll have to walk and talk. The illusion runs out soon, right?"

"You're infuriating, and you're going the wrong way." He ran a hand through his hair and put a hand on her shoulder, guiding her to the left until they reached the entrance. "Now tell me, what do you want?"

Amy raised her chin. "Information will cost you. If you tell me what Opal wants from my sister and I, I'll tell you what you want."

Dusk gritted his teeth together. "Fine, don't tell me." He opened the door and shoved Amy in. "Sit," he pointed at the chair.

She shuffled to the chair and lowered herself into the seat which was damp with sweat. The metal cuffs on her feet dug into the skin on her ankles.

"This feels too easy. What are you planning?"

She turned up her nose. "I thought we established that I wouldn't tell you?"

When he wrapped the chains around her torso, he tugged them so tightly that she wheezed. "Are you trying to kill me?"

"No. I'd just like for you to feel as uncomfortable as you've made me feel."

Amy put her hands into her lap and dug her nails into her black yoga pants. "Well pardon if my blackmail was uncomfortable for you. You know what else is uncomfortable? Being hunted and chained up like some sort of…" Her voice trailed off.

"Oh, what made you stop? Let me guess you were going to say animal." he snickered.

Her face flushed, and she muttered. "No. Well. Maybe."

Dusk shook his head. "It's okay I am one, but it's not because I'm a shifter." His gaze flickered to the camera and back to her, a silent warning. His face fell back into a stony-faced gaze. "I'll be back with your food later, prisoner."

"Oh boy. Just what I want, poisoned food," she joked.

He covered his mouth with a hand and turned his back to her. "You haven't changed a bit."

If only you knew how wrong you are. Amy waited while he typed in the pin. When the door slid shut behind him, she slipped her hands out of the cuffs on her wrist and worked on the chains constricting her chest with her hairpin. She hunched over while she worked, throwing a furtive glance up at the camera behind her to see if she was in its line of sight.

When the chains slid off her waist, she glanced around the room, looking for any way to avoid the camera's notice while opening the door or any alternate way out of the room. There was no doorknob or lock to pick from the inside. And the air vent on the ceiling was enchanted with Jet. Not to mention even with the chair, which was fused to the floor, it was too high up to reach.

The only chance she had was to crack the code on the door. She touched her finger to the golden hair pin but stayed in the chair. Once she got up, it was only a matter of time before reinforcements came. She'd have to get the code right quickly and be gone before Opal could send anyone to tie her up again.

The first numbers were one and zero. Maybe that's her birth month since her Choosing was on Halloween, and he typed in four more numbers. What would Opal type? The day of her appointment ceremony? No, that would only be four digits total. Her full birthday? That could work, but it seems too obvious.

Amy looked down at the loosened shackles. *She cared for Dusk before he'd become Dusk. During the "War of the Twin Swords." Maybe his birthday is included somehow? When was his birthday again?* Amy dug her fingers into her palm. *Think. You can figure this out.*

Maybe it's her birth month, Dusk's birth month, so June and when she lost Joan which was November third. So, 100603 or maybe 100111. Might as well try before one of them comes back.

Amy got up from the chair and ran to the door, starting with Opal's full birthday. 103194. The door hissed but didn't open. She punched in 103103 next, but it locked up and started a ten second timer. A loud chirping noise came from the keys. "Come on. Please be this one."

100611. The chirping ceased, and Amy hissed out a "yes" as the door opened, but her victory was cut short when she came face to face with a guard.

Amy shoved his chest with all of her strength and raced towards the frantic hum of her familiar's gem as the guard shouted. "The prisoner has escaped. If you find her, capture her. Alive."

The humming got louder as she rounded a corner. A shout went through Amy's mind. *Dusk has me. Be careful.*

Amy slid to a stop as thudding footsteps approached. She crept back around the corner and pressed her back against the wall.

Dusk's dark chuckle made her wish she could use illusion magic to disappear. "I had a feeling you'd try something like this, little lynx. You can reveal yourself or I can take you back to your cell by force."

Shit, she thought as Dusk approached. The familiar clink of gemstones punctuated each step he took towards her. Amy tugged her shoe from her foot. "Then, you should know I always have to do things the hard way." She threw the shoe at him, but he dodged to the side.

"Nice try, but a shoe isn't going to stop me."

Amy slid her other shoe off and threw it at him. He turned his head, watching it fly through the air. Amy slid along the smooth floor and snatched the pouch from Dusk's pants with a snap before careening down the hallway.

Dusk reached out for her arm, and talons grazed her skin, but he didn't get a good enough grip to stop her. "Who said the shoes were meant to stop you? Goodbye old friend." She waved and disappeared down the corridor.

Her heart pounded in her chest as she ran towards the exit. She kept glancing back to see if Dusk had followed her.

Once she couldn't see or hear him anymore, she fell to her knees and gasped for air. Her lungs burned, but she couldn't stop yet.

Amy sprinted in a random direction, but walls rose up all around her. A dead end. She dug into the pouch looking for anything that could be helpful and saw the stone Dusk had once used to communicate, the calligraphy stone. And she'd given one to Iris. Perfect. *Hopefully, they still have it.*

Amy channeled her energy into the stone, and it glowed. It would only hold a sentence or two, so she had to be concise. She traced the words "Opal's weakness. Malachite curse," onto its surface. It glowed a golden brown to let her know that the message was received.

Amy clutched the gemstone to her chest. *Now I just have to find a way out of here.*

CHAPTER 9

a chill slithered down Amy's spine, and she caught a flash of silver hair in her peripheral vision. Amy bit her lip. *Please don't let this be who I think it is.*

An airy laugh echoed through the corridor, and Amy turned her head towards the noise. Gold and silver swirled in the air. As Opal approached her, she forced her slack jaw into a smile. *Don't show weakness. You can't afford to.*

"Well if it isn't the Amethyst killer in the flesh. What are you doing out of your cage?"

Amy hocked up phlegm and spat on the sparkling tile floor. "Getting my sister so I can get out of this hellhole."

Opal screwed up her nose and unsheathed her sword. "You're going to regret that. I will cut you down where you stand."

Amy's heart lodged in her throat, but she forced venom into her voice. "If you wanted to do that you would have already done it ten times over, but you still want something from me. Am I wrong?"

Opal's hand went to her gem pouch. "Yes. I want to know how you staved off Dusk with an amulet that turns things to gold and how you threw back that soldier in the heat of battle.

Neither of those things were Enchantress magic. What kind of monstrosity are you? I'd like to know what I need to exterminate."

Amy's jaw dropped. If that's what Opal wanted, she would kill Amy the second she knew what the amulet was, but Opal didn't know that Amy knew the amulet's origins, yet.

Amy shrugged. "Unfortunately for you, I can't give you that information. I don't even know what I am."

Opal's smile didn't waver. "I find that hard to believe, but it doesn't matter. I can turn you over to the same people I hired to 'experiment' on Iris. They could figure out what you are or torture you until you give the information over just to make the pain stop."

Amy's face went paper white, and her hand dipped into the gem bag at her hip without breaking eye contact with Opal. Opal drew her sword as Amy stared down at the gem she'd managed to grab, a blocky golden pyrite crystal, but before she could even start on a spell Opal struck.

Wind whooshed past Amy's ear as the sword arched down, cutting through the air. The roar of a dragon accompanied Opal's movements.

Amy reached out to her familiar. "Violet, please help. Distract her." The bracelet glowed and changed shape until what stood before her was her lynx familiar with rough purple crystals coating her like fur. Amy jumped back as Opal's blade came down again, grazing her face. Her skin stung, and she put a hand to the fresh wound. It came away wet with blood.

Don't touch my enchantress. Violet bared her fangs and hissed. She rammed into Opal, knocking her back, but Opal latched onto one of Violet's crystals to stabilize herself and stabbed Violet's back. Silver and gold magic spiraled down the sword's blade and went through Violet's body, making her shudder.

"Violet, get away from her!" Amy shouted.

Violet leapt back. The sword made a sharp tss and a loud ripping sound as it raked along her familiar's torso. Violet bared her fangs as Opal approached, but one of her hind legs collapsed.

The lynx limped back to Amy, standing in front of her. *Hurry. Finish the spell.*

Amy gulped and focused on the golden flecks of the pyrite in her hand. *I need to thoroughly oxidize the stone, or it won't work. Can you buy more time?*

Violet nodded. *I'll do my best.*

Opal ran towards them again. The gem glowed and warmed in Amy's hands, but she dropped the stone when Violet grabbed onto Excalibur's blade by the teeth, and her body slammed into Amy, tail first.

The gem went flying, landing just behind Opal. It glowed and let out a bright flash, and pop instead of a large explosion.

Opal kicked the stone away and swung the sword at Amy's leg, but a girl with stormy blue eyes ran up to Opal and tugged on her sleeve. Opal turned her head, sword at the ready, but stopped when she saw the girl. Her features softened, and she turned her back on Violet and Amy.

Violet cocked her head to one side. *That girl just spoke to me. She shouldn't be able to do that. We're not contracted.* Her ear twitched. *Why is someone who is omni tongued with Opal? Did she kidnap her?*

Amy glanced at the doorway and shuffled towards it as Opal signed something to the girl. The girl nodded and signed something back.

Opal turned back to see Amy at her side and grabbed her by the shirt. "You are a tenacious one. Luckily for you, she's asked for me to leave you alone for the time being, but don't think that means you're safe." Opal wiped the bloody sword on her already blood caked black pants and sheathed it.

Violet padded up to the girl. Amy shouted. "Violet what are you doing? She's allied with the enemy."

"Maybe she's decided to leave you because you're too pitiful to protect her," Opal said and snickered.

Violet gave Opal a soft warning growl before turning back to the girl who patted Violet on the head. The girl looked up at Opal and in a hoarse voice said, "Why did Violet ask if you kidnapped me?"

Opal glared at Violet but crouched down and signed something to the girl.

Violet rubbed against the girl's leg, asking for more pets. *Violet doesn't like anyone. Who is she?*

Violet's thoughts came to her. *She's a guardian of magical creatures just like the enchantresses were the guardians of Gemstone Forest. Her name is Raven.*

Amy's thoughts on how this young girl was a guardian were cut short when Opal stomped over and grabbed Amy by the elbow. Amy reared her arm back and elbowed Opal in the face. Opal didn't flinch even as her cheek started to swell.

Raven let out a short gasp. "Opal, don't hurt her."

Opal didn't release her steely grip on Amy's arm. "You heard her. Stop resisting."

Amy flailed in Opal's grip as Opal pulled lead cuffs from the belt on her pants and slapped them on Amy's wrist. She snatched the gem bag from Amy and tossed it to Raven.

The girl caught the bag and placed it under the crook of her arm.

Opal signed something to Raven that Amy imagined was some lie about how she was dangerous and that she shouldn't give back the gem pouch for any reason.

Raven nodded and signed something that resembled the sign for okay that Night had taught her years ago.

Amy's head swirled with unanswered questions as she was dragged along back to her cell. *How did she get that young girl and Dusk on her side? I'm starting to feel like the bad guy here.*

Amy shoved that last thought down as Opal guided her

towards the jail cell. Amy shook her head. *I killed one person in an accident. Opal killed thousands. We're not the same.*

Fragments of memories from just before the War of the Twin Swords flashed through her mind. Opal's burning eyes and the feeling of Opal splitting skin when Amy had held her hands in surrender. Opal's wild smile and burning eyes coupled with the words, "You'll have to do better than that if you want to survive a war," were permanently etched into Amy's mind.

Amy eyed the green veins creeping up on Opal's left hand. *She didn't notice me sneaking away before, but why?* Amy risked a glance up at Opal.

Opal's gaze scanned the corridors as they walked. When her left eye moved, her right eye didn't follow. *Strange. Maybe the eye is fake?*

If it was, she might have a shot at getting out of here. Her hands were bound, but she still had free use of her legs and teeth, but she'd need to locate an exit if she didn't want to get captured again.

When Opal turned down the next corridor, Amy saw a big door with the words "emergency exit" in red letters. It was now or never. Amy dug in her heels and winced when she had to put weight on her injured leg. She bit Opal's wrist and the taste of copper invaded her mouth. Opal gripped the chains tighter, so Amy stomped on Opal's foot. Opal yelped and dropped the chains. Amy bolted for the door despite the blood running down her left leg.

When she looked back, Opal's unmoving eye faced her. The sight of it sent a shiver down her spine. The color was more of a dull grey than the silvery color in her other eye. If she hadn't seen that attack coming, it had to be a fake.

The pain grew sharper as her feet pounded against the tile floor, and Opal shouted, "Get her." but it was drowned out by the roaring of blood in her ears as Amy focused on putting one foot in front of the other.

She glanced back at Violet who yowled out for her. Hopefully, she would stay safe or at least transform and get away.

Those hopes died when she ran into someone's chest and looked up to see dark hair and yellow eyes. "Looks like you've been caught, little mouse."

Amy lowered herself into a crouch and rammed into him with her full body weight. They both toppled to the ground, and she crawled on her hands and knees to get behind him and wrapped the chains around his neck, pulling them taut by criss crossing her arms.

Amy shouted. "Stand up," as she pressed her chest against his back.

He grumbled, but didn't speak as he stood up stiffly, and gagged slightly when the chain dug into his throat. Opal walked towards Dusk, but Amy tightened the chain against his throat. "Come any closer, and I'll make sure he suffocates. If you want him back alive, let me go free."

Amy's words came out sharp, but her heart felt like ice. She pulled his body flush against her chest and kept a foot on the back of his heel. His magic flickered, and his illusion magic began to fade.

Dusk froze against her. His eyes searched Opal's. "Opal?"

She cocked her head to one side. Gold and silver threaded her gaze, but she didn't step any closer. "Go ahead, Amethyst Killer. Do it. I'll find another assassin."

Opal licked her lips, and Amy's breath caught in her throat. Her instincts told her to pull the chains taut. Call her bluff and use him to escape, but her heart squeezed at the thought of hurting him, at letting his magic flicker out so he'd face the same fate she would. Amy released her grip on the chains, and Dusk stepped out of her clutches. Amy held out her arms, her gaze steely. "He's not worth killing. If I'm going to claim my title, it will be for killing you."

Dusk rounded on Opal. "Were you planning on letting her kill me?"

Opal placed a black painted fingernail under his chin. "Of course not. I knew she wouldn't do it. She'd rather die than prove me right. Besides, you should be able to handle one enchantress on your own. Now carry her back to her cell."

Dusk rubbed at his throat. His voice shook, "I'm not your gambling chip. Why don't you carry her back to the cell?"

Opal grabbed his neck and squeezed. "That was an order, not a request. Unless you'd like to share her fate."

"You don't scare me," his talons slid out.

"I should, shifter," She snarled.

His gaze flickered to Amy who shook her head. "Fine. I'll do it."

Opal released him, and he gritted his teeth. "Come with me, prisoner." Dusk grabbed Amy by the arm and hauled her to her feet.

"And make sure she doesn't get away this time," Opal spat.

Dusk bared his teeth in a grin. "Yes, madam Council leader."

Opal's nostrils flared, "You know I hate being called that. Get out of my sight. Now."

"Gladly." He glared daggers at Opal and dragged Amy back to the cell. Once they were out of Opal's sight, he whispered. "Why didn't you do it? If she'd seen what I was, she probably would have killed me herself."

Amy pursed her lips. "I don't owe you an explanation."

"You could have called her bluff or exposed me, but you didn't. I want to know why."

Amy swallowed over a lump in her throat. "She calls me Amethyst Killer. I don't want to be the person she thinks I am. I don't want to be the person you think I am."

Dusk glanced down at his palms. "I knew she'd changed, but I never thought she'd turn on me. She'd never been that way with Cat, but I think if you had wanted to, she would have let you kill me."

Amy stiffly patted his shoulder. "I'm sorry you had to

find out this way. But I think you did mean something to her. Otherwise, why was your birthday part of the passcode?"

Dusk frowned. "That was Cat's birthday. She loved Cat, but I don't think she would love Dusk."

Amy let out a long sigh. "I loved you both as Cat and as Night. And I think both of those pieces of you are still in there somewhere. That's why you haven't thrown me into the cell yet. Am I wrong?"

Dusk's face flushed. "I… I've gone too far down a dark road."

Footsteps thudded down the hallway. "One right choice, one light could make the dark road a little less dark."

"If she suspects I've been helping you, she'll kill me."

Amy jangled her chains. "We can make it look like an accident, but it would have to be quick. Someone's coming."

The footsteps came closer. Dusk leaned into her ear. "No matter what happens, play the part of the rebellious prisoner."

Amy grinned. "With pleasure."

The guards turned the corner and pain lanced Amy's spine as her back was shoved into the metal door. "If you try anything else, you'll be going back to the cell in pieces."

Talons dug into her arm and Amy squirmed underneath his grip. She kicked and flailed as the guards approached. "You don't scare me, baby bird."

One of them eyed Amy. "Is she giving you trouble? We can help you subdue her if you'd like."

The guard licked his lips, and she grimaced.

Dusk placed a hand to her neck and squeezed. Amy gasped for air and clawed at her throat. His other hand plucked the pin from her hair. "She tried to break out of her chains with this," he held up the golden pin with his free hand and bile rose in her throat.

She frantically reached for the pin, but he kept it out of arm's length. "Give it back!"

"No. I think I'll keep it as a souvenir. Now let's get you in the cell."

His hand reached for the door, and Amy stomped on Dusk's toes. His grip tightened on her throat, and he lifted her up off the wall. "I guess you had too much air. Let's see you try to struggle when you're unconscious."

Amy's vision blurred, but his grip loosened ever so slightly. She took that as a cue to shut her eyes and go limp in his arms as he punched in the code to open the door.

When the door clicked open, one of the guards said, "You seem like you've got this handled, but call if you need anything." before the two guards' footsteps faded into the background.

Once the guards were far away, Dusk released his grip on Amy's neck. She took small sips of air to refill her lungs but didn't open her eyes even when cool metal was tucked into the waistband of her pants.

After the door slammed shut and chains were wrapped around her torso once more, the room went quiet and Dusk spelled a word on her palm. "Key."

That must have been what he'd given her. She waited a full twenty seconds before opening her eyes again.

"What the hell was that for?" She screamed.

"You were being difficult. Be lucky Opal needs you or I would have killed you myself."

Amy's nostrils flared. "You're a sick bastard. You know that?"

"Why thank you."

"It wasn't a compliment," she grumbled.

He dug his talons into her skin. "If you don't want to die, then learn to listen. Opal will be back for you, and she'll kill you if you try anything else. I have another matter to attend to, so try to stay out of trouble until then."

She pouted. "But I'm oh so good at making trouble. It's a hobby of mine."

"You're hopeless," he scoffed and strode out of the room.

She waited a few moments after Dusk's departure to dig the key from her waistband and pulled the cuffs close to her chest and away from the camera's gaze to undo the metal shackles. *Hopefully, she hasn't had a chance to change the code, yet.*

Amy slid up from the chair and over to the keypad. She held her breath while typing in the pin. When the door hissed and opened, Amy sighed. *Thank goddess.* The exit had just come into view when the sirens blared and guards ran after her. Amy took a quick glance back but didn't stop even when a guard threw a knife at her already injured leg.

She threw open the first exit door she could find and ran into the suffocating hot, humid air. Amy squinted in the blinding sunlight. Her lungs burned as she ran into the depths of the Everglades.

The sound of Violet's screams sawed at her brain. *Opal knows you've escaped. Don't stop no matter what.*

Amy swallowed over a lump in her throat. *Damn her. I might have just gotten two more people killed for daring to live.*

Pain shot through Amy's leg, and she bit her lip to keep from crying out. Amy didn't dare look back. Violet's screams echoed through her mind, and she covered her ears instinctively, but there was no blocking it out.

When the path of trees gave way to the muddy water of the Everglades, Amy waded into the muck, and her feet got sucked up. She jumped whenever a branch brushed against her ankle.

Her lungs threatened to explode as she waded through the muck, but she kept moving even as black filled the edges of her vision and the scenery blurred. Noises turned to static in her ears. Her left leg went numb.

I have to keep going. I need to get far enough away that she won't find me. If they're going to find the fortress and save Garnet, they'll need me.

That thought kept her pushing forward as the sun burned her skin. When she looked over at her shoulder, it was pink, so

Amy reached down and grabbed mud and rubbed it on her shoulders and face.

As adrenaline turned to exhaustion, her left leg collapsed. When a group of tourists passed by in a boat, she cried out. "Help!" before all the energy drained out of her, and she fell face first into the mud.

WHEN AMY WOKE, it was to the sounds of unfamiliar voices. "You found her in the Everglades like that?"

"Did you see anyone who could have done this to her?"

"Was she attacked by a gator? She has a huge gash on her leg."

Amy's eyes fluttered open, and the coolness of a metal table pressed against her back. The pain in her leg had subsided a little, but when she sat up the world spun around her.

An unfamiliar man looked at her. "I wouldn't recommend getting up too quickly. When we saw you out in the Everglades, you'd already lost a lot of blood. You're lucky to be alive. What happened to you?"

Amy's gaze scanned her surroundings, and her shoulders slumped when she took in the fake gators surrounding her. *It's just a gift shop.* The lie rolled off her tongue with ease. "I was wandering around the swamp and like always my shoes got sucked up. No surprise there. The gash well...I'm sad to admit I had a run in with a gator that was a little too close for comfort. It got in a good swipe at my leg."

A younger man with dirty blonde hair let his bangs fall over his eyes and smiled. "You should've run in zig zags to get away. We get taught that the moment we're old enough to walk 'round here."

Amy smiled. "I'm not from around here. I'll have to keep that in mind for next time."

The older man laughed. "You're planning on going back for round two?"

Amy shrugged. "I have to pay it back for getting my leg," Her lips curved up in a grin.

He shook his head. "You really should be more careful out there. It can be dangerous in the Everglades if you don't stay on the path. Do you need someone to take you to the hospital?"

Amy glanced down at the bandage on her leg. The gauze was wrapped tightly to stop the bleeding, and her leg tingled with pins and needles when she moved it, but it looked clean. She held up her hands. "That won't be necessary. I can't afford it anyway. No health insurance."

He clicked his tongue. "I hear ya. Well let me at least drive you back to your car. You're in no condition to walk out of here."

Amy ran a hand through her hair. "Actually. I walked here."

His eyes widened. "You what? You really must be out of your mind. Well, if you aren't too far let me drive you home."

Amy's shoulders slumped. She had a feeling he wasn't going to let this go without a fight, and she didn't want Opal or Dusk finding her, but even now she wasn't sure if these people were friend or foe. Any of Opal's allies could be hiding amongst the humans. Her gaze drifted to the floor and her hands gripped the table underneath her.

"I'm not sure I should be getting into the car with someone I've just met."

A first-aid kit sat on the table beside her. The man caught her glancing at the supplies. "I can assure you I don't bite, and you're better off with me than walking home. I'll have to insist on either letting me drive you or calling one of your friends to pick you up."

At the mention of friends, Amy thought of Tiff. She was

probably still at the store. "Actually, do you have a phone? I have a friend I can call."

He dug his hand into his jeans pocket, pulled out an old cellphone and placed it into her hand. "Hopefully, you remember the number."

Amy's brow furrowed. "I think I do." She rubbed at her temples. Her mind felt foggy from the loss of blood as she punched in Tiff's number.

A chirpy voice answered, "The Gem of the Forest. This is Tiff speaking, how can I help you?"

Amy put the phone in the crook of her shoulder. "Hey Tiff, it's Amy. Can you close up shop a little early and come get me? I'm out in the Everglades."

"How did you get all the way out there? I thought you were supposed to be halfway to Israel by now."

"It's a long story, but I need you to pick me up."

Tiff's sigh made the phone crackle, and she had to pull it away from her ear. "Alright. I'll be right there. What's the address?"

Amy turned to the man beside her and shoved the phone at him. "Here. She might need some directions."

He fumbled the phone and scrambled to keep it from dropping it on the floor. "This is George's Gators. I assume you're this young lady's friend. Are you heading here from the north or the south?"

North. Amy answered in her head. As the man rattled off the instructions, Amy's mind wandered off to Iris and Naru. *Hopefully, they're both doing okay.*

CHAPTER 10

*I*ris gawked at the town square. Cars zoomed down the streets at dizzying speeds, but alongside them, you could spot people riding atop Allocamelus, camels that had the heads of donkeys, as they traveled along the stark white sand.

The town square was dotted with shops. Several boasted ice creams made with ice magic, and in the window of a barbecue shop, Iris spotted a fire elemental charring a massive hunk of meat on a huge spit that towered several feet high. The scent of cumin and coriander tickled her nose.

Iris tapped Luna on the shoulder. "Did you know about this place?"

Luna's gaze skimmed the shops as well, but she turned to Iris. "No. I had no idea an alliance like this existed. We rarely venture outside of the four walls of our clan especially after the incident with Kito."

Iris blinked and rubbed their eyes when Enzo led them to a massive clearing with a statue of Freya at its center. The woman wore an amber necklace that looked a lot like Amy's. Iris pointed at the statue. "Enzo. Not to pry, but why is the statue of an enchantress idol in the center of your town?"

Eiji put a hand across his throat, begging Iris to stop talking, but curiosity had gotten the better of them.

Enzo whirled on Iris and flashed them a predatory grin. "She wasn't an enchantment mage, and we have her up there because if it weren't for her, none of us would exist. She's a deity, not an idol. She's very real and she still lives, so I would watch your tongue if I were you."

Iris held up their hands. "Sorry. My mistake." *I doubt that they're still around. If they were as real and powerful as we've been led to believe, they wouldn't have allowed Opal to rampage like she has,* Iris thought, but they didn't push Enzo any further.

A sea green canal just past the center of the square ran through two rows of tinted glass and clay homes. The waterline was flanked on either side by torches designed for fire elementals. A handful of cobalt blue and cloud white boats sat along the bank of the water, waiting to be used. At the end of the canal, a massive stained-glass house glinted in the sunlight.

Enzo stepped into this largest boat, making it bob in the water. He pointed to the large glass house Iris had been eyeing. "If we're going to talk about strategy, I'd like for us to meet there."

Eiji put an arm around Enzo's shoulder. "You just want to show off the new house you made, don't you?"

Enzo blushed and kissed Eiji on the cheek. "It's not like that. I just want to make sure we won't be overheard. Especially since the crows started popping up recently."

The words *what crows?* were on Iris's lips, but before they could utter them, a caw sounded above, and black wings swooped overhead.

One of Enzo's guards pulled back his bow string and loosed an arrow. He caught the bird in the wing, and it went down.

Enzo's lips curled up in distaste. "One of the Magic Council's spies. Let's get going before another one comes."

Eiji helped the archer lower himself into the boat. The guard took up the rear and Eiji plopped down next to Enzo.

Iris and Luna followed behind them. Iris's body relaxed as they moved along the water, and they leaned into Luna's shoulder and inhaled the scent of sandalwood that always lingered on Luna. Iris tilted their head up to look into Luna's eyes. "Do you think we stand a chance in this battle?"

Luna's body tensed beneath Iris's. "I think you already know the answer to that question, but you're still choosing to fight anyway."

Iris pursed their lips. "I couldn't just leave Amy to die."

Luna lowered her voice to a whisper. "So, you sent everyone else to die in an attempt to save her?"

Iris reached out for Luna's hand. "She's a friend and whether she knows it or not, she might be our best chance at defeating Opal and the Magic Council. I think she's a deity descendant," Iris said, dropping their voice to a whisper.

Luna's eyebrows shot up. "What makes you say that? The last time someone was deity blessed was during Merlin's era."

Iris placed a finger to their lips. "Keep your voice down. I don't want to reveal too much in case we're being watched. When Amy was packing for Israel, she was wearing an amber necklace just like the one on the statue of Freya here."

Luna muttered something that sounded like "brigerben," before dropping her hand from Iris's. They continued down the canal in silence as colorful houses with powder blue, sunflower yellow, and coral pink glass passed by. The residential housing tapered off and the man-made canal narrowed as they approached the massive glass house.

Enzo's guard pulled the boat over to the side and everyone else followed suit. Crowds of people gathered around. An old woman gawked at Enzo.

A young boy approached him. "Are these new members of the clan?"

Enzo bent down so he was at the boy's level and ruffled his

hair. "They are just visiting, so make sure you're on your best behavior, okay?"

The boy gave a serious salute that looked comical from someone who barely reached Enzo's waist. Then he scurried off to kick a clear ball around with the other children.

The younger glass mages openly gawked at the group of shifters. The older mages glared and muttered under their breath when they thought Enzo wasn't looking.

Iris's heart raced, and they felt a tail tug at the back of their pants. They clasped their hands over the forming tail. Luna placed a hand on Iris's shoulder and whispered. "Remember. We can't let our emotions rule us or the change will take hold."

Iris squeezed Luna's hand and steadied their breathing as Enzo led them down the cobblestone path. Instead of focusing on the people, Iris stared down at the ground, focusing on the feeling of the stones underneath their feet. They ran a thumb along the calligraphy stone absentmindedly, wishing they had a way to communicate with Amy to see if she was okay and if she'd escaped.

Enzo's glass fortress of a home loomed closer. The place looked as heavily warded as the Council's death row prison cells judging on how much glass had been used in its construction. *I hope Amy's not in one of those prisons because she tried to send us a message.*

When they reached the front entrance, Enzo ran his hands along the top of the glass door and the edges of it glowed. He pulled out a glass shard that was attached to the top of the door by a metal chain. "In order for the magic to recognize you, you'll have to touch this piece of glass. I can give you access by using your magic fingerprints."

Blood rushed through Iris's ears. *Will the device be able to recognize my magic after all of the experimentation?*

Iris hung back as the others pressed their fingers to the glass and walked through the barriers effortlessly. Eiji was the first to go through the door and the magic shimmered a rainbow hue as he stepped through the door. Next up came Shophan who pressed his index finger to the glass and then skittered through. Abir came in just behind him. He didn't break eye contact with Enzo until he was inside.

Once everyone else had made it past the barrier, Luna gave Iris's hand one last squeeze and whispered. "I'm sure it will be fine." before pressing her finger to the glass and stepping through the barrier.

Enzo smiled. "Last but not least."

He held the glass shard out to Iris, but they shook their head. "I don't know if it will recognize me. My body and magic were permanently altered. My physical form is unstable, and my magic might be the same way." Iris held up their thumb, showing its smooth surface.

He pursed his lips. "We'll try it with blood and if the barrier doesn't recognize you, you may have to wait outside. I can't risk taking the barrier down completely."

Iris pricked their finger on the edge of the glass shard. Their violet blood welled, and they allowed a few drops to fall onto the glass. It sizzled and glowed yellow.

When Iris rushed towards the door, it let them through effortlessly, causing Iris to lose their balance and tumble to the black and white tiled floor.

Everyone gawked at Iris like they'd just lost their mind, but Iris just brushed at their pants. "I'm just clumsy. Don't look at me like that,"

Enzo came through the barrier just behind Iris and cleared his throat. Iris turned to face Enzo as Iris hastily pushed themself off the floor. "I know better than to think this is a visit for pleasure. Eiji, do you care to explain what brings your allies here?"

Eiji crossed his arms behind his head. "I'd rather they explain why they're here. It's more interesting that way."

One of Eiji's fangs poked out when he smiled. *I'll repay you for this later.* Iris thought as a claw poked out of their pinky finger. Iris's gaze locked with Enzo's. "One of our allies has been captured by Opal, and we hope to break her free from the Council's clutches."

Enzo clenched his hands at his side and spoke through gritted teeth. "You expect me to send my men on a suicide mission for one mage. You've seen what Opal did to her own clan. Give me one good reason why I should risk my clan's safety for this mission."

Iris opened their mouth to speak, but Luna stepped in front of Iris, putting a hand across their chest. She turned back to Iris. "Let me handle it from here."

Iris's hands went clammy as Luna's voice turned silken. "Amy is not just any enchantress. She could be the key to stopping Opal for good. Iris suspects the girl is a descendant of one of your Gods."

Enzo's mouth dropped open, and he turned to Iris. "What artifact does she carry?"

Iris shrugged. "I'm not sure, but it was a gold necklace with an amber pendant and anytime I was near the artifact, it felt warm like being bathed in sunlight."

Luna added. "There you have it. She has Brísingamen, Freya's necklace. Now, do you want to help us, or would you rather end up on the wrong side of history?"

A hush settled over the room. When Enzo spoke again, his voice was hard. "I will send my men, but if she isn't what you claim her to be, I will have you killed for treachery."

His tone was so cold that Iris shuddered. Their voice came out weak. "Yes sir."

"That's commander to you." He snapped. His forehead wrinkled, transforming his young face.

Iris bowed their head "Apologies. I spoke out of turn, Commander. I can give you my word that she is in fact holding one of the artifacts."

He straightened his back and strode towards Iris until they

were nose to nose. "I can't afford to send my entire army, but I will offer you several of my best soldiers. Don't make me regret it."

Then he spun on his heel and his features softened as he strolled over to Eiji. Enzo rubbed a hand over his face and Eiji placed a hand on his shoulder. "Why don't we sit down for a moment," Eiji crooned and guided Enzo over to the couch.

Eiji gestured to the armchair, and Iris sat in the chair with their legs pulled to their chest as Luna perched on one of the arms. She placed a hand on Iris's thigh. "You're doing the right thing even if it might not feel like it," she whispered.

Eiji rubbed at Enzo's back while Enzo buried his face into Eiji's shoulder. Iris was jealous of the ease in their affection. As much as they wanted to be vulnerable around Luna, they couldn't risk what would happen if they lost focus. They'd already nicked Luna once.

However, when Luna rubbed at Iris's legs, a growl built up in their throat, and they allowed their head to rest on Luna's shoulder. Luna ran her fingers through Iris's short hair and for several minutes, they just sat there without speaking to one another.

It was Abir, the ox shifter, that broke the silence. "Should we leave you all alone? You're looking rather cozy."

Enzo's head rose from Eiji's shoulder and he stood back to his full height, so that he was eye level with Abir. "That won't be necessary. I will go ahead and ready the troops. In the meantime, it might be best if you stay here for the night. There are several rooms, so I'm sure you can find one that's to your liking."

When Enzo rose from the couch, Iris followed suit. "I can't thank you enough for your help."

Enzo gave a weak smile. "I hope it's worth it," he said before rushing out of the door. When he walked through the barrier, something thumped against the house and a caw reached Iris's ear, sending a shiver down their spine. Several of the other shifters stiffened and Luna turned to Iris. "Did you hear that?"

Iris nodded. "Let's hope that little spy didn't hear our conversation. Otherwise, we're dead."

The caw sounded again, and the bird pecked at the house. Iris's skin tingled, and when they reached up to touch their head, they felt pointed ears. Iris sighed. "I'm going to go ahead and lock myself in the upstairs room so I can just ride out the change."

Luna placed a hand over Iris's. "I'll come with you."

Iris walked up the stairs as claws grew from their feet and scraped against the soles of their shoes. Iris kicked off their shoes and carried them upstairs as fangs pricked at their lips. By the time they'd reached the second floor, fur grew from their arms. When Iris and Luna saw a door, Iris opened it and filed in. Luna followed just after. Iris slammed the door shut behind them.

The fabric of Iris's shirt itched at their skin, and they tried to pull it off, but they had more claws than hands. Luna pulled Iris's shirt over their head for them.

When Iris frowned down at their pants, Luna helped slide them off. "You know in different circumstances this would be kind of hot." Luna said and her lip titled up in a grin.

Iris opened their mouth to say something, but it came out as a low rumbling growl. Without the clothing to restrict them, the change happened much faster this time. The ground rushed up to meet Iris as their limbs shortened.

Iris formed a barrier around their mind as their paws stretched out in front of them. Luna sat down beside Iris and a whine escaped Iris's mouth.

Luna stroked Iris's fur covered back. "Don't let the ones who hurt your body take away that fighting spirit I've always admired. If you do that, they win. If this is your new normal, we'll take it one day at a time. Together."

Iris lifted their head and nuzzled Luna.

"You can talk to me, you know? There's no need to be ashamed."

That made Iris tilt their head up to look Luna in the eye. They reached out a tentative thread to Luna's mind. "I feel defective like this. How am I supposed to help fight a war when I can't control my powers?"

Luna's voice echoed in Iris's head. "Maybe this time your role is to lead, not fight. Even now you might feel out of control, but you've been able to control the change somewhat. When you use the breathing exercises, it seems to help you."

"Only for a short while, and I still can't stop it." A whimper escaped Iris.

"You're thinking about the negatives, but I saw several positives as well. When we were in danger, you changed into something that resembled an Encantado and scared the mermaids. I sincerely doubt that it was an accident."

Iris's ears perked up. "I guess you're right, but I haven't been able to replicate what happened there. It was probably just a one-off thing."

Luna placed a hand on Iris's head. "If I know you, you'll figure out a way to make this work in your favor. You're the most resilient shifter I know."

"Thank you, and you're the bravest person I know."

Luna's gaze fell to the floor. "I wish that were true."

Iris rested their head on Luna's lap. *It is true whether you believe it or not.*

When Iris skimmed the room, they caught a glimpse of Enzo's orange underwear lying on the floor and a pair of handcuffs with one cuff still attached to the headboard. Judging by the pictures of Enzo hanging around the room and the rumpled sheets, this was not one of the guest rooms.

Luna's gaze followed Iris's. "Do you want to change rooms?"

Yes please. I don't need to be reminded of Enzo's sex life or my lack thereof. Iris curled up their snout, revealing pointed teeth underneath.

"Valid."

Luna stood up and grabbed Iris's clothes before opening the door. They both stepped out in the hallway and walked along until they found another door. But it revealed a pristine bathroom that gleamed white. "Well, that's not a guest room either. I swear I feel like I need a map to navigate this place," Luna mumbled before shutting the door and heading down the hallway.

The next entrance led to a bedroom the size of a walk-in closet with a sunflower yellow comforter and powder blue walls. The flooring underfoot was a light wood paneling and Iris's claws scrambled against its surface. "Easy there," Luna said and held Iris upright when they almost clattered to the floor.

Luna went over to the bed and patted it.

Iris let out a low growl. *I'm not a dog, you know?*

"I mean technically we're cousins of dogs."

Iris did their best attempt at narrowing their eyes, but Luna just laughed. "It looks really weird when you do that, please stop."

Iris shook their head and then hopped up onto the bed, curling up on the soft duvet. But the sound of glass shattering made their ears prick. *We need to go now,* Iris hopped off the bed, their paws scrambling for purchase on the floor.

Luna turned her ear to the sky. "Did you hear something?"

I think I heard glass shatter from downstairs. Maybe they broke something?

Shophan's scream pierced Iris's mind. Iris's ears pinned back, and they snarled. Iris paced over to the door.

Luna's eyes widened. "We have to help him."

Iris nodded and Luna threw the door open just as they

both felt a sharp pain in their brain like a fraying nerve. Iris and Luna raced down the hallway and towards the stairs.

From the bottom of the stairs, talons scratched on the wood floor. A melody meant to entice mages grated on Iris's sensitive ears.

Iris glanced up at Luna. *It's one of the Sirins. Cover your—* Luna's eyes glowed pink. *Too late.*

Luna walked towards the downstairs with halting footsteps like she was being tugged along on marionette strings. Iris lunged for her, grabbing at Luna's pants leg with their teeth. *Cover your ears. Now.*

Luna looked back at Iris with narrowed eyes. Claws sprouted from Luna's fingertips, and she slashed out at Iris's side. Iris jumped back, and lunged at Luna's other leg, trying to grab her shoe or pants, but Luna kicked out at and caught Iris in the nose. *Just know that you brought this upon yourself,* Iris backed up and then ran towards Luna at full speed and tackled her.

Iris's claws dug into skin and Luna toppled over. She squirmed underneath Iris, her hands pushing at Iris's fur. The pink glow in her eyes faded. "Why is there 120 pounds of wolf sitting on my chest?"

Great, so you're back. Cover your ears. There's a Sirin here.

Luna clasped her hands over her ears and Iris backed up off of her. "How the hell did a Sirin get in here?"

Iris snorted. *I don't know. Why don't you ask her when she's done tearing you to pieces?*

"No thanks."

The Sirin's gaze locked with theirs and its wings flapped as it crept closer on taloned feet. Iris's gaze skimmed the downstairs area, and their heart sank as they caught sight of Shophan's mangled body. Claw marks raked across his skin, and his eyes were open, but no one else was visible from the stairs. Iris reached out to Abir's thoughts. *Is everyone okay?*

Abir's mental voice was scratchy and his thoughts scrambled. *I don't. I'm not. No. Shophan's gone. My fault. He was here because of me. He heard the Sirin first and warned me. He pushed me out of the way. How did the Sirin get through the barrier?*

Iris pinned their ears back. *I'm not sure how she made it through the barrier, but I think the crow we heard earlier was what sent her.*

Ayla growled. *Damnit. I didn't think it could hear us here. If we'd left sooner, Shophan might still be...* Her voice trailed off. She couldn't bring herself to finish the sentence. *What do we do now?*

The connection went silent as the Sirin came within arm's reach of Luna. Iris shuffled several paces back, but the Sirin advanced four steps for every two Iris took. Each flap of their wings helped propel them forward even as Iris struggled for purchase on the floors. *She's speedy for a walking bird woman.*

Iris glanced at Luna. *Find some water. We need to drench her wings so she won't fly off. She should be weak to electricity and fire too. I'll look for fire.* Then Iris did the one thing they were taught to never do. They ignored their screaming instincts, turned their back on the Sirin and ran through the hallway.

Iris searched for a flame or anything that could create electricity, but not being able to open the doors made that tricky. Every closed door made their heart thump louder in their chest.

When another hallway led to a dead end, Iris tried to back track, but the Sirin was there with her fangs bared. Iris's hackles raised, and they let out a growl, but the creature only hissed back. Iris glanced at the window, but it was closed and too high up to jump out of without risking serious damage.

Iris's back pressed against the wall, and their blood chilled in their veins. *Someone help. She's got me cornered,* Iris shouted out to anyone in range, but they got no reply.

Every muscle in Iris's body screamed to run, to not get any closer to that Sirin, but no one was answering their call and they had to act soon if they wanted to get away.

When Iris caught a glimpse of Luna coming up behind the Sirin with a bucket of water, they pounced.

Iris curled their lips back revealing fangs, and they snarled before rushing in and snapping at the creature's leg. The Sirin pivoted out of Iris's reach, so Iris lunged to the side and grabbed hold of the creature's other leg and yanked it back with their teeth. The Sirin's nails scratched at Iris's haunches, and Iris yelped but kept the hold and tugged, putting all their weight into bringing the creature down.

The Sirin fell on the floor with a thud. Iris shouted, *Now.* And Luna dumped the water on the creature.

Iris skidded past the fallen Sirin, beelining for the stairs with Luna just behind them. Iris kept looking back to see if the Sirin was following, but they hadn't seen the creature yet.

When a pair of hands grabbed Iris, trying to pull them into a room, Iris turned around with teeth bared, but they stopped short at the sight of dark black hair and eyes as white as the moon. It was Luna.

"Trying to bite me. I'm offended. Especially considering I just saved you back there." She joked.

Sorry. I thought you were the Sirin. We need to get out of here before she comes after us again. Our best bet is heading into town to meet Eiji and Enzo. Iris nodded towards the exit.

"Alright, but we'll have to move quickly, so I'll shift as well." Luna stripped off her clothes and crouched down. Her snout grew longer, and her limbs shortened until she was standing before Iris covered in midnight black fur.

I think that creature was after you. When you ran off, she ignored me and went straight for you. You must have really pissed Opal off.

Iris nodded. *That makes sense considering I'm putting together a rebellion to free her prisoners.*

Iris ran out of the room and down the hallway. The Sirin was close behind. *Everyone. Meet us at the front door. We need some help opening it.*

"Got it," Abir replied and raced down the stairs. When he

saw the Sirin approaching, he threw the door open and recovered his ears.

Iris and Luna leapt over the last few steps and raced out of the door.

Iris's heart dropped as they approached the square. Off in the distance, smoke rose from several buildings, and a fire ravaged the pristine city. The dome surrounding the city was cracked and charred in several places. *This has to be Opal's doing. We have to find Eiji and Enzo. Now!*

Iris's paws flew across the cobblestones. Crows circled in the sky. Weather mages at the center of the square stirred up dark storm clouds that shot lighting at the glass mages. Each glass mage was in an organized group with elemental mages flanking either side.

The fire mages super-heated the sand the glass mages carried and then the ice mages pelted the glass with a thick layer of frost. Iris watched in amazement as the mages turned tiny glass bubbles into massive shields that they used to barrel through the chaos. Magic bounced off the glass and projectiles shattered on impact. At the back of their glass bubble was a small tail that trailed behind them as they moved.

The elementals shot fire from their hands and the weather mages struck out at them with hail and lightning. Black clouds coated the sky and heavy hail rained down. The elemental mages raced towards the glass tail to protect it, but they were too late. A golf ball sized piece of hail hit the tail. Spiderweb cracks filled the glass sphere and it exploded with the mage still trapped inside.

A sad howl tore from Iris's throat.

Luna snapped. *Stop, they're going to come after us if you...*

A weather mage turned towards the two of them. A dark cloud loomed over Iris. Their hackles raised as the mage stirred up magic. They jumped to the side just before a bolt of lightning seared the ground. *That was too close for comfort.*

Iris searched the crowd for Enzo and Eiji. Iris and Luna

ran behind one of the buildings to get out of the weather mage's direct line of sight.

When Iris glimpsed white blonde fur, they ran towards it to see Eiji with his fox ears perked up and fangs bared. Several versions of him, illusions, stood side by side in the courtyard with balls of blue fox fire in their palms.

A massive wolf, a Fenrir, held Enzo's neck in his teeth. The vicious beast stank of rotting fish, and Iris's lips curled back.

Enzo pelted the creature with orbs of glass that shattered and embedded into the creature's skin, but it barely flinched.

Eiji snarled. "Put him down or I'll make you regret that you ever dared cross me."

The Fenrir shook Enzo in its grip like he was a chew toy. Enzo kicked out wildly at the wolf in an attempt to break free.

Luna sprinted towards Eiji and blocked him from the Fenrir. She let out a deep warning growl and the massive wolf's ears pinned back. The Fenrir dropped Enzo to the ground and lowered its head. Then it charged at Luna.

Iris darted past Luna and sank their teeth into the monster's massive side. It threw Iris off like a bothersome fly with a shake off its head. Then it turned and grabbed Iris's neck in its teeth. Iris whimpered and threw their body weight around, trying to get out of its grip. Its teeth tore Iris's flesh and took off chunks of fur. Waves of pain crashed over Iris as they bucked and flailed, but it was getting harder and harder to breathe.

Iris felt warmth and thought it was blood until the sulfur scent of burning fur stung Iris's nose. The Fenrir's grip slackened. Hands pulled Iris back, and they turned around to bite their new attacker, but a familiar rumbling chuckle stopped Iris.

"I'm trying to help you, not hurt you, Iris." Eiji's sand colored hair came into view.

The other mages yelled. "The Fenrir is down." before Iris's vision went fuzzy.

Eiji shook Iris, or at least they thought he was, but it felt far away. Iris's body felt cold despite the heat coming from Eiji's hands. Even though their bones were cracking, and they knew they were changing, they didn't feel any pain, just numbness.

Tears streamed down Eiji's cheeks, and Iris wanted to move to brush them away, but their body refused to budge. "Don't cry. I'm okay," they wanted to say, but their mouth refused to form words.

Is this what the end feels like? It's more pleasant than I thought it would be. They thought as their vision faded to black.

CHAPTER 11

A guard bowed to Opal with terror in his eyes. "Council leader. I apologize, but the prisoner has escaped."

Opal tightened her grip around the amethyst lynx's neck. She snarled. "Which prisoner?"

The guard gulped. "It was Amy. She got out of her cuffs. It appears she swiped the key to her cuffs somehow."

Opal raised her sword, and the guard shut his eyes, "Open your eyes, coward. I won't kill you, yet. I'm using my leverage." Opal yanked the lynx upright by the scruff of its neck and sliced its back, close to its core. The blade cut the animal like it was made from flesh instead of gems. The animal whimpered as blood sizzled and hissed against her sword's magic. She dug the blade deeper into the lynx, hoping the threat would lure Amy back, but Clarent whispered in her ear. *We need the lynx alive if you want her to come back for it. That enchantress girl should feel her pain. The sting she feels through their connection might at least slow her down if it doesn't convince her to return.*

When a gasp sounded from Opal's side, she turned to Raven who was peeking out from one of the steel walls, her eyes wide. Raven signed. "Why are you hurting Violet? I like her," she pointed to the lynx, and Opal cursed under her breath. Opal dropped the familiar, and its limp body slid to the floor.

"I had to. That girl is an enemy. She wants to hurt us."

"But Violet was nice to me. She told me you hurt that girl's friends. Is that true?"

Opal's jaw clenched. It was hard to forget sometimes that she was omni tongued. "I did what I had to in order to protect you and my people."

Her dark blue eyes, like sapphires stared into Opal's soul, and a dark curl fell in front of Raven's face, reminding her of Joan in a way that made Opal's heart clench. She eyed Opal with distrust as she took cautious steps to the lynx and encircled it into a hug. She raised her hand and signed. "Well Violet didn't do anything wrong, so leave her alone."

Opal didn't know what Raven mentally murmured to the beast, but she imagined Raven was saying something along the lines of "I'll protect you."

Clarent's voice whispered. *I still don't understand why you saved this girl. She's a liability, a weakness that your enemies can exploit. You should kill her.*

Opal's hand gripped the sword. *You can't have her. She's one of the few important people left in my life.*

Clarent's voice turned sickeningly sweet, coating Opal's mind like honey. *Caring for Joan's cousin won't bring back Joan. Not even a necromancer can revive her. Her soul has moved on and so must you.*

Opal shouted at the dragon. *That's not what this is about!*

The dragon's wicked laughter curled around her mind like smoke. *Whatever helps you sleep at night, but saving one girl doesn't make up for the thousands you killed seeking revenge.*

You can destroy me thoroughly, but I'll never allow you to kill my friend. I will find a way to rid myself of you and this curse.

The sword glowed silver. *The curse within you was potent enough to kill Merlin herself. She died to seal me away.*

Opal clanged the sword against the ground and the force vibrated up her arm. *Well then, I will have to be more powerful than Merlin.*

What makes you think a weakling like you who came seeking my power can defeat a curse Merlin couldn't? The dragon hissed.

Because I might have found something more powerful than the curse, she thought

You mean the girl who slipped through your fingers. I have no doubt that you will fail to retrieve her.

Shut up, Opal yelled, and the dragon went silent, but her laughter echoed through Opal's mind, taunting her.

Opal crouched before Raven and placed a hand on the girl's shoulder to get her attention. She signed. "I'm sorry, Raven. I'll be gentler with Violet, okay? I'm going to take her to someone that will bring her back to her mage companion, okay?"

Raven signed. "She says she doesn't want to go with you. That you're lying." And hugged the lynx tighter.

Opal ran a hand along her face and signed. "Raven. Her owner is dangerous. She tried to hurt me. I know this is hard to understand, but I need Violet to help me find her. I won't hurt her as long as she doesn't attack me again. Can you tell her that for me?"

Raven glanced down at the creature and signed back "Okay."

She nuzzled the lynx who huffed.

Raven signed. "Violet said she will go with you, but she still hates you. Why does she hate you?"

Opal shook her head and signed. "The accident."

Raven's mouth opened in an "O."

Opal stroked Raven's hair with one hand and signed with the other. "I need you to go back to your room until I come get you. If Amy escaped, it is dangerous for you out here."

Raven nodded and walked away in the direction of her room. Once she was out of sight, Opal glanced at the lynx as it struggled to stand. "I guess I'll have to carry you if you can't get up." When she reached for the lynx, Violet hissed at her. Opal raised an eyebrow at the creature. "I'm trying to help you since you can't move. Don't even think about biting me." Opal hauled Violet up onto her shoulder and dragged her along as she searched for Dusk.

Opal pulled out a sparkling dark red and turquoise Chalcopyrite pendulum and placed her palm to its jagged surface. The stone gave off a silvery white aura, and pulled slightly to the left, so she went down the corridor.

The signal was weaker than expected. Usually, it would tug her around corners like a large dog in desperate need of a walk, but this was more of a gentle pull. *Did he fall asleep on the job?* She thought as she headed towards him.

Her footsteps clunked on the metal floors and echoed through the corridors. As she grew closer, the aura grew stronger, and she saw something she hadn't planned for.

Leaning against the wall was someone with dark black hair like Dusk's plastered to their face with sweat, but with a slighter stature and longer, thinner arms. They wore the black pants Dusk always wore, but a familiar pocket watch with a glittering black cat's eye at its center stared back out at Opal. Their lips were full and pink and the black stubble on their chin was gone. When they looked up, their amber eyes widened, and she caught a glimpse of a brown device on their ear. "Opal. It's not what it looks like."

Now she knew why she'd been drawn to Dusk when they'd first met. *Dusk was really Cat.*

When Cat's gaze caught hers, she crossed her hands over her chest. The familiar features morphed, the full lips thinned, and her figure lengthened. The familiar image vanished before her eyes. The hearing aid disappeared. Dusk was standing before Opal once more.

Her blood boiled. *Why would Cat lie to me?*

His, no her, lip curled up in a faint grin. "Hi Opal. How long have you been standing there?"

Opal's arms crossed over her chest. "Long enough. When were you planning on telling me about your little secret, Cat?"

Cat leveled a cold stare at Opal. Her voice came out low and rough. "I'm not Cat. I never was. That was who my mother wanted me to be, who the clan wanted me to be."

Opal shook her head. "If that's true, why didn't you just tell me who you were instead of tricking me?"

Cat bit her lip. "Because I had a feeling you wouldn't accept me for who and what I am and based on your reaction just now I was right." Cat shoved her hands in her pockets.

Anger swelled in Opal's chest. "You're wrong. If you hadn't lied, I would have accepted you."

Cat dug a hand from her pockets. Talons grew from her fingertips. "Fine. You want to know the truth? I'm not just an enchantment mage, I'm a shifter too just like I told you when you found me that day. I didn't lie, I just told you what I needed to so you wouldn't kill me on the spot." Cat glanced at the floor. "My mother spouted the same lies when I told her I was an enchanter, not an enchantress. What I did doesn't void my eligibility for acceptance. It's your own stubbornness that did that." Her hands shook at her side.

Opal gritted her teeth. "You have some nerve. If you don't want me to toss you to the Magic Council, you'll go and fetch Amy for me and take this wretched creature with you," She took the lynx off her shoulder and slid it across the floor to Cat as the creature panted heavily.

Cat grabbed the lynx by the scruff of its neck. Her eyes narrowed in a glare. "How do you suggest I find Amy?"

Opal banged the Chalcopyrite into the wall and several pieces fell off and clattered to the ground. "Amy's familiar is connected to her, so it can be used to track her. You're an enchantress and a shifter, so use the familiar's blood to track her. Maybe you can use one of the birds to track her. They should flock to you since you're a bird shifter."

Cat picked up the gemstone. She spoke to Opal with her face frozen in a frown. "As you wish, Argentum."

"That's not my name." Opal hissed.

"And Cat isn't my name." She answered and strode out of the room head held high.

Clarent's dragon familiar whispered in her ear. *I didn't even have to intervene that time. You played the part of villain excellently there. Perhaps I'm beginning to rub off on you.* Opal looked down at the green marks creeping along her sword arm and dug her nails into them.

"Shut up." Opal boomed.

Excalibur's voice was a weak whisper in her mind. *You could make it up to him if you went and apologized.*

"I'm not apologizing, she's not a him, and I'm not a villain. Will you both just shut up?"

Opal slammed her fist into the wall and strode out of the room, trying to banish the image of Cat's features contorted in a grimace. *I'm sorry Cat. I failed you just like I did back then.*

CHAPTER 12

*W*hen Tiffany arrived, Amy stumbled out of the gift shop and into her car. "Sorry you had to come get me on such short notice. Did any of the customers complain?"

Tiffany shrugged. "Just the one with the Karen haircut that thinks vaccines cause autism."

Amy rolled her eyes. "That's okay. She'll live for a day without her essential oils."

Tiffany laughed. "I'm glad to know I'm not the only person that finds her infuriating. You look like shit. Did someone hit you with a bus?"

Amy let out an awkward laugh, "Try bitten by a hungry gator."

Tiffany hissed through clenched teeth. "Ouch. Maybe you should've just gone to Israel."

Amy rubbed her shoulder. "You know that was the plan, but life had something else in store for me. Let's get back to the store before any more of the customers get upset."

Tiffany shrugged "Alright, but you might want to let me grab the step stool, so you don't have to climb up." She said as she led Amy to her beige SUV.

Amy limped to the passenger door and climbed up to the passenger's seat, plopping down unceremoniously into the leather chair.

Tiffany gaped at her with the step stool in her hand. "You couldn't have waited five seconds?"

Amy blew a strand of hair out of her face. "I hate using step stools just like I hate using ladders, and I just want to get out of here. The sooner the better. Oh, and did you bring the pouch of gems like I asked?"

Tiffany turned the key in the engine. "First of all, the customers can wait. You're injured. Second, I know you're afraid of using them, but I think the hospital is even less fun." Tiff shrugged. "And yes Ms. messed up priorities, I brought the gem bag you wanted. Although, I'm still not sure why you didn't have me bring a first aid kit or something."

Amy crossed her arms over her chest. "I just feel better having them here."

Tiff shook her head. "I mean whatever makes you happy boss, but if those wounds reopen, don't come crying to me."

As the SUV's engine roared to life, Amy's mind drifted off. Her hand reached for her bare wrist. She gripped the gem pouch in her lap like a lifeline. *Once I'm alone, I'll have to contact the others.*

They'd been driving in silence down 95 for several minutes when Tiffany turned to her and said, "So are you going to tell me how you went from going to Israel to ending up in the middle of the Everglades with a massive injury on your leg? I have a feeling you're not telling me the whole story."

Amy gave her a mischievous grin. "If I told you, I'd have to kill you."

She snorted. "You watch too many movies. Be as cryptic as you want, but I'll figure it out eventually."

Amy rubbed at her wrists which were still raw from the metal cuffs. "Trust me when I say you wouldn't believe me even if I told you."

When Tiff turned off the highway that led back to the shop, golden eyes appeared in the rearview mirror. Amy yanked the handle of the seat and threw her weight back, dropping out of view. Her vision blurred, and white dots danced in front of her eyes.

"What the hell are you doing? You're going to hurt yourself," Tiffany said.

Amy gulped in a few breaths. "Sorry. I think I saw one of my exes. Did you see a guy with golden eyes and dark hair on the side of the road?"

Tiff's gaze moved to the left and then the right. "I don't see anyone. Are you sure you aren't imagining things?"

Amy bit down on her lip. "I could have sworn I saw him. Maybe the blood loss is getting to me. I'll go ahead and rest down here until I feel less woozy."

She let out a dry laugh. "Alright, but you might want to prop the seat up a little higher in case one of the cops pulls us over. Unless you plan on paying for the ticket."

Tiff's laughter stopped, and she muttered an "Oh shit." and swerved the car to the right, slamming Amy into the door ribs first.

Amy's gaze snapped to Tiff. "What happened?"

Tiff let out a sigh. "Sorry. I think I might have hit a bird. I'm going to pull over, so I can go check on it."

Amy's head shot up. "Did you see what kind of bird it was?"

Tiffany shook her head and pulled over to the shoulder of the road. "I'm not sure. Maybe a falcon or something?"

The car bumped and moved beneath Amy, making bile rise into her throat. She swallowed. "Maybe we should just leave it. It's probably fine without us."

Tiffany yanked the emergency brake up and shook her head. "How can you be so heartless? What if the poor thing is injured?"

Amy gripped the cup holder on her door with white

knuckles. "Then it's the circle of life."

Tiffany covered her mouth with her hand. "Remind me to never let you pet sit. I'm going out to check on it."

Tiff reached for the door handle, and Amy grabbed onto her arm. "Don't. I'll go check on it."

Tiffany shot her an incredulous look and pulled her hand away. "Five seconds ago, you wanted to leave the bird behind. Why do you suddenly have to be the one to do it?"

Amy pursed her lips. "You'll just have to trust me when I say it's for your own safety."

"I'm starting to think more than just your leg was injured," Tiffany said and pointed to her head.

Amy's shoulders slumped. "I know you probably won't believe anything I'm about to say and you'll think I've lost my mind-"

"I already think that." She interjected.

Amy rubbed her fingers on her temples. "That bird out there might be a shapeshifter and a dangerous one at that. He's after me because I'm an enchantress. Why do you think everyone comes to me when they want to fix their luck and broken relationships?"

Tiff waved away Amy's comment. "Now I know you've lost it. I'm going to check on the bird whether you like it or not."

She stepped out of the car and stomped over to the bird with Amy trailing behind her. Amy heaved out a sigh of relief when she saw it was just a regular mottled brown bird with eyes that were black rather than gold. It had a black anklet on one of its legs that looked like a tracker. *Maybe it escaped from the bird sanctuary?*

Tiff pet the bird's head and it leaned into her touch. "See the bird isn't some dangerous shapeshifter, and it seems to be friendly with humans. Why don't we drop it off at the bird rescue just around the corner?"

Amy crossed her arms over her chest. "Fine. You were

right. Happy?"

Tiff rolled her eyes. "I'd be happier if you hadn't made up that weird story in the first place to keep me from helping the bird." Tiffany glanced down at the anklet. "Weird. It doesn't look like any tracker I've seen before. Maybe it's new tech. Mind if we take it to the sanctuary before I drop you off at home?"

Amy picked at her lip. "I guess. I mean it's not like I have much choice since you're driving." When Tiffany picked the bird up, it chirped happily in her arms, and they wrapped it up in one of her jackets before transporting it.

The tension in Amy's muscles eased, but stars still danced in her vision with any sudden movement. She desperately needed some food, drink, and rest, but she couldn't do any of that yet. She still had to let the others know that she'd escaped and find out if Naru and Iris had been able to gather enough mages for a successful rescue.

"Can you just take me straight home after this please? I have something I need to get before I go to the hospital."

Tiffany raised an eyebrow. "You lost a lot of blood. Shouldn't you go to the hospital first?"

She shook her head as she scrambled for an excuse. "I need to bring my medication with me. They probably won't have my prescription there, and I need it."

Tiffany shrugged. "Alright, but if you pass out, I will call an ambulance and you'll have to foot the bill."

Amy gulped. Paying for an ambulance ride would wipe out a sizable portion of her savings. "Fine, but if I end up getting hospitalized, you'd have to deal with all the Karens by yourself."

Amy grinned as she looked at Tiffany, but Tiffany's face paled and she slammed on the brakes. The car jerked forward, stopping halfway into the parking lot.

"Tiff. What happened this time?" Amy jostled Tiffany's shoulder. Tiffany just pointed forward, and Amy looked in the parking lot to see Opal's silver-grey hair flowing freely in the wind. She held Violet by the spiny scruff of her neck. Violet's panicked screams reached Amy's mind. *Get out of here. Now. She intends to use me to capture you again!*

The bird they'd picked up chirped wildly. Its bracelet beeped, and she saw flickers of magic coming from the tag on its foot. She squinted her eyes at the anklet and saw the black tag had streaks of dark red, turquoise, and violet. Tiny chips of chalcopyrite were embedded into it. *Damnit. Tracking magic. She made a fool out of me with fools gold.*

A weight pressed against Amy's chest, and she looked down to see the amber pendant. The one she'd bought from the market stalls in Delray. *Strange. How did that get there?* It felt warm against her skin.

Tiffany turned to Amy. "Y-you weren't bullshitting me earlier, were you?"

Amy's eyes locked with hers. "I wasn't, and that woman there wants me dead. She tracked us with the bird you insisted on helping. I suggest leaving it here and driving in the opposite direction."

Tiffany gaped. "I'm not throwing an injured bird out into traffic. We'll find somewhere safe to drop it off once we're far away from this shit show." She moved her hand blindly towards the gear shift. Amy's eyes remained fixed on Violet as Tiffany threw the car in reverse and slammed on the gas.

The car lurched backwards, but Opal ran towards them, inhumanly fast.

A long honk sounded as a car whizzed past. Tiffany screamed and jerked the car to the side, slamming Amy into the passenger door. She gritted her teeth together as pain radiated through her shoulder. The guy flipped her off as he sped by.

"Hurry," Amy glanced through the front window to see Opal only a few dozen feet away.

"I'm trying." She slammed the car into drive and hit the

gas. They careened forward, but cars rushed right at them.

"Wrong way. Wrong way," Amy shouted and put her hands over her eyes. The car jerked forward. When Amy heard a thump and Tiffany screamed, she peeked through her fingers. The metal of the hood of the SUV had been dented, but the other car wasn't as lucky. Most of the other car's hood had collapsed in on itself and it spewed smoke. The man they'd collided with scowled and slammed the door shut behind him before it fell off its hinges.

Amy shook Tiff's shoulder. "If you want to have a chance at living to tell this tale, I recommend getting as far away from here as you can." She opened the door and hung out of the passenger's side of the car.

"But what about the guy? I don't want to get in trouble for a hit and run."

Amy sighed. "You're really worried about that right now? I will take care of him, but you need to leave. Now." Amy leapt out of the car.

Tiff's glance jumped between the angry driver approaching the car and Amy. "How are you going to get back?"

Amy held up a hand, blocking Tiffany from making any more comments. Opal gave an airy laugh that sent a shiver down Amy's spine. "I'll figure it out. Now go!"

Tiffany slammed the door shut behind Amy and revved the engine. Her tires squealed as she backed away from the crushed car and swerved back into the correct lane and down the street.

Amy threw up her hands, "All right. You've got me. Now what are you going to do with me? I'm not going back there with you. You'll have to kill me first."

Opal didn't smirk or make a retort. She gave a dry laugh and drew a sword that looked like Excalibur, but she couldn't feel any magic coming off of it. Opal's chin dipped to her chest, and she slouched.

Amy bit her lip. *Opal would never slouch like that and that sword doesn't feel real. Is that really Opal?* She reached down to the amber necklace and bright light fanned out around her. Opal jumped back like a cat avoiding getting sprayed with water. Grey eyes turned to golden yellow.

Got you. Amy stepped towards the fake. "What are you doing here, Dusk? Why are you still helping her?"

Violet's voice shouted. *What are you doing? Run. Opal sent him to bring you back.*

I'm not leaving you behind again, and he's not what you think he is, Amy thought.

Violet squirmed in Dusk's grip, clawing at the air as she tried to break free.

Dusk pressed a knife to her throat. "Move any closer, and I'll kill your familiar."

Amy shrugged. "Funny. I thought Opal had already done that. What's stopping you? I did leave her behind."

Dusk's eyes darkened and the hand holding the knife shook. "Opal thought bringing you back would require leverage. If you don't want her to take her last breath, come with me."

Amy's gaze met those familiar yellow depths. "You don't have to do this. I would have died back there if you hadn't helped me."

Dusk clenched his teeth together. "There's no going back for me. I've killed and hurt so many people for her," his eyes shone with unshed tears.

Amy took a step towards him, but he backed up. His grip tightened on Violet, making her hiss. "I won't say you were blameless, but you looked up to her, and she took advantage of that. Opal is the irredeemable one, not you. You still have a choice, Dusk. Choose to forgive yourself. Choose to take a better path. One where your allies don't consider you disposable."

Dusk looked between Violet and Amy as indecision warred in his eyes.

Amy took a step back and raised her open palms. "I don't have any gems in my hand. I just want Violet back. Please think about how you'd feel if I threatened you with Kuro."

Dusk glanced at the frazzled familiar, and he let out a long sigh. He dropped Violet. Violet gave a low growl and ran to Amy's side. "Go before I change my mind," Dusk boomed. Any trace of Opal's face vanished, revealing his angular jaw and dark black hair.

Violet rubbed up against Amy, but still bared her teeth at Dusk.

Dusk cocked his head to the side. "How did you know I wasn't Opal?"

Amy licked her lips. "Opal would never lower her head like that; she's far too prideful, and she wouldn't hesitate to put me down with a snide remark. The sword was the biggest indicator because it just didn't feel right."

He shrugged. "And here I thought you were going to say the power of friendship or some nonsense like that."

Amy stroked the spiny fur of her familiar, and her hands came away with blood. "I'm glad you're okay, Violet." She turned to Dusk, and her face fell into a frown. "Why did you let her go?"

He placed his hands in his pockets, and the silver from his pocket watch glinted in the sunlight. "I imagine the same reason you didn't expose me to Opal or kill me when you had the chance. Not that it matters now."

"What do you mean by that?"

His nose wrinkled. "I made a miscalculation. Opal is more perceptive than I gave her credit for."

Amy reached out a hand for him. "You can come with us. You don't have to fight for her. You don't have to die for her."

He smacked her hand away. "Don't talk like you know her. You talk like she's nothing but a monster, but she's not."

"How could you say that after what she did to our people, to you? She was supposed to lead us, and she turned our town to a smoldering pile of rubble. She was willing to gamble with your life."

He balled his fist at his side. "But she also saved Joan's sister and believed in me in the War of the Twin Swords when no one else did. Even if you weren't the one who handed me over, you abandoned me."

Amy clutched her shirt just near her chest. "It wasn't like that."

"Then why didn't you ever look for me?"

Amy's gaze drifted to the floor.

He scoffed. "That's what I thought. You gave up when she captured me, but when your sister goes missing, all of a sudden you're ready to become some revolutionary. Be honest with yourself. You only care when it affects you personally."

Amy bit her lip. "That's not true."

He crossed his arms over his chest. "Then please enlighten me. How am I wrong?"

Amy shifted her weight from foot to foot. "When Opal captured you, I tried to find you at first. When I came up with nothing, I thought you were dead. I should have done anything possible to get you back or to at least find out what had happened, but I was too scared. But I'm not going to make that mistake again. I'm going to fight, and I won't let anyone stop me. Not even you."

A smile brightened his eyes. "I haven't seen a fire like that in your eyes since the first day I met you." His finger lifted her chin, so that she was gazing into his citrine yellow eyes. "You didn't run like I warned you to. I could take you back to her now, but you've intrigued me." A shiver ran down her spine at that word. It made her think of how Opal had described her, *intriguing*.

Dusk lowered his hand. "But I have to go now. Take this chance to run as my parting gift."

He turned his back on Amy. *He can't leave. If he leaves, he'll die.* She reached for his wrist, but he walked so quickly that she reached for air. Her injured leg gave out, and she tumbled forward, smacking into him.

Dusk turned around and yelled. "What are you doing?"

Her full body weight slammed into him, making him lose his balance mid turn. She fell to the floor on top of him, her legs straddling his chest. His eyes were wild, and he searched the ground.

Her gaze was drawn to his ear and then to the ground beside him. A brown device lay on the asphalt. She'd knocked out part of his hearing device. Amy pulled her dagger out and placed it over his chest, but her hands shook. "It's still not too late to join us."

He grabbed the hand that held the dagger. "You think they'll just let me join you? They'd probably kill me slowly and painfully after what I did." He grabbed onto the blade of the dagger, his hand dripping blood and yanked it sharply upwards.

The handle hit her in the chest. As she was gasping for air, He grabbed hold of the handle and twisted it to the side, wrenching it from her grip.

Dusk bucked her off and tossed the dagger. It slid across the asphalt. "Why are you so determined to have me join you?"

Amy craned her neck, so her lips were in full view. "Because I can't let you waltz back to your death like you don't matter. You matter to me more than you know...old friend," She gave him a lopsided grin and felt around the asphalt for the hearing aid that had fallen.

When Dusk caught the movement, he grabbed her wrist with blinding speed and squeezed. "Was that some form of trick to get me to drop my guard?" Amy shook her head and opened her palm to reveal the device.

149

He ran a hand through his hair. "Oh." He loosened his grip. "Sorry."

Amy dropped the device into his hand. "It's okay. I understand. I'd be wary too after what Opal told you." She placed her hand on his. "I'll make sure they don't hurt you. I'll vouch for you. You just have to trust me. Can you do that?"

Dusk put the hearing aid back in and covered his ears with his hair. The device disappeared into his magic. He took her hand. "That I think I can manage."

Behind her, Violet hissed and snarled. *This must be a trap. Finish him and let's get away. Opal killed your people. She killed so many of my own kind. Helping him is as bad as helping Opal, and you promised me you'd kill Opal. Why not start by killing her assassin?*

Amy's gaze turned to her familiar. *He's my friend, and you heard him. He's going to work with us. I won't hurt him.*

Her black tipped ear twitched. *He's an enemy and a liar. If you won't finish him, I will.*

She lunged, but Amy jumped in the way, her arms held out in front of her. Gemstone shards ripped into her arm and Violet hissed.

I don't understand what's gotten into you, but I want no part in it. Until you come to your senses, I'm abandoning our contract.

Amy ran towards her. "Please don't leave. Just trust me," she shouted.

Violet bared her fangs in a snarl. *Trust you? We all trusted your clan and look where that got us. There are thousands of dead familiars scattered about Gemstone Forest. Your people have been reaping the benefits of our magic, but they abandoned their duty as protectors when it mattered most. Our home is a smoldering ruin because of Opal. I won't aid someone who's a sympathizer to our killer. You promised to end Opal, but now you take in her ally. If you won't kill her, I'll do it myself even if it kills me.*

She turned her head and loped away, leaving Amy alone with Dusk.

hen Iris's eyes fluttered open, Eiji hovered over her. He rubbed at his tear-stained eyes and clutched her hand. His voice cracked when he called out. "Enzo. Iris is awake."

Iris bit her lip as she took in her surroundings. The sibling shifters she'd seen when her eyes had fluttered open earlier were gone and a snake shifter with slitted pupils had taken their place, hanging back in the shadows of the room. Iris tried to push herself up, but the room spun, and Eiji pushed her back down on the couch. "Take it easy there. You were pretty seriously injured."

Iris's voice came out raspy when she spoke. "What happened? Is everyone okay?"

Eiji bit his lip. "Not everyone."

Her heart sank. "Where is Luna?"

Eiji turned to Enzo and then looked back at her. "She has some serious injuries, but she'll be okay. She won't be joining us in the fight."

"Oh, thank Dagon she's okay," Iris said and then put a hand over her mouth.

Eiji rolled his eyes. "It's okay Enzo isn't going to take offense to your differences in beliefs."

Enzo cleared his throat. "So long as our differences of beliefs don't create a difference in morals, it makes no difference to us."

Iris's cheeks heated. "How bad were the casualties? How did we fight them off?"

Enzo raised an eyebrow. "We didn't fight them off. They retreated. But, I'm afraid I lost many soldiers, so I can't offer you much assistance. I need to protect my clan after all and repair the dome."

Iris dug her nails into her palms. "That's okay. I understand," Iris's stomach dropped and her breath hitched. Their odds of rescuing Amy and Garnet were looking worse by the moment. *If we can't build a strong enough army, we won't stand a chance against Opal, especially with her wielding Excalibur and Clarent.*

Eiji tapped Iris's forehead with a finger. "I can see you spiraling, Iris. We'll figure this out. He will still be sending us a handful of soldiers. We're better off than we were. Take some deep breaths, okay."

Iris took an overly exaggerated breath in and groaned when she breathed out. "There. Satisfied?"

Eiji smiled. "Yes. Feel better?"

Iris groaned. "Not really. What are we going to do?"

Eiji placed a hand on her shoulder. "We'll find a way to win this fight, somehow."

"And if we don't? If it's impossible to win?" Her voice cracked.

"Then we retreat so we can live to fight another day."

Iris hunched her shoulders, but Eiji lifted her chin. "I know as wolf shifters you're a prideful lot, but there's nothing wrong with running to survive."

Iris swallowed over the lump in her throat. "That doesn't make it easier, Eiji. I'm not exactly keen on abandoning my friends despite what the pack thinks. Let's gather the troops."

He blinked at her. "Are you planning on going to the human world now? You haven't even finished healing."

Iris braced her hand against the couch and stood up. The floor swayed beneath her, and she blinked against spots in her vision but stayed upright. "I'll heal soon enough. One of the...perks of the experimentation," she wrinkled her nose at the word *perks*. "Think about it this way. How long do you think she'll keep Amy and Garnet alive?"

"As long as it benefits her." Eiji said, his voice flat.

Iris raised her gaze to meet his, "Precisely. Which is why we need to act quickly. She could have already tortured out whatever she wanted from Amy and Garnet. Once that happens, she might wait to get approval from the Council to execute Amy, but that's if we're lucky. We need to act quickly."

He sighed. "I see your point, but many of us were injured including you. Shouldn't we at least wait until you've all had some time to heal?"

Nausea battered her stomach, but she stood her ground. "If we wait, our only chance at rescuing a powerful ally in defeating Opal might disappear forever. We can't take that risk. We need to move now. The sooner the better."

Eiji looked back to Enzo who frowned. Enzo said, "I'll gather the troops, but they won't be pleased by this turn of events."

"That's okay. You can blame me," Iris said with a strained smile.

Enzo turned on his heel and left Iris and Eiji alone. Her thoughts shifted to Luna. Images of her covered in purple bruises whirled through Iris's mind. As if Eiji had seen her thoughts, he said. "I take it, you want to see Luna?"

Iris nodded.

He gave her a grin that showed a hint of fangs. "All right, but take my arm. We can't have you passing out on us again."

"Thank you," She whispered as he looped an arm around

her waist, supporting her as she stumbled up the stairs to one of Eiji's guest rooms.

On the way there, they passed the remainder of the Sirin with its mouth permanently open. Glass shards skewered its body and its empty eyes looked up at the sky lights. "Who did that?" Iris whispered

Eiji bit his lip. "That would be Enzo. He was less than pleased when he found it in his home uninvited."

Her eyes widened. "Enzo did this? I didn't know a glass mage could be that powerful."

"Why do you think he keeps their alliance and the true state of their city a secret? The other mage clans won't go out of their way to take out what they think is a weakling clan that isn't competing for riches or attention, but if they knew about this city or the potential the mages here held, the place would be swarmed."

When they reached the door, Eiji placed himself between her and the guest room. "Before you go in there, you might want to brace yourself. She's a bit worse for wear."

Eiji's tails swished behind him in an anxious flurry. Iris pushed past him. "I don't care. I have to see her now." Iris shoved the door open to see Luna's shadow black hair plastered to her face from a thick sheen of sweat. Her face was paper white, but her eyes lit up when she saw Iris. "I'm glad you're okay, love." The thin sound of Luna's voice was enough to make Iris's knees buckle.

Iris crossed the room in two long strides. Her eyes raked over the bruises covering Luna's body and the blood-soaked gauze wrapped around her torso. "What happened to you?"

Luna bit the inside of her cheek. "I may have gotten on the wrong side of a charging Minotaur when I heard you scream."

Luna tried to push herself up, but her body shuddered, and she fell back down into the bed. "Sorry. It still hurts to move too much. Eiji, you'll have to look after…" Luna trailed off and looked up to Iris.

Iris stroked Luna's hair. "It's a she day."

Luna placed a hand over Eiji's. "Right. Look after her for me, Eiji?"

Eiji placed a hand on Luna's shoulder. "I'll do my best to keep her out of trouble,but no promises there. You know how she can be."

Luna gave a slight smile. "I do, and I want her to come back. Alive."

Iris scoffed. "I'm right here."

"Am I wrong?" Luna gave Iris a pointed look.

Iris brushed some of the sweaty hair back from Luna's face. "You're not. I'll make sure to come back alive for you, but in the meantime." Iris leaned in and pressed her lips to Luna's. Luna looped her arms around the back of Iris's neck. Her lips felt rough and warm, but when Luna brought her hands up to tangle them in Iris's hair, her breathing came out ragged.

Iris reluctantly pulled away and placed a kiss on Luna's forehead instead. "A parting gift in case I don't come back."

Luna clucked her tongue. "You'd better come back and not after six years like last time. If you want to leave a parting gift, I'll need some…steamier memories to get me through the nights,"

Luna winked, and Iris's face flushed. "You probably have several broken bones and that's what you're thinking about?"

Luna ran her tongue along a fang. "Yup."

Iris rolled her eyes. "That sounds like you." Despite the battle looming in the near future, Iris cracked a small smile. "How about I save that gift for when I come back so I don't break the rest of your bones. It'll be motivation for me to, you know, not die?"

"I supposed that's fair, but before you leave, I need you to come a little bit closer so I can tell you something."

Iris craned her neck down, and Luna wrapped her arms around Iris's neck with a surprising amount of force. Luna's teeth grazed Iris's ear.

"Only you would try to flirt at a time like this."

"I haven't seen you in six years and you're already leaving. Can you blame me? Now go defeat Opal but come back safely. And keep Ayla and Ze'ev safe too."

Eiji cleared his throat. "Are you two quite done yet?"

"Yes, sorry. Goodbye, Luna," Iris gave Luna's hand one last squeeze before getting off the bed and heading to the door. Eiji followed behind, his feet squishing as he tread on the plush carpet.

When they made it back to the guest room, Iris took stock of the remaining troops. She gulped when she saw Abir alone, his head hung low. Iris bit her lip. "With Shophan. Did the Sirin...?"

Abir nodded and wiped tears from his eyes. "The wound was too severe. He didn't make it."

Iris bit her lip. "I'm so sorry, Abir. I know you cared about him."

His jaw popped. "I'll kill that bitch for sending the Sirin here."

Iris placed her hand on his. "We'll make sure she pays for all she's done, Abir." Iris turned to Ayla. "What about your brother? Is everyone else okay?"

Ayla combed her fingers through her hair. "Ze'ev is okay, but suffered some minor injuries when he pulled me away from the Sirin after I tried to attack her for killing Shophan."

Iris's hand balled into a fist at her side. She boomed. "You did what? Both of you are supposed to be staying away from the fighting. What do you think would have happened if that had been Opal?"

Ayla's eye twitched. "What am I supposed to do, let everyone else die while I just stand by and watch?"

Iris's fingers twitched. "What you're supposed to do is let the older more experienced shifters and mages handle the situation. Death is inevitable in a battle. If you can't handle that without endangering your life, you can't be here. Understand? I can't protect you like I promised Luna if you don't listen!" she snapped.

Ayla smacked her fist into the couch. "Luna did the same thing I did and so did you."

"And We are both adults who can make our own decisions," Iris snapped.

"But-"

Iris held up a hand to cut her off. "End of discussion. Abir, I want you and the glass mages to keep Ayla and Ze'ev as far away from the front lines as possible. If there's trouble, drag them away."

Ayla stomped her feet. "That's not fair,"

"That's exactly what you signed up for. Luna and I were both against you coming with us. It's dangerous for two pups like you. Now stop fighting me on this unless you want to get sent home."

Ayla ground her teeth together. "Fine."

Iris straightened her back and lifted her chin as she addressed the room. "I know we lost people we care about, and I wish I could tell you we won't lose any more, but that would be a lie. We're doing this because we need to win before Opal and her Council destroy anything else. If we can't save Amy, what happened here will just be the beginning. We will lose far more people. Is that what you want?"

A chorus of "No." erupted from the group. Ayla didn't join in the chant. She only rubbed her arm and glanced at the spot where Shophan had been with tears in her eyes.

Ayla blinked back tears. When she caught Iris staring, she said, "Don't give me that pitying look."

Iris nodded. "I understand. I'll miss him too." She looked up at the rest of their group. "We need to come up with a search and rescue plan. Has anyone ever been to the Magic Council's base?"

No one spoke up.

Iris rubbed the back of her neck. "In that case, we'll be going in without a map." Her gaze flicked to Abir. "We need someone who can wander around unseen and give us the layout of the place. Once we know where to go, we can send the rest of the troops there. Are there any shifters here who can turn into something small?"

A shifter dressed in dark clothes that blended to their skin stepped forward. Abir scooted away from the shifter with wide eyes. The shifter held out their hand. "I'm a snake shifter. You can call me Nyoka, and I go by they/them pronouns. I can probably get through the vents without being noticed."

Iris placed her arms on the table. "Then you'll sneak in first. If they catch you, you'll run or hope Opal doesn't know what you are."

Nyoka blinked at Iris. "I suppose you bring up a good point. Do we have a backup plan in case that doesn't work?"

Iris frowned at Nyoka. One of the elementals with orange hair stepped forward. "I'll take that as a no." He crossed his arms over his chest.

Iris threw up her hands. "Do you have any better ideas?"

The orange haired shifter pointed at Iris. "As a matter of fact, I do. If Opal is our main obstacle, maybe we can draw her away from her fortress."

A loud laugh rattled Iris's chest, and she gripped her stomach. "That's a good one." But his face remained impassive, and her expression sobered. "Oh, you were serious? She's never going to leave her base. All of her protection is there, and if she loses her hostages, she risks losing power. If you tried to be any sort of bait, you'd end up bathing in her dragon familiar's fire."

The man shuddered. "Well when you put it that way, it does seem outlandish."

Iris scanned the crowd. "Anyone else have any other ideas?"

A glass mage with lime green hair, a silver earring, and a leather collar on his neck raised his hand. "What is the plan once we learn the layout? Are we just going to charge to our deaths?"

Iris picked at the skin near her nails but didn't meet his eyes. He sighed "Wow, such a brilliant plan. Can we get a real strategist over here please?"

Iris huffed. "Rude but fair. Eiji, did you have any ideas for us?"

Eiji's gaze darted to her. "Ah. Assuming I'm a brilliant strategist because I'm a Kitsune, huh? That's a stereotype and you do know how I abhor those. You're lucky you're cute or I'd be mad." He smiled in a way that showed off his lone dimple.

Iris tapped her foot. "You know damn well that's not why I asked you. Your brother was the top strategist for your clan."

Eiji batted his eyelashes. "Okay, you got me there. I couldn't help it. You're just too fun to tease."

Iris's face reddened. "Can you just tell us your plan, please?"

"Okay, but only because you asked nicely. Nyoka is going to go into the vents to search for any potential weak spots in their security and check for magic dampening metals. Since metal dampeners only affect enchantment type mages, we can take down the guards in those areas. The glass and elemental mages will look for any places with weakened defenses that can lead us to Amy and her sister. We avoid contact with Opal at all costs. If you see Opal, abort the mission. You cannot win in a fight against her. Understand?"

"Yes sir." They all said in unison.

Iris strode over to him and clapped him on the shoulder. "Thanks, Eiji. And how are we going to know where Amy and Garnet are being kept?"

He pushed hair back from his face. "As a former Council leader's brother, Kito had been teaching me a few things about the common locations for the execution and interrogation rooms for the Council headquarters..." He trailed off. His gaze dipped to the floor.

Iris placed a hand on his shoulder. "We'll kill Opal and whoever hurt him."

He gave a tight-lipped smile that didn't reach his eyes. "I appreciate the thought, but that won't bring him back. I'd rather not think about him right now. Let's just focus on how we're going to win this battle or at least minimize casualties."

Iris nodded. "Pack some clothes and essentials and make it quick. We're leaving for the human world tonight."

Ze'ev shot her an incredulous look. "We can't leave Luna behind, and she isn't healed yet."

Iris dug her fingernails into her palm. "We don't have a choice. We need to get there before Opal kills Amy and Garnet. If they die, our chance of overthrowing her and the Council will drop to nothing. We can't wait days or even weeks for injuries to heal. I don't want to leave her behind either, but we have no choice."

Ayla gaped. "She's our leader. We can't go into a battle without her."

Iris tugged at the collar of her black shirt. "If you want to stay behind, I'll understand. Pack comes first."

Iris's heart sank when a wolf shifter with golden eyes whispered "I'm sorry." and strode to the room Luna was staying in.

Iris straightened her back, determined to project confidence despite the seemingly insurmountable task they were about to face. "Anyone else?"

Ayla stepped forward. Her lips pressed into a thin line. "Pack first means we do what's best for the pack, and in this case what's best for the pack is completing this mission. We need to stop Opal before she harms anyone else. Are we all in agreement here?"

Iris's stomach fluttered.

When Ayla faced the group, Abir and Nyoka nodded in agreement.

Iris's vision misted. "Thank you. I know it won't be easy, but I'm grateful for everyone's help."

Ayla frowned. "This isn't for you. It's for Luna and the rest of the pack."

Iris flinched. *Is it this easy for them to reject me? Pretend I never stood beside them, led them, helped forge alliances to protect them?* The tears in her eyes spilled over, and she wiped them away with the back of her hand. "You have an hour. Grab whatever you need for our journey."

Once the room cleared out, Iris sank into the sofa. Eiji placed a hand on her shoulder and sat down beside her. "You did the right thing."

"Then why do I feel like shit right now?" Iris's voice cracked.

He shrugged. "Because sometimes doing the right thing sucks?"

Iris raised an eyebrow, and Eiji laughed. "Hey. I might be a Kitsune, but I'm not some wizened old elder, at least not yet anyway."

"I guess you have a point. I just need to know if Amy's okay. If she was able to contact us, that means she tried to escape, and if she failed, Opal caught her." Iris gulped. "I doubt she has much time left."

Eiji bit his lip. "If I were you, I'd keep any mention of her possible escape to yourself. If they think she's gotten away, there's little chance of them going in there to save Garnet. Garnet is just another Enchantress to them, not an important part of the revolution."

Iris's gaze went down to her feet. "I know."

Iris pushed herself up from the couch and shook out her legs. "I'm going to go take a walk. I can't stay cooped up here anymore."

He got up and stood beside her. "I'll go with you. The town was just attacked. There's no telling what the Council might send after us next."

She let out a sigh. "Fine, but then who's going to tell them where we went?"

He shrugged. "Oh, I don't know, maybe leave them a note. You can write, right?"

Iris rubbed at her chin. "Fair point." She scrawled down a quick note and then pasted it to the refrigerator.

WHEN IRIS and Eiji got back several minutes later, Ayla and Ze'ev paced by the door while the rest of the group waited with arms crossed, towing small suitcases behind them. Ayla rubbed at her wrists when she glanced at Iris. "We were starting to wonder if you'd gotten impatient and left without us."

"I just needed some air. Luna may be your leader, but she's my mate."

Ayla's features softened. "I suppose that's fair. Lead the way."

Iris's miniature army left Enzo's house and made it about five feet from the door before they were met with Enzo who had a hand on his hip. "When I saw you leaving the house, I remembered what Eiji told me about you taking the long way to get here. You do know there's a bridge going over the forest, right Eiji?"

Eiji rubbed his neck. "Oh, that's right. I almost forgot. Mind showing us how to get to it again?"

Enzo rubbed at his temples. "I swear you'd lose your head if it weren't attached. Follow me and let's make this quick. I have to repair quite a few buildings, you know. The glass here might be tough, but not Fenrir tough." He pointed to a shop in the distance with a shattered store front and a splintered wooden sign hanging from the archway.

Enzo led them to the mouth of the forest and Iris glanced around at the misty thicket. "Okay am I missing something here? Where is the bridge?"

Eiji tapped her on the shoulder. "Try looking up."

Iris turned her head to the sky. Rainbow colors reflected on the massive sheet of glass high above. She squinted up at the bright light. "How are we supposed to get up there?"

Enzo knocked his fist against the air. It made a clink and Iris rubbed at her eyes. "What is this?"

"It's a stairway made of thick glass. That's how you get to the bridge. We cloaked it of course. You can take this all the way back to shifter territory. We usually go there to gather sand."

Iris gave a slight bow. "Todah rabah." When Enzo gave her a blank stare, she flushed and tucked a stray hair behind her ear. "I mean thank you very much for everything," she said.

Iris headed for the stairs, but Enzo held up his hand. "Wait. I think you might need this to get back. Eiji said money was tight, right?" He held up a canvas bag.

Iris tilted her head to the side. "Is that human money? How?" When he held out the bag for her, she took it.

"Collecting sand isn't the only reason we venture into your territory. The human world import network is rather lucrative, so we trade some of our glassware there and bring back the money for interested collectors."

Iris placed a hand to her chest. "Thank you. I'm not sure how I would have gotten us back otherwise."

He shook his head. "Don't worry about it. Just don't tell anyone the truth about our clan," he said and placed a finger to his lips.

Iris mimed zipping her lips and then grabbed onto the banister and climbed the glass stairs with wobbling legs.

She kept her gaze forward, but her heart pounded in her chest as she walked across the transparent bridge. Her palms dripped sweat until she exited the stairwell and her feet hit the sand at the entrance to the desert. Iris knelt to the sand and kissed it. "Oh, thank Dagon, solid ground."

Eiji snickered behind her, and she elbowed his knee. "Sorry I just find it hilarious that you hate heights but will fearlessly face a Fenrir."

Iris narrowed her eyes at him. "Considering I can't control my shifting, I don't want to test my luck falling from something that height, okay? It's a valid fear."

He held up his hands in surrender. "Sure. Whatever you say."

Iris huffed and stomped all the way over to the portal. When Iris crossed over the barrier, a mixture of a howl and a human cry sent shivers down her spine, but none of the portal creatures dared attack such a large group of travelers.

When they stepped into the human realm, heat came up from the sand in waves, and the sun beat down on Iris's back. She turned to their small group. "We're going to catch the next flight back to the U.S. Make sure that in the meantime you avoid any use of magic. We don't want humans growing suspicious of us. Understood?"

The others nodded, but a finger tapped Iris's shoulder, and she glanced up to see Eiji dangling the magic pendant Amy had given her. "Speaking of avoiding magic, you may want to put this on in case the change takes over again."

Iris's face flushed, and she snatched the necklace from his hand. "Thank you. I'd nearly forgotten about it."

He gave an overly formal bow. "You're welcome. Now will either you or one of the elementals who are familiar with the human realm lead us to the airport?"

Before Iris could speak up, a fire elemental cleared his throat. "I know where it is. Follow me."

They followed him through town, and the entire way Iris's

head swiveled, searching for potential threats. She clutched her pendant tight against her chest when her ears pricked up and placed a hand on her head to cover them.

Eiji scoffed. "Don't be embarrassed, I think it's rather cute." Iris elbowed him, and he rubbed his arm. "I was just teasing you."

Iris dropped her voice to a whisper. "How about you focus on keeping an eye out for people from the Magic Council."

His brows knitted together. "You don't think she'd attack somewhere so public, do you? There would be numerous human casualties and it would expose us to humans."

Iris sighed. "She doesn't believe in subtlety, and I doubt she'd care about human casualties if she razed entire cities for daring to stand against her."

He held up a finger. "Good point. I'll take the rear, and you take the front?"

Iris placed a hand over her chest. "I wasn't aware you were attracted to me like that."

Eiji sputtered and blushed. "I'm talking about defending our group. You aren't exactly my type."

"Now who's sensitive about getting teased?" she said with a smile and jogged up to the front of their group.

THEY ALL MADE it to the airplane and onto the flight without a hitch. Once Iris settled into the seat, her mind wandered off to Naru. Iris hoped she'd had better luck finding troops.

CHAPTER 14

"*I* just need your help. Please," Naru shouted as Ren scurried up the old oak tree next to his house.

"No. The last time you came around asking me for help, I got caught in the middle of a game of tug-o-war between a hell hound and a wolf shifter. I'm maxed out on my helpfulness quota for life."

Electricity sparked on Naru's fingertips. "All right, you leave me no choice. I hope you like the electrocuted hairstyle."

Ren gripped the tree with his nails and several branches wrapped around his wrist, rooting him to the spot. "You wouldn't dare. This is my favorite tree, and I'm allergic to lightning."

Naru rolled her eyes. "Then get down from there and help me."

His lip quivered. "But you've seen how powerful Opal is. How are a few elemental mages going to make a difference against her? We can't beat someone using Excalibur and Clarent."

Tears formed in Naru's eyes, and her voice cracked when she spoke. "But if we don't do anything Amy...Amy will be."

Ren dug his nails into the tree. His back stiffened. "She got Amy?"

Naru nodded, and her lip quivered. "Mhm."

He blew a strand of dark hair from his face with a sigh. "I know how you feel about Amy, but you can't go charging into battle anytime she's in trouble."

Naru kicked the tree. "Well, what do you suggest I do, let her die?"

"I don't know Naru, but I can't help you."

Naru glared up at the tree. "It's hard to believe you're the child of two revolutionaries."

Ren pressed his face against the tree's bark. "I guess I got the recessive gene for cowardice then. I'm not going."

Naru tilted her head to one side. "Final answer?"

He huffed "Yes."

"Wrong answer." Naru pointed at a small branch above Ren's head and shot electricity at it, making it snap off and land on his head with a thunk.

Ren's mouth dropped open. "I can't believe you did that."

"I can't believe you won't help me! You didn't seem like the type of person to let someone die, but maybe I misjudged your character." Naru crossed her arms over her chest and stomped away from the tree.

Branches rustled and a hand grabbed her wrist. She turned to see Ren's dark brown eyes. "Wait. Is saving Amy really that important to you? I thought you were staying away from her after you know." He waved his hands.

Naru stared down at him. "Yes, I was avoiding her, but that doesn't mean I stopped caring. If you aren't willing to help, I'll do it alone. Take a good long look because this may be the last time you ever see me."

Naru yanked her hand from his, but he grabbed her shoulder. "Wait. I'll help. I know a couple places where we can find some other mages in the area."

Naru shook his shoulder. "Why didn't you just tell me that? Where are they?"

"There's an elemental hangout in a museum in Delray, but you'll need me to get in."

She cocked her head to one side. "Why is that?"

He rubbed the back of his neck. "The hideout is kind of sort of hidden with wood magic. You need wood magic to break the spell."

Naru cracked a grin. "Thank you. You're the best. Can I hug you? I feel like this is a hugging moment."

He rolled his eyes. "Don't go singing my praises just yet. We still have to get in, and I'm not sure how keen they'll be on letting someone in when their elements are fire and wind."

Naru bit her lip. "Fine. I'll be on my best behavior. Now let's go."

Ren dragged his feet to the car. "Are you sure you can't just let her go? We can find someone else for you to pine after you know." Naru pinched his shoulder, and he rubbed at the skin. "Ow. That wasn't necessary."

"Neither was your comment," she sneered.

Ren twirled his car keys around his finger. "Just remember I'm the one driving us there and I can just as easily drop you off somewhere in the Everglades. Maybe you'll be a good snack for the gators."

Naru gave a sharp laugh. "You wouldn't dare."

"Try me." Ren got in the car, and she tugged on the handle. Instead of unlocking it, he rolled down the window. "What was it that I wouldn't dare do again?"

Naru clenched her jaw. "Ha. Ha. very funny. Now let me in."

He cupped a hand to his ear. "What's the magic word?"

"Fuck you," she said through gritted teeth.

"No thanks. Try again."

Naru rubbed at her temples. "Will you please let me in?"

He batted his lashes. "See. Now was that so hard?"

Naru climbed into the car and slammed the door shut behind her.

Ren snort laughed. "Easy there, firecracker. I don't have money for a new car door."

She smacked her fist against the dash. "Look. I know you're trying to cheer me up, but right now I just want to get there so we can find as many mages as possible. Okay?" Naru slumped down into the seat and rubbed at her watery eyes.

He placed a hand on her shoulder. "Sorry. I know you're worried. I just don't want you risking it all for someone who doesn't have your best interests at heart."

Naru looked down at her hands. "That's the thing. She does in her own convoluted way. She told me what I was and helped me find a mentor to control my magic. I know Amy's probably pushing me away to protect me. I suspect she was trying to keep me from getting kidnapped like her sister."

Ren gave her a knowing look. "If that's the case, there's a very real possibility that what you want from her may be something she's never willing to give you."

Naru ran a hand through her long, dark hair. "I know. Now can we just go?"

"Of course," he started the car and headed south west until they reached trees and a massive off-white building with a small forest behind it.

Naru did a double take when she caught sight of the building up ahead. "Ren, why are we going to the Japanese Cultural museum? Is the hideout hidden in a painting or the bamboo in the gardens or something?"

He parked the car and then turned to Naru. "You're half right. This place was acquired by a powerful water and Earth elemental years ago. We never moved the bases despite how many people come here because of the technology he built. There's even a water elemental hideout the original owner put in the middle of the lake."

Naru's jaw dropped, "He put a hideout in a lake? How?"

Ren gave her jazz fingers, "Magic."

Naru rolled her eyes. "Really?"

He shrugged. "Ask dumb questions, get dumb answers."

"Okay but wouldn't they eventually run out of magic and the whole thing would get flooded? That seems inconvenient."

Ren opened the door and started walking to the museum and Naru followed behind him. "He was like our Merlin. There's a massive wall and a dome covering the hideout that keeps the water physically out. The water magic hiding them is only needed during business hours when people are actually at the museum."

Naru pulled open the door to the museum. "That seems like a lot of trouble to make something that's in plain sight when they could just pick somewhere less populated like, I don't know, a nature trail?"

He nodded. "There are some there too, but I didn't want to risk you burning down a full-sized forest if our attempt to incite rebellion doesn't go well."

She grabbed his shirt collar and lowered her voice. "What do you mean if it doesn't go well?"

Ren threw sidelong glances at the ticket counter. "Let's just say a lot of the mages here are self-taught and a bit rough around the edges, so accidents happen. Do you remember what you used to do before you had a mentor?"

Naru dropped him. "So, they use their magic for personal gain and have probably experimented with their powers to see what they can do. Based on how you're acting I'm guessing it's worse than me rigging the crane games to win stuffed animals."

He shot Naru with a finger gun. "Precisely."

"Great. Will they have booze and gambling?"

He tapped a finger on the bottom of his chin. "Maybe, but I'm not letting you drink, lightweight."

She pouted. "Why not?"

"FIRE mage in a tree, drunk. Does that seem like a good plan?"

She crossed her arms over her chest. "What about the water hideout?"

He shifted on his feet. "I don't know any water mages and we'd need one to get in and out."

Naru pushed some hair behind her ear. "Just go get our tickets."

"That's what I thought," Ren said and shoved open the door to the museum.

Cool air chilled Naru's face as they both made their way over to the ticket clerk.

Once they had their tickets, they walked out the back door and past the café. They meandered along the walking path near the lake until they reached the entrance to a small nature trail thick with trees and bamboo. They followed the path to the end and then Ren turned to the left and said, "It's here."

Naru glanced around. "Where? I don't see it."

He pointed at the wall of bamboo and trees in front of them. "It's behind all of this. Just take my hand. You'll need it to get into the fortress."

"Okay." Naru placed her hand in his, and the wall of trees twisted and turned before her eyes, opening up into a mass of mages. Bartenders coaxed branches into sliding beers across the counter to waiting customers. A water mage forced water down their stumbling friends' throats.

In the back Naru spotted a Pacman game, and her eyes widened. She shook Ren's shoulder. "Can I?"

He glanced at the rows of games. "Sure. I'll join you. I'm just going to get a virgin pina colada first, okay?"

"Mhm." Naru said with her eyes fixed on the machines.

She maneuvered over to the Pacman game as Ren whispered. "She probably didn't hear a single thing I said."

"Yes, I did," Naru called back and winked at him.

Ren shook his head, and Naru made her way over to the

abandoned arcade game. She'd just pressed start for a one player round when a male mage with short neon blue hair leaned on the machine and gave Naru a thorough once over that made her skin crawl. "Room for one more?" He asked.

Naru glanced over at the bar, but Ren had his back turned. She plastered on a tight-lipped smile. "I just started a one player game, but you can have the machine after that if you'd like."

She turned her attention back to the game, but he inched closer until his cinnamon and alcohol infused breath went right into her nostrils, making her gag. "I was hoping we could play together and maybe I could push your buttons later."

Naru bunched her fists at her side. *Don't make a scene. Don't make a scene. We're here to make allies, not enemies.* She gulped down her anger and forced cheeriness into her tone. "I'm not interested in men. Sorry."

Without missing a beat, he slid a hand through his overly gelled hair and said, "I can change that."

Naru dropped her hand from the game as her cheeks flushed. "You know, you can have the machine. I'll just be over there." She muttered. "Far away from your dumb ass."

He grabbed her wrist. "What did you say to me?"

Naru bared her teeth at him. "Nothing that you need to worry your pretty head about if you'd like to not have your limbs extra crispy."

She tried to yank her hand free, but he tightened his grip. "You think you can insult me and get away with it, bitch?"

Naru spat. "Just know you brought this upon yourself." She focused on just her hand and separated out the fire and air magic that lived in the electricity she always used. As she focused on the fire, flames flickered to life along her hand.

The creep flinched away, wooden gauntlets covered his hand. "Who the hell let a fire mage in here?"

She spat on the ground in front of him. "If we use common sense, which I know you're lacking, we can deduce that my friend let me in since you know I actually have friends. Now unless you want two charbroiled hands, you'll leave me alone. Now."

He loomed over her; his nose wrinkled in disgust. "You think you're some hot shit, don't you? Who needs you, bitch."

Naru flipped hair over her shoulder. "You're missing the bad in bad bitch. Bye now."

Just as the mage stormed off with his shoulders bunched up in knots, Ren shuffled over to her with his virgin pina colada in hand, sipping from the neon pink straw. "What happened to not using magic because you could burn the forest down?"

Naru rubbed at her arm. "He refused to leave me alone, and you were taking too long, so I dealt with him."

Ren slurped up the drink. "Suddenly I'm wishing this were a real pina colada. Too bad I'm the designated driver."

"I mean you could always let me drive the car back."

He glared at her. "Remember what happened the last time you drove my car?"

Naru bit her lip. "Oh right. To be fair, he cut me off and almost crashed into your car."

"And so, you thought that losing your temper and frying my car battery would be better? No thanks. I can't afford any more repairs right now."

Naru hid her face under her dark bangs. "I'm sorry. It wasn't on purpose. Now can we play some Pacman together?"

He sighed. "Sure, but only if you'll play Galaga with me after."

"It's a deal," She pushed the start button and crushed him in a couple of rounds of Pacman before they moved on to Galaga.

They were halfway through a rematch so Naru could redeem herself when Ren tugged on her shirt. "Hey. Stop for a second."

Naru kept her gaze on the screen. "What, because you're losing? Not a chance."

He nudged her shoulder. "Not that. Some of the more powerful mages just showed up, and we need powerful mages, right?" He pointed out a cluster of mages that had just walked in. Half of them were dressed in so much leather they looked like they were in a biker gang and the other half looked like they'd crawled out of a video game with their neon colored hair and clothes.

"Those are powerful mages? They look more like angsty high schoolers."

He placed a finger to his lips. "Don't let them hear you say that. We could use their help."

Naru threw her hand up in surrender. "But do we stand a chance of getting their alliance? I mean, have you ever talked to them before now?"

He tapped the toe of his shoe against the ground. "Not exactly, but I thought maybe we can convince them."

Naru pressed her lips into a fine line. "Have you thought about how we'd do that?"

He folded in on himself. "No. I didn't think that far."

Naru grabbed his shoulder and tugged him towards the group. "Well, no time like the present to get acquainted. Let's go say hi and hope for the best."

He dug his heels in. "No. No. No. Not again. If this goes south, I'm leaving. I refuse to be a punching bag."

"Don't worry it'll be fine," Naru elongated the word "fine."

Naru yanked Ren behind her as she walked up to the group and waved at them. "Hi. The name's Naru. I heard you all were the most powerful mages here. Is that true?"

A girl with neon blue hair twirled her hair while beaming at Ren. "That depends. Who's asking? You, or the cute mage beside you?"

Naru turned to see Ren half hidden behind her shoulder and snorted. "You mean him?"

She nodded. "Yes. Why is he yours?"

Ren glanced at Naru and gagged. "Never in a million years."

Naru elbowed him, and he stepped out from behind her, "We wanted to introduce ourselves. I'm Ren and this is Naru."

A pink haired woman dressed in a black leather jacket looked Naru up and down. "She doesn't look like a wood mage, so what element is she?"

Ren waved his hands in front of himself. "Well, you see. That part is a little complicated, but her element isn't what's important." He shoved Naru forward. "You tell them what happened."

Naru shot a sidelong glare at him and blew a strand of hair out of her eyes. She focused on the pink haired mage clad in the leather jacket and collar. "A friend of ours was captured by Opal, and we're sending in a team to help her. We need help, and we could use more powerful mages like you."

Roots clawed up from the ground and pointed at Naru's legs. "You should consider your friend gone because there are few mages insane enough to crawl into that dragon's den."

Naru clasped her hands together. "Please. We'll pay you, give you whatever you want. Just tell us what you need in exchange."

The blue haired girl wrapped her arm around Ren's shoulder. "What about a night alone with your friend here? He's rather cute."

Naru looked at Ren's uncomfortable expression and coughed. Ren placed a hand on the woman's shoulder "I'm flattered, but somehow, I don't think you're looking for a night of Webflikz and chill minus the chill."

She let go of his arm. "Well. Can't blame me for trying. Right, Tera?"

The pink haired woman, Tera, rolled her eyes. "I can

blame you for trying with everyone. Sorry, but if you're lacking a bargaining chip, we're not interested."

Naru held up her hand. "Wait. Our friend is an enchantress. We could offer you as many enchanted gems as you'd like in exchange for your help."

Tera raised an eyebrow. "You have my attention. How skilled is she?"

"She was able to take down an armed sorcerer with her enchantments by age twelve by herself. She had her Choosing at ten."

Tera held out her hand. "Okay, but if we find out you're lying we'll take your friend as payment instead."

Naru took her hand. "Deal."

Ren's brow furrowed as he looked over the group of mages before them and muttered " Four, Five, Six. Not enough."

Naru tapped him on the shoulder. "Are you okay there?"

"Even with using me and Amy as a bargaining chip, we only have six mages. I think I may need to call in my favor for us to have the best chance for success."

Naru looked to the mages in front of her and then back to him. "And you neglected to tell me about this favor before now because?"

Ren wrung his hands. "Uhmm...about that. They may have gotten themselves into some trouble."

Her tone turned stern. "How much trouble are we talking about here?"

He batted his eyelashes. "They may be in a halfway house on the other side of town."

Naru pinched the bridge of her nose. "Before we do this, I have one question. Did they kill anyone?"

He pressed his lips into a thin line but said nothing. "Well, Amy killed someone, but you're friends with her."

The blue haired mage looked over at them chatting and smiled. "I'd say lovers quarrel, but I know that's not the case. What are you two talking about?"

"Can I tell them?" Naru whispered.

Tera stepped between Naru and Ren and stared down at Naru with a forced grin. "Tell us what?"

Ren put an arm up to hold Naru back. "I have a few friends that can help us, but they're in a halfway house near here."

Tera looped an arm around Ren's shoulder, and he tensed. "In that case let's go get them. I'm willing to bet we can persuade a few to escape with us."

Naru held out her hand. "Lead the way."

Ren walked to the thicket of branches and shoved a few of them away before placing his hand on the massive wood barrier. The barrier parted so they could walk through the exit.

Naru trailed behind as Ren led them out of the museum. They piled as many mages as possible into Ren's car.

Ren scratched his head. "I hope the rest of you have cars. We'll need at least two more vehicles to transport my friends."

Tera gave a small smile and walked over to a massive pickup truck and rapped her knuckles on the door. "This one is mine." She opened the door and climbed the stairs that led into the truck. "We'll follow you there," Tera said before leaping into the driver's seat and slamming the door behind her. The mage with bright blue hair followed behind her.

On the way there, they passed several busy streets, each one with more broken glass and dilapidated buildings than the last. Sirens sounded and a cop whizzed past on their right hand side.

When they took a turn down yet another deserted avenue with several abandoned buildings sporting broken windows, Naru's heart sank. Naru shoved her hands in her pockets and glanced over at Ren. "Are we almost there? I'm getting child-hood flashbacks."

He reached over and gave her hand a squeeze. "We're almost there. There's the closest parking garage." He pointed at a tiny, deserted parking garage with a crumbling building to the left of it.

Her gaze scoured the streets for any potential threats, but she doubted there was anyone here that could genuinely hurt them.

When they parked the car and exited the garage, they passed a man lying on the concrete, his head resting on a pack stuffed with clothing and with a toothbrush peeking out. A tin can sat beside him, and Naru opened her wallet to grab a few dollars.

The pink haired mage wrinkled her nose. "Put that away before someone notices."

Ren turned back and plucked her wallet from her hand. "Don't do that. You know better than to flash money here."

"What's that supposed to mean Ren?"

"It means you're going to attract unwanted attention from unsavory types."

Naru tugged at the collar of her black t-shirt, and her whole body warmed. She felt sparks crackle on her fingertips. "I think you forget I used to be one of those unsavory types, so watch your tongue."

Ren hunched his shoulders. "Sorry. I just meant I don't want someone to see the money and try to attack us."

Naru held out her hand that popped with electricity. "They can try, but then they'll be the one getting injured."

He lowered his voice to a whisper. "You can't do that. There are magic hunters around here, and if they find you, Opal will become the least of your problems."

Naru rubbed at her arms. "There are magic hunters here?"

His eyes darkened. "Yes, so be careful if you don't want to end up as a hunting trophy or tortured for information in a rhodium and lead coated magic prison that saps your magic." He turned to look at the pink haired mage. "All of you. It may be better for just me and Naru to go to the front entrance. You all should sneak in through a back entrance once we have them distracted."

The pink haired mage smiled. "We have names. I'm Dahlia and the two behind me are Alder and Ash."

Ren raked his fingers through his hair. "Okay Dahlia, can you call the rest of your group and let them know the plan? Naru and I will pretend to be related to my friend Ryu. If we can get him, the others will follow. Remember magic should be a last resort. Okay?" He said while throwing a glance at Naru.

Naru crossed her fingers behind her back and gave a slight smile. "Fine. I'll be careful."

He beamed at her. "Great, then you won't mind wearing one of these." He held up a handful of slightly scratched rhodium rings.

Naru blinked at him. "Where did you get those, and why are you giving them to us?"

He shrugged. "Let's just say my parents got them from people who weren't happy about parting with them. But these will keep the magic hunters from tracking your magic signature. Only take these off if the escape attempt goes awry."

Naru snatched the ring from his palm. "Fine. I'll wear it, but just know I'm not happy about it."

He gave Naru a smug smile as she slid it on her finger. Dahlia slid hers on with a grimace. "I'm starting to regret agreeing to this. How much farther is this place?"

Ren pointed his chin to a large beige building. "That's the facility just up ahead. You, Alder, and Ash should go around the back and wait near the fence in case we fail to get my friend out unnoticed."

Ash brushed auburn bangs from his face. "Got it. Come on Dahlia." He pulled Dahlia away by the elbow as a small yard with yellow-green patches of grass and dirt came into view.

People wearing rhodium ankle bracelets milled about the yard with eyes lowered.

When a boy with a shaved head caught sight of their rings, he gasped and walked towards the fence. He flinched when his hand grazed the metal and took two steps back.

Hair raised on Naru's arms and she leaned over to whisper into Ren's ear. "What is going on? I thought this was a regular halfway house. Why are they wearing magic dampening equipment and isn't the fence a bit much? This isn't a prison."

Ren bit his lip. "The co-founder of this house is a Magic Council member. The human staff members think it's a regular ankle bracelet."

Naru's forehead wrinkled. "Is it?"

"Yes and no. It's not GPS, It's magic. But it serves the same function. We'll have to destroy them when we break everyone out."

Naru placed a hand on her hip. "And how are we planning on doing that?"

"When you forced me to come along with you, I called up one of my parent's connections in the rebellion. They sent over forged release papers with my picture and a fake name. According to the paperwork, I'm his brother Hotaru. Remember he's in there because he was framed for arson and several of his family members got injured. His sister died, so you're his friend and came with me to escort him home."

"But what if they don't believe us? Does he even have a brother?"

"He has an older brother, and the lady that usually works the front desk has never met his real brother. She assumed I was his brother last time I was here, and I never corrected her, so I doubt she'll question us."

"And if they call security?" Naru asked.

Ren shrugged. "Then we call the others and fight our way out. Make sure once I have her distracted that you meet with Ryu first. Last I saw him, he had his hair dyed neon yellow, so he should be easy to spot. Just do your best to be convincing once we get inside."

She threw up her hands. "I'll do my best, but I'm a god-awful liar. It would be best if you do most of the talking."

"I plan to." Ren grabbed her hand, and they pushed open the heavy metal door at the entrance.

An older woman with blood red lips and a severe expression on her face eyed them with distaste. "Who are you, and what are you doing here?"

Ren feigned a shy grin. "I'm just here to pick up my brother, Ryu. I was told he was getting released today."

Her nose wrinkled. "And which of these low lifes is your brother?"

Naru couldn't help it, she leaned over the counter and spat. "Just because he made a mistake doesn't make him a low life."

The woman rolled her eyes. "You people are all the same."

Naru's blood ran cold. "Excuse me. What do you mean by you people?"

Naru moved her hand to slide the ring off her finger, but Ren placed his hand over hers. "I'm sorry about that. She's just very emotional. We've been waiting a long time to see Ryu after the incident with the fire. Right, Naru?"

Naru's lip bled when she bit down on it to keep another retort from escaping her mouth. Instead, she gritted her teeth and forced a smile of mock politeness. "He's right. I'm sorry, ma'am."

She eyed them suspiciously. "I don't remember him having a sister."

Ren held up his hands. "We're not related. This is Ryu's friend."

She looked to the cameras behind her and then back at them. "Sure. I'm just going to double-check the release paperwork. I'll be right back."

Once she walked away, Ren turned to Naru. "I'll stall her. You gather as many of the mages as you possibly can. Okay?"

Naru nodded and snuck through the hallway and out the door that led to the courtyard. She pressed her back to the wall and peeked her head out to see a couple of guards standing watch. One of them carried a taser on his belt. *That's odd for a halfway house. If they're carrying weapons, I'll have to be careful.*

Naru pressed her foot against the wall near the entry doors. *Maybe I can create a distraction?* She glanced towards the group of mages and cupped her hand around her mouth and chanted. "Fight." A girl with spiky violet hair joined in the chant. She turned to Naru and winked before shoving one of the boys.

"What was that for?" The boy yelled and pushed her back. They soon started fighting in earnest. Two other mages started chanting "Fight" and mages crowded around the scuffle in the center of the courtyard.

The unarmed guard swore under his breath and stomped over to break it up. The armed guard followed suit.

Now's my chance. Naru snuck through the crowd, going directly for Ryu. When he caught her smile, he frowned.

"You're not a new member of the halfway house and you aren't Ren. Who are you and what are you doing here?"

Naru grabbed onto his wrist. "I'm Ren's friend and a mage like you. We're here to break you out, but we need to go before one of the guards figures out what I'm doing and stops us." She pointed at the taser on the guard's hip.

Ryu shook his head. "That's too dangerous. All of us are in here because we lost control of our magic. If the prison system doesn't get us for escaping before the end of our sentence, the Magic Council will. And I don't know about you, but I'd rather not get on their bad side."

Naru tugged his hand. "It's a little late for that. Opal's already declared a war on multi clanned mages like us. She's captured a dual clanned Enchantress and plans to execute her and the sister that harbored her."

He ripped his hand from her grip. "That mage is not our problem. We just want to live in peace."

"If you think the leader who calls us impure half-breeds will stop with one dual clanned Enchantress, you're sorely mistaken. Look at how The Council has you locked up. Are you okay with this?" Naru's voice caught.

He pressed a finger into her chest. "Yes. My *freedom* endangered the people around me. Do you even know why I'm here?"

Naru shifted uncomfortably on her feet. "Ren said you were arrested for arson. Several people in your house sustained severe burns and your sister died."

He blinked. "If you know that, why are you trying to help me escape? I'm a killer. A danger to those around me."

Naru glanced over at the guards to make sure they hadn't noticed her. "I mean Ren warned me you killed someone, but he said it wasn't on purpose. Right?"

Ryu's gaze fell to a brown patch of grass. "Mhm. I had a thing for incense and candles, but I never knew why, and I liked to run my hand over the flames to see how many times I could do it without getting burned. After a while I realized I could stick my entire hand in the flame and the flames didn't burn me."

Naru dug her nails into her palm, knowing what came next. She'd nearly electrocuted her mother in the bath when she was younger. When he hesitated, she placed a hand over his. "You don't have to tell the whole story if you feel uncomfortable."

He shook his head. "It's okay. I want you to know exactly what happened." Ryu gave a shaky breath. "One day, when I was playing with a candle flame, my hand caught fire. When I tried to put the flame out by smothering it with a damp towel, the towel caught fire too, and I panicked. I went to open the door to my parent's room to warn them, and I accidentally set the door aflame."

He gulped. "If my screaming hadn't woken half the neighborhood up, I don't know what would have happened to my parents. I was too scared to call anyone and too panicked to warn them or put the fire out. One of our neighbors called the fire department, but they were too late to save Mei. She died from smoke inhalation. When I lied and said I'd set the fire on purpose, I went to jail for arson and after I got offered an 'alternative' halfway house by a Magic Council member who came to visit me in jail. They offered to help, but at the price of my magic."

"I'm so sorry. I was in a similar situation, and my mother has the scars to prove it, but we can get you help if you come with us."

Naru's gaze scanned the crowd, and she gestured at the other mages. "What about the others?"

He pressed his lips into a thin line. "Most are here by choice. For many of us, our magic resulted in injuries or worse. The Magic Council approaches a lot of mages in jail and gives them an alternative. A place where we have some freedom, but in a more controlled environment that can handle an out of control mage."

Naru gulped. "And those who didn't choose to come here?"

Ryu rubbed his arms. "Some of the younger ones here are mages without families that were snatched off the streets. I suggest you try to persuade them to leave instead. I'm not willing to risk hurting someone, not again."

Naru tugged at Ryu's arm and dug her heel into the dirt when he didn't budge. "I'm not leaving without you. We need all the mages we can get, and we can train you. We have an advanced mage that can teach you control like they did for my friend and me." Naru crossed her fingers behind her back hoping he didn't catch the partial lie.

He crossed his arms over his chest. "And why would you help me?"

Naru stumbled for words. "Because I was a lot like you once, afraid of my own magic. Because of a friend, I got help, and I want to help you too." That much at least was true.

"Fine, I'll go. But if it gets too dangerous, if I get too dangerous, I'm coming back here and turning myself in. Deal?"

Naru nodded. "Deal."

Ryu nodded to a guard's key ring. "You take care of getting the keys from a guard so we can get these anklets off. I'll see who I can grab from the crowd."

Ryu weaved through the crowd of mages as the guards struggled to break up the fight. Ryu gathered the mages hanging towards the back of the crowd and led them to the door while Naru swiped an unsuspecting guard's keys and unlocked ankle bracelets and guided handfuls of mages to the door that led back into the building.

Naru was kneeling down in the grass unlocking the sixth mage's ankle bracelet when a guard locked eyes with her. He held out a hand and shouted "She's helping the residents escape. Get her."

Naru grabbed Ryu's bracelet. "Run and tell Ren to get out of here as quickly as possible."

His whole body tensed. "Are you sure that's a good idea?"

Naru glanced back at the approaching guards. "I'm just going to buy us time. Go!" Naru turned towards the fence and shouted. "I could use some help over here."

Roots shot up from the ground and Dahlia vaulted herself over the fence. Alder launched Ash over the fence and then went to the car to get it ready for a getaway.

Naru slipped the rhodium ring off her finger and electricity sizzled at her fingertips. "Alright you've caught me. Now what are you going to do to me?"

She stepped toward the guard. He gawked at her wide-eyed and pointed at her hand. "W-what is she doing? Is that real?"

Another guard wearing an Opalescent badge with a dragon on it shoved the normal human guard aside. "Go tell the owner what happened."

The human guard scrambled back and ran into the building. The magic hunter pulled out a taser "How the hell did you sneak in here, mage?"

Naru held her sparking hand out. "If you want to find out, you'll have to catch me first." Naru faced her palm towards the guard and electricity shot from her fingertips, hitting him in the arm. The guard's entire body shook, and he fell to the ground.

Another human guard approached Naru with his hands up. "I don't want any trouble. I'm just doing my job."

Naru's voice gained a playful lilt. "I'll give you five seconds to turn and run before I change my mind."

His unblinking wide eyes met hers. "You'd really let me go?"

Something about his sudden willingness to surrender struck her as odd. She heard footsteps behind her, and something cool pressed against her ankle. She kicked behind her as pain shot through her arm, and her lightning fizzled.

Naru reached back and grabbed onto a guard's hand. She caught a flash of an opalescent dragon in her peripheral vision, another magic hunter. Her fingertips brushed against the cool metal of the badge. Naru balled her free hand into a fist and struck at the man's jaw with such force that his head snapped to the side.

"You little runt. You'll regret that." The electric hum of a taser caught Naru's attention as the first guard started running towards her.

Ash shouted, "Not if I have anything to say about it." and raced after the guard.

Naru put a hand across her throat in a "cut it out" motion as the human guard with the taser moved towards her.

The magic hunter near Naru shouted. "Wait don't it won't-"

His words were cut off when the human guard fired the taser gun. The probes dug into Naru's flesh and electricity vibrated through her body. A headache pushed at her temples as the magic got blocked up in her veins, unable to come to the surface. Then, with a pop like an overinflated balloon, the buzz of electricity broke through the dampening metal.

A sharp crack sounded, and the destroyed anklet fell to the floor. "I think your comrade was trying to warn you that I can harness the electricity in that taser. Oops?" Naru ripped the electrodes from her skin and yanked the wire.

The guard tumbled towards her, and she jabbed the probes into his flesh. His body convulsed, and he dropped to the floor in a trembling heap.

The other magic hunter stopped in his tracks. "The other magic hunters will be coming for you after this stunt, so you better watch your back."

Naru rolled her eyes. "Two of you buffoons couldn't even take down one mage. What makes you think you stand a chance against us?"

He smiled. "We have Clarent and Excalibur on our side,"

Naru's blood froze in her veins. *The Magic Council member controlling this place is Opal? Why is she keeping elementals?* Naru forced her expression into what she hoped resembled amusement.

"We have something even more powerful than her. Our leader, Amy."

He sneered. "That girl is just a brat who ran away from home. If I were you, I wouldn't be so proud of being on her side."

Naru struck him down with a jolt of electricity. "You know people say the same about me and yet you're the one on the ground." Naru spat and turned to the door to see everyone had already filed out of the courtyard.

"Have fun explaining to the Council that you lost to a brat." She stuck her tongue out at him and raced to the entrance. A handful of mages shoved their way through the front door as Ren stared down at her skin crackling with magic. "What happened to laying low?"

Dahlia appeared behind Naru and placed a hand on Naru's shoulder. "She got caught sneaking the others out, but we took care of the guards, right Naru?"

Naru rubbed at her arm. "Ya, but one of them got away. He was sent to alert the owner whoever that is, so we should go."

Ren nodded. The woman at the front desk's eyes widened when she caught the massive group of mages. "Guards. Guards!" She shouted.

Naru smiled. "About that. They aren't coming." Naru turned to Dahlia who curled open her hand to reveal a green leafy branch. "Laurel hedge fumes are pretty potent. You might want to leave for this part. I'll take care of her."

"Thanks Dahlia," Naru said and then the mages from the halfway house piled into Ren's car and the cab of Alder's pickup truck. Dahlia came to them running and sweating and hopped into the back of the truck before shouting "Drive, drive, drive!"

"Alright alright." Ren answered and slid out of the parking lot as his tires screeched in protest. As they sped towards Amy's home to meet with the rest of the team, Naru looked back at the people they'd gathered and hoped this wouldn't be the last time she'd see them alive.

CHAPTER 15

*D*usk gaped at Amy. "Where is your familiar going? Can she do that?"

Amy's shoulders slumped. "Violet doesn't see shades of grey morally, so she sees siding with you as me siding with Opal. She said if I won't kill her, she will."

Dusk cocked his head to one side. "And you're not going to stop her?"

Amy rubbed a hand across her forehead. "She won't listen to anything I have to say."

His gaze drifted to the floor. "Sounds like she and Opal are perfect for each other."

Amy stifled a laugh as she glanced at Violet's retreating back. "Careful. Violet really will kill you if she hears you say that." Amy clapped a hand on his shoulder. "But in all seriousness if you want to join us, I need you to tell me everything. What happened after I escaped and why did you join Opal's side to begin with?"

Dusk picked at his lip. "You won't want me on your side if I tell you everything."

Amy grabbed his hand. "I'm just going to listen. I need to

understand what happened if I'm going to vouch for you with the others. Okay?"

Dusk nodded. "Okay." He took a deep breath. "After you escaped, my magic fizzled out, taking my glamor with it. I was on the way to my quarters when I ran into Opal. That's when-" His mouth opened, but no sound came out. He nibbled at his lower lip.

She squeezed his hand. "It's okay, Dusk. What happened next?"

Dusk sucked in a breath. "Sorry the next part is difficult to talk about. You know about the name I used to go by before I escaped to the human world?"

Amy's jaw clenched. Her gaze burned into his. "What. did. she. say?"

Dusk turned away from her as he spoke. "She refused to see me as Dusk. She kept calling me by my old name, so I called her by hers. She didn't like that and well you know what happened next."

Amy's mouth opened in an O, and she grabbed Dusk's chin so that he was looking at her. "If Violet doesn't kill the bitch, I will."

Dusk placed a hand over his mouth. "Amy."

"Don't Amy me. Now tell me how she convinced you to join her."

Dusk sat down on the grass and drew his knees into his chest, looking like he could sink into the grass at any moment. Cars whizzed by them as they talked while sitting on the grass in the median. "The day that Opal found me in the hotel, I felt the angry footsteps approaching. I'd had my talons out and a glamor on when Opal opened the door. She took one look at me and said a little birdie told her she could find a shifter here. She gave me two choices: side with her or die. I'd insisted you'd come back for me, but then she said you were the ones who'd sold me out."

Amy frowned. "And you believed her?"

He shook his head. "Not at first. I'd only caved when she'd opened the blinds and pointed Garnet out in the parking lot as she led you to the car. I knew Garnet didn't like me, so I thought maybe she'd convinced you to leave me behind. I didn't know you were unconscious."

Amy squared her shoulders. "She manipulated you then. I wonder how her heart functions when it only pumps ice."

He shook his head. "It wasn't entirely manipulation. I'd looked up to her. She was kind to me before the war, the one that destroyed everything."

Amy wrinkled her nose in distaste. "Maybe she appeared kind, but only because her abusive tendencies weren't directed at you."

He blinked. "What are you talking about?"

Amy chewed the metal chain on her necklace. "When we were training for the War of the Twin Swords, she tried to convince me to stay out of the battle. I refused, so she got overzealous." Amy shivered as she felt phantom cuts along her skin.

Dusk placed a hand on her shoulder. "It's okay. She isn't here now."

Amy sucked in a breath. "Sorry. It's hard to talk about. Sometimes, I can still feel the cold blade ripping through my skin and hear her hissing complaints about me."

He bit his lower lip. "I didn't know. She'd been so kind to me then, making sure I could follow what was going on by signing for me and mentoring me in my magical abilities. And after the war, she saved a child from the sorceress clan that was like me."

Amy's voice shook. "But then she decimated our entire village. Can you honestly defend her after that?"

Dusk clutched his stomach. "I know what happened was awful, but she wasn't in control. It was the swords. Her voice and eye color had changed. Right before the explosion she got this panicked look in her eyes and told me to run, to evacuate

191

the clan to the human world. Because of her warning, I managed to escape with several members of the Enchantress clan before the portal and the village got magic bombed."

Amy bit her lip. "Like what happened with my magic in the first war, but on a large scale. But if you evacuated, how did so many die in the explosion?"

He dug his nails into his palm. "Many refused to believe me or didn't want to abandon their home. My mother died because she refused to listen to a lowly enchanter that could have had the rank and benefits of an enchantress."

Amy rubbed at her creased forehead. "Oh. But you have to realize that regardless of her reasons for doing so, she's killed too many. Unchecked, she could kill off entire magic races. You might have to kill her if you join our side. Do you think you can handle that?"

Tears filled Dusk's eyes, and he wiped them away as he choked out sobs. "I don't know. She was my mentor and my friend."

Amy awkwardly patted Dusk's shoulder. *How could he have become an assassin?* He seemed so helpless sitting on the grass, crying his eyes out. It seemed strange. She needed to know why.

"Dusk. This may be a bad time, but how did she convince you to be her assassin? I'll need a way to justify your actions to the group so they don't kill you on sight."

Dusk's eyes darkened. "Opal told me the targets were dangerous, but looking back I think she lied. One was a Kitsune that was supposedly running dangerous experiments on shifters, but after I'd killed him, I didn't find any evidence of the experiments or any technology capable of what she'd claimed. When I confronted her about it, she said he must have known I was coming and hid everything away."

Amy wrinkled her nose. "That sounds like a filthy lie."

He hugged his arms around his chest. "I think it was all lies. A wolf shifter tried to stop me. She was crying out as he took his last breath. I can still hear her screams when I sleep. What I did was unforgivable."

Amy ran a finger along her ear. "You have a lot to atone for, and there's a chance they might never forgive you. You'll have to win their trust, our trust."

He curled up into a ball, his chin pressed to his knees. "What do I need to do?"

"Tell us everything you know, any weaknesses we can use against her. Help me get my sister back."

"What if they don't accept my help? Then what?" His voice cracked.

Amy dug her nails into her palm. "Regardless of what they say, I'll be there with you. You won't be alone, but you have to trust me. Can you do that?" She stood up and held out a hand for him.

He rocked forward. "That I think I can do."

Dusk took Amy's hand, and she helped him up. "Then let's go find Iris and Naru. They still don't know I escaped, so we need to warn them before they go charging into the Council's lair. My guess is they went to my house to regroup since it has the most magical protection."

Amy held out her hand and Dusk took it. She helped him up from the asphalt and they walked to the nearest bus stop. They rode to her home in silence. She kept her back straight and her eyes fixed on Dusk the entire way, still wondering if this new truce would last.

Dusk relaxed into the seat and whispered in her ear. "Opal's weakness is that girl you saw with her, Raven. If you can capture her, she will give up any fight without protest...just promise me you won't kill her. She hasn't done anything wrong."

Amy's hand twitched. *Opal would really let go of a battle because of a girl? No, it had to be more than that.* "Any idea why she's so attached to Raven?"

He rubbed his thumb against his cat's eye pocket watch. "I

think she was related to Joan. They have the same eyes and facial features, but she's more than just a sorceress."

Amy sighed. Opal had cared so much about Joan that she'd razed entire cities, but the girl was probably harmless so long as no one made the mistake of killing her. "That I can promise you. I have no intention of harming a child. I'm not Opal."

He placed a hand on her arm, and she flinched. He jerked his hand back. "I didn't mean to scare you. I just wanted to say thank you. I couldn't live with myself if Raven died because of me."

Amy gave a slight smile but hid it under a curtain of her purple hair. *Perhaps some of the old him is still there underneath all of the pain.* She hoped that would be enough. "When we get there, let me talk to the others first. I don't want them killing you."

Dusk looked her over in a way that made her flush. "Whatever you say, rebel."

The bus approached their stop, and Amy pulled the string to notify the driver. As they shuffled off the bus, her heart sank into her stomach. A handful of cars were parked outside her home.

When Amy got to the front door, she held up a hand, stopping him. "Wait just around the corner. Stay out of sight until I signal you."

He nodded. "Got it."

Once he'd turned the corner, she pushed the front door open to reveal a small group of about thirty people. A ragtag mix of shifters, glass mages, and elemental mages stood in her living room.

Amy stepped over the threshold to see Iris with dark circles under their eyes and jagged red marks along their arms and legs. Iris leapt up from their spot on the couch and ran over to Amy to envelop Amy in a hug. "You're alive! I was so worried you got yourself killed trying to send me that message."

Amy shoved at Iris's chest as her ribs got squeezed and her breaths quickened. "It's good to see you, but I need air."

"Oh, right, sorry." They released their grip on Amy. "How did you get free? Is Garnet with you?"

Amy rubbed at her neck. "It's a long story, but I couldn't take Garnet with me. I barely got away myself. I had some help from an old friend, and this amulet must have unlocked some new magic because I was able to make a pin levitate and pick the locks on the cuffs."

Amy pulled back and glanced down at the angry red marks on Iris. "What happened to you?" Amy glanced up at the group behind them. "And where is the rest of the army?"

Iris turned to Eiji behind them and twirled a rainbow curl around their finger. "We lost several allies when we were attacked in the glass mage village, and we only had a few recruits to start with. We didn't know you'd escaped, and we wanted to get here as quickly as possible before Opal killed you."

Iris bounced on their heels. "But how did you figure out you could make a pin levitate?"

Amy's gaze drifted to the floor. "It was a wild guess. I remembered when I was in the war, I threw people back from my shields sometimes before they touched them, so I thought maybe telekinesis, but I can't control it very well."

Amy glanced up to see Naru shift from foot to foot as she stared down at the ground, her face flushed. "I'm glad you're okay. I know you don't like hugs, but." Naru held out her arms.

Amy ran over to Naru and placed her head against Naru's chest. Amy planted a kiss on her cheek. "Sorry for worrying you."

Naru gulped and shook her head. "No, I'm sorry I couldn't find more people. I also may have had to bribe some of the ones here by offering them your gemstone services."

Dahlia elbowed her. "Is that your girlfriend?"

Naru's heart rate quickened as Amy lay against her chest. "Uh. I wish."

Dahlia jerked a thumb at Amy. "Speaking of which Isn't this the mage we're supposed to be saving? If she got out, what do you need us for?"

Amy removed herself from Naru's embrace and approached Dahlia with a set jaw. "Because if you want whatever reward Naru promised you, I'm going to need my sister back, alive."

Amy raised her gaze to the rest of the group. "For those of you wondering why you should still help, just know that I won't deliver what you were promised unless you help me first and that means getting my sister back."

A wolf shifter sauntered up to Amy with a scowl. "If we're going to help you, I want to know you're the real deal. Where's that God's pendant Iris told us about? I want to know you're not just any old enchantress."

Amy's brows drew together. "What's a god's pendant?"

Iris cleared their throat. "The pendant you got at the market. The amber one."

Amy opened her mouth in an O. "You mean this pendant, the amber one?" Amy placed a hand to the necklace warming her chest.

Iris gave a curt nod. "Yes, that one."

Amy pulled it over her head and handed it to the shifter with sandy hair and skin the same tawny hue as Iris's. When she held the pendant out, it glowed a bright orange yellow like the sun's rays. The shifter squinted against the light. "The name is Ayla and yes that pendant. Glass mages, you're the expert on relics. Can you take a look at it?"

A glass mage stepped forward and held out his hand. "May I?"

Ayla nodded and placed the pendant in the mage's hand. He squinted at it as it glowed brighter in his grip. He examined each bit of gold encircling the amber with care and then placed the pendant back in Amy's hand. "It's genuine. It holds an insignia of Freya on the side."

Amy slumped her shoulders. "Now are you all willing to help or not? We need as many people as we can get if we're going to survive this."

Naru wrapped an arm over Amy's shoulder. "You already know I'm in, and the elementals with me are too, but one of them will need some basic advice on controlling magic. Iris, do you think you can help Ryu over there?" She nodded at a mage that slouched in the back with his hands in his pockets.

Ryu ran a hand through his hair. "How is a shifter going to teach me to control elemental magic?"

Iris held up a finger. "Because the principles of magic control are the same for most magical species, and since our magic takes hold at the youngest age, we have the most practice."

He crossed his arms over his chest. "I was hoping for an elemental mage as a mentor, but I suppose I'm open to help either way."

"That's the spirit," Naru said with a smile.

Amy rubbed the bridge of her nose. "Naru, I thought elementals were as abundant as salt in the sea here, so why are there so few here and ones without magic control at that."

Naru grumbled. "Because we had to integrate into a society where our parents think magic is fake and there's rarely anyone to teach us that we have powers let alone control them. Several of the ones here were in a mage prison disguised as a halfway house."

Amy cocked her head. "And why were they in a halfway house?"

"Uh several of them accidentally hurt others because of lack of magic control. They got arrested and the Council approached them to go be in their facility nestled in the middle of magic hunter territory. Before you scold me for going somewhere so dangerous, I got some interesting information for you while we were there."

Amy leaned into Naru's shoulder. "I'll scold you in private. What's the information?" She trailed her fingers along Naru's arm.

Naru flushed and cleared her throat. She spoke loud enough so everyone could hear. "It appears Opal owns a magic prison and has several magic hunters as guards. She's collecting elemental mages, but we don't know why."

"In that case, we will have our work cut out for us. Any idea why she is working with the magic hunters?" Amy asked.

"No, but the facility staff had normal humans and magic hunters working there," Naru said.

Amy placed a hand under her chin. "In that case, we'll need to be especially cautious to avoid running into magic hunters. No doubt they'll be after you if you took mages from Opal's prison. We'll stay here tonight since there's already some barriers in place and the glass here is shatter resistant. The glass mages here might recognize it since it was specially ordered from the magic world. I'll reinforce the wards with our new ally's help."

Naru cocked her head to one side. "What new ally?"

Iris glared at Amy. "If they're an ally, why can I smell anxiety wafting off you in waves?"

"He's a very recent ally, but an old friend. Before he comes in, I need all of you to promise you won't attack him. He's the reason I was able to escape, so behave. Got it?" She raised an eyebrow at Iris.

Iris crossed their arms over their chest. "Don't look at me. I'm not the one you should be worried about," They said and pointed a thumb at Naru.

"Rude, but fair." Naru said. "You can bring him in, but if he betrays us." She dragged a hand across her neck. "No mercy."

Amy's eyes darkened. Her words felt heavy on her tongue.

"Iris. This new ally talked about something he did on Opal's behalf, and I want you to know he regrets it before you meet him. Based on his story, the victim might have been living with wolf shifters. Just try to remember he was sent there under false pretenses. Opal hurt him too, and he wants revenge. We'll need his help to take her down."

Iris's lips pulled back from their teeth. "I don't like the sound of this. Who is he?"

Amy gulped. She couldn't look at Iris. "He was Opal's assassin, Dusk."

In a flash Iris was on her, hand grabbing at the collar on her shirt. "I will not ally with him. He killed someone I loved. Kito suffered a slow and painful death because of that *monster*." She spat.

Amy placed her hands atop Iris's. "Please just give him a chance. She abandoned him for who and what he is. She lied to him, manipulated him into working for her. Please. He was my friend before she took him. He sided with her based on the lies she fed him."

The outline of Iris's jaw popped as they clenched their teeth together. Amy's vision blurred as Iris shook her. "Last time he was here, he kidnapped you and took you to Opal. How do you know he won't just turn on us?"

Amy gripped Iris's hand, her knuckles going white as she tried to pry Iris's fingers off her collar, but they had an iron-clad grip. "I can use an enchantment on him to prove his intentions. That place is a maze, and he knows it far better than any of us. We'll need his help to navigate that place."

Iris ground their teeth together. "Fine, but if I so much as suspect his betrayal or if he puts anyone in danger, I will kill him myself. You understand?"

Amy nodded. "Yes. I'll go get him."

Iris released Amy who sucked in a breath. Iris rubbed at their temples. "Bringing my lover's killer in front of me and not letting me kill him. That's cruel," Iris grumbled.

Amy went over to the window in the living room and waved at Dusk, signaling for him to come in.

She went to the door and gave him her hand so he could walk through the barrier that had been designed to keep him out. As he stepped through the door, he tripped over the ledge and bumped into Amy's chest. He pulled himself back, so their chests didn't touch. "Sorry. Are you okay?"

Naru bristled in the corner and muttered. "She's just fine. You know, you may have helped her escape, but you also brought her to Opal a few days ago."

Amy snickered and looked at Naru. "Relax, Naru. He just tripped."

Naru cut a glance at Amy's hands which were still clasped with Dusk's. Amy flushed and untangled their fingers. The tips of Dusk's ears turned pink, and he cleared his throat. "I take it this means they won't be killing me just yet."

A strangled laugh escaped Amy's throat. "Let's just say Iris is less than thrilled that you'll be joining us, but they agreed as long as your intent is pure. I'm going to use an enchantment to test your intentions, okay?"

He blinked his wide golden eyes. "Okay." He leaned into her ear and whispered. "Are you sure that's a good idea?"

Iris's upper lip curled back "It's an excellent idea. If you have any objections, you can leave now."

Dusk held up a finger. "How did you hear that?"

Iris tucked a strand of hair behind their ear. "The shifters in this room have enhanced hearing, and you're not that good at whispering."

Dusk gulped, and he held out his hand. "Fine, do you want one of my rose quartz since that's the closest to your familiar's gem, or are you planning to use something else?"

Amy rummaged through her pack and pulled out a smooth, round light pink stone with white inclusions and curled her fingers around it. "That's okay, I have my own." The gem glowed a faint lavender around the edges as she placed it in Dusk's hand. "What do you intend to do if you have to choose between me or Opal?"

Dusk shrugged his shoulders. "I intend to stay with your side. I have a better chance of survival here, and you know and care for the real me. Opal gambled with my life and refused to accept me. She wasn't who I thought she was."

The stone glowed white, and Dusk dropped it into Amy's hand. "Is that good enough for you?"

Every instinct in her screamed not to trust him, and her fingertips already tingled with the start of magic exhaustion from that small spell. She wanted to believe him, but she needed to know one more thing. "Not yet." She placed the stone back in his hand. "Do you intend to hand me over to Opal?"

He forced a smile. "No. I'd sooner chew off my own arm."

The gem glowed white, and her fingers twitched as she took the pink quartz from Dusk's hand. The glow of her magic faded, and her hand lost its grip on the Rose quartz. Dusk plucked it from the air before it could fall to the floor.

She curled her right hand against her chest as pins and needles shot through her fingers. Between the magic she'd used to escape and losing Violet as an external power source, two truth spells severely depleted her mana.

Amy gestured to the room of mages. "There you have it. He doesn't intend to betray me, so unless you know anyone else here that is adept in illusion spells and that can navigate the Magic Council HQ, he's our best chance at finding Garnet and getting her out safely,"

Amy's knee buckled, and she pitched forward. Dusk grabbed her shoulder to steady her. "Careful. The wound on your leg still hasn't healed. Maybe it would be best for us to leave tomorrow night?"

Amy raised her head to look at Iris. "What do you think?"

Iris opened their mouth to speak, but the Kitsune beside them answered instead. "I know you don't know me, but I think you're right. Although I'm sure Iris will insist on jumping into the fray while still injured."

Amy twisted a ring around her finger. "Thank you...uh."

"Eiji," He offered.

"Thank you, Eiji, but I want to hear from Iris as well."

Iris picked at their cuticles. "Of course, I want to go as soon as possible because we don't know how long Opal will keep any given captive alive. It would be rather pointless if we broke in and lost comrades only to find your sister has been executed."

The knot in Amy's chest loosened. "That I can understand. I want to go there now too, but Eiji is right. We're not in any condition to attempt a rescue mission today. We'll go tomorrow the moment the sun sets. If we hear any news of a public execution, then we'll leave sooner. She's my sister, so they may try to make a spectacle of her death because she was harboring me."

Iris's voice came out strained. "I suppose you have a point."

Amy turned back to Dusk. "Good. Now that we're agreed, we'll get everyone healed up." She grabbed Dusk's hand. "Come with me. I'll walk you through a healing spell for Iris and me."

He ran a hand through his midnight hair. "I'm not great at healing spells, but I'll do my best."

DUSK GLANCED down at their joined hands as Amy led him to her workshop and rummaged through a dresser drawer brimming with a plethora of stones. She handed him a green stone shot through with red. "You'll need this to clean the blood and avoid infections. It's a bloodstone."

She dug through the contents of the drawer again and pulled out a red Beryl. "Aha. I thought I might have one somewhere. This should be easier for you to use for the actual healing part since it's a Beryl like your Cat's eye familiar." *You remember that but didn't recognize my face when you first saw me as Dusk. Oh, Amy.*

Dusk took the gems from her. "Okay, but how do I use it?"

Amy bit her lip. "First, you're going to hold it over the wound, but don't touch it with the stone. There should be less than a fingernail's distance between the gem and the wound for this to work."

She placed a hand over Dusk's and guided his hand to her leg wound. "Next, I'll take off these bandages." She carefully unwrapped the bandages wound around her leg until the angry red wound was exposed.

"Now what?"

"Instead of sending out energy, you're absorbing it like a straw from the stone to almost magnetize it so it will latch onto the impurities in our blood. If you need a verbal spell to focus your energy try this. Sanen desde las raíces y limpien la sangre."

Did she forget that I don't use verbal spells? Dusk closed his eyes and clamped his hand around the bloodstone. "I'll try, but my spells use signing. Remember?"

Amy pursed her lips. "Hm. That's true. Maybe you can try one of the more physical ways to focus a spell instead. Here, take my hand."

Dusk's face flushed. "Why?"

"It's for grounding. Just trust me. Each gem has its own vibration to it. Like the physical ones you feel when you used the whiskers spell to feel the enemies near you during the War of the Twin Swords."

He placed one hand against Amy's and held the stone with the other. "What does that have to do with me completing the spell properly?"

She traced a circle on his palm. "Those vibrations are easier to notice when the magic has something to ping off of.

In this case, my palm. Go ahead and try a familiar spell first so you can get the...feel for it," She snickered.

He rolled his eyes. "Did you really just make such a cheesy pun."

"Yes, yes, I did. Just do it."

He waved her off. "All right, All right."

He pulled a golden stone with a pupil-like stripe down its center, a cat's eye, from his gem bag, and palmed it. He pursed his lips together. "I'm not sure how to do this since the spell requires my hands. I guess I can try the one-handed version of the spell."

Amy glanced up at the ceiling and then back to Dusk. "It should work as long as I'm touching a part of your body or the gemstone. It doesn't have to be your hand, just a part of your skin that's sensitive enough to pick up the feel of the spell."

"Okay in that case, I guess place your palm on my foot."

Amy wrinkled her nose. "Alright, but your feet better not stink."

He shook his head and slipped off his socks and shoes. Her hand pressed against the sole of his foot as he gripped the golden cat's eye in one hand.

"I'm going to do a simple illusion spell to change my hair color." He did the sign for blonde and then used the sign for hair to activate the spell.

A soft yellow light came from the stone, and Dusk's hair changed from black to a pale blonde. He felt a short sharp vibration against his foot like what would happen if you dropped something heavy into a tub of water.

He cracked a small smile. "Hey, it worked. Now how do I apply this to the healing spell?"

"We'll do the same thing, but this time with the bloodstone. Once you know the right frequency of that stone, each spell is just an increased or decreased intensity of the same thing. Healing and other support spells are usually a slightly softer frequency and attack spells are more intense, faster frequencies. Does that make sense?"

He blinked. "Yes, but how do you know all of this?"

Amy's expression darkened and she bit the inside of her cheek.

Dusk placed a hand on her shoulder. "Oh...Was it Garnet?"

"Mhm. She was...is...great with linguistics. She taught me spells in as many languages as she could. Her familiar gave her knowledge instead of power."

Dusk swiped at his bangs as they changed from blonde back to black, "I understand. I still don't trust her, but I know she's important to you. We'll get her out somehow, but first let's focus on this," He pressed his hand to hers, and she interlaced their fingers.

"Do you know any spells for bloodstone?" Amy asked.

He shook his head. "No, can you do one?"

Amy closed her eyes. "I don't have much magic left, but this one I should be able to manage. It's a simple enhancement spell, so the frequency should be similar to healing. Coraje."

The stone pulsed between their palms with a steady thump like that of a vein pumping blood. He supposed that made sense.

Amy winced and sweat dripped down her forehead. Dusk took the bloodstone from her and disentangled their hands. "Maybe you shouldn't cast any more magic for a bit."

"I'll be fine. I pushed myself far worse in magic school when they all thought I was some prodigy," she said, her voice breathy.

"Well, we can't rescue your sister if you're useless, so let's take care of your wound. Scoot closer."

Amy slid along the carpeted floor until her leg was an inch from Dusk's hovering hand. His pulse quickened as he gripped the bloodstone. *Her being this close is dangerous. She looks beautiful even all muddied up.* He squeezed his eyes shut. Inky darkness coiled around the gemstone and her wound as mud and other debris extricated itself from the cut and fell to the carpet in a greyish blob.

When he opened his eyes, he grimaced at the dirt that had been left behind. "Well now I see why you wanted me to clean the blood first. I'll take care of Iris next. Can you bring her in?"

Amy rubbed at her hair. "They probably heard you. Iris, you can come in now."

The door creaked open to reveal a scowling Iris. Her ears were prominent and pinned back against her head. "Iris, can you come here so I can heal you please?"

Iris bared her teeth, her pointed canines showing. "I don't want your filthy hands or your magic touching me."

Amy huffed. "Well, my magic is extinguished, so you can let him help you or go into battle with what looks like a pretty severe wound."

Iris snapped. "Fine. I'll allow you to heal me this time, but if we meet again after this, we will meet as enemies."

She's testy for someone asking for help. You think she'd be more grateful.

"First of all, at least for the moment, I'm using they/them pronouns. Second of all, your thoughts are obscenely loud. As a shifter, you may find it beneficial to guard them."

Dusk's eyes widened. "Sorry. My mistake, they are testy. Wait, does that mean you can hear all my thoughts?"

Iris licked their lips. "Yes, when they're emotionally loud or if we're purposefully trying to communicate. Yes, I heard *those* thoughts too. Don't worry, I won't share them, yet."

Amy cocked her head to one side. "What thoughts?"

Dusk flushed. "Just about how they're ungrateful for not accepting my help, right Iris?"

Iris shrugged. "Sure. We'll go with that," and they sat down next to him.

Dusk hovered his hand over Iris's wound and tuned into the feel of the gemstone under his fingertips, upping the intensity of the spell as it snagged on several layers of magical residue. His chest heaved from the effort as he pulled out small shards of glass and bits of concrete.

Once Iris's wounds were cleaned, he picked up the Red Beryl on the ground. "I know exactly what spell to use to test the frequency for this one. Amy, can you hold my hand for this?"

He held out the hand holding the gemstone towards Amy, but she gave him a wary look. "Why?"

"Because this spell requires two people and hand to hand touch. It's supposed to help you find something in common with another person by lighting up an object or showing a word."

She held out her hand. "Oh. I wonder if it will tell us something obvious like that we both use gemstone magic."

Doubtful since it tells you how you can become closer with someone you like, he thought.

Iris covered their ears and mouthed. "Loud."

Dusk ignored them. He used his right hand to poke his chest with the tip of his middle finger twice, and the stone pulsed in his hand. This one had an ebb and flow to it like the tide in the ocean.

A tendril of magic went down into his pouch, and he dumped the gemstones on the floor. A blood red ruby glowed between them.

"Well, that's disappointing," Amy said. "I was hoping it would give us a word or something. Does this just mean we have our magic in common?"

Or that I need to be loyal and compassionate to win you over. Dusk nodded and grabbed hold of the ruby. *But I can't let her know that.* He pressed the gem to his chest. "It means we're both creative. That's what we have in common."

Iris raised an eyebrow. *That was a creative lie.*

He glared daggers at them.

Amy folded her hands in her lap. "I'm not all that creative. I just look at other people's designs and copy them."

Dusk placed a hand over hers. "But I'm sure your jewelry had its own unique twist to it too."

Iris tilted their head to the side. "Are you sure it's creativity and not l-"

Dusk elbowed them. "Zip it, mutt."

They twirled rainbow hair around their finger. "Sure thing, baby bird."

Dusk shot them a glare. "Let me heal Iris first, so they can leave."

Iris nodded. "Ah so, you two can be alo-"

Dusk placed a hand over their mouth, cutting them off. "I'm sorry for insulting you. Please don't."

Iris removed Dusk's hand and pretended to zip their lips. "I won't say another word. Heal away."

He muttered. "I think I prefer you being angry at me." He hovered a hand over the wound that ran along Iris's leg and widened at their stomach. His other hand clutched the red Beryl. He squeezed his eyes shut and clung to the thrum of its magic like the ebb and flow of the ocean and slowed its tides.

He pictured that magic sweeping over the body, tugging skin together and smoothing out torn muscles. Energy ebbed out of him, and when he opened his eyes, Iris's wound was healed, but the room spun. He pitched forward, and Amy grabbed his shoulder, steadying him. "Easy there. Don't use up all of your magic when you have a familiar that can help you."

Dusk bit his lip. "I'll ask, but I won't demand. They're meant to be partners, not energy drinks." He prodded at his familiar's mind. *Can you loan me some of your powers?*

Kuro let out a loud yawn. *Of course, but you don't need to be so reluctant to ask for help. I know you're not out to abuse my magic.*

It still feels wrong after what you told me about the alliance.

Fair enough, but the solution would be to tell Amy that, not try to do everything yourself. Dusk's magic threaded through with amber the color of his eyes. *That should be enough. I'm going back to sleep. Don't wake me again unless someone is dying.*

Dusk mumbled. "You act more like a sloth than a cat."

Amy bit her lip, but he still caught the hint of a smile. "Sorry. Kuro isn't keen on being woken up from his cat naps. Now hold still so I can heal your leg."

Amy stretched her leg out in front of him, and he hung his hand over the wound. Tuning into the calming wave of the gem's magic was much easier the second time with Kuro's magic guiding him. When he cracked open one eye, the gash was mostly closed aside from a pale pink mark that stretched along the length of Amy's leg.

Amy grabbed his hand, but his gaze stayed fixed on her thin pink lips. "Thank you for helping me twice now...Old friend."

He snorted at the use of the endearment. "I called you that partially out of spite, but oddly enough it was still true."

"Not was true, is true. We'll mend that friendship together. Right, Iris?"

Iris made a face like she was trying to hold back a laugh. "Sure. Friends. Uh. Let's get back to the others before one of your other friends comes bursting in here worried."

Right on cue, the door swung open to reveal the girl from before that had given him spiteful looks. Her gaze fell directly on his and Amy's intertwined hands. "I was wondering what was taking you so long, Amy. I suppose the enemy is a safer bet than me?"

Amy jerked her hand from Dusk's grip, and he deflated a bit when Amy's back straightened and her face flushed. "It wasn't like that. I was thanking him for healing me. This is the second time he's helped, so I think it's fair to say he's not an enemy anymore, Naru."

Naru turned up her nose. "Well, I still don't trust him. I'll be keeping an eye on you, assassin," she said and pointed to Dusk.

Dusk's shoulders slumped. "I suppose you have a point, and I don't blame you for being cautious around me, but I will earn my place here regardless of what you think."

Naru crossed her arms over her chest. "Well, a good start would be explaining to the mages and shifters out there exactly what invaluable information you'll provide."

Dusk pushed himself off the floor. "Of course. I'll go address the group now, so we can plan our attack."

He strode out of the room, pushing past Naru who recoiled at the brush of his fingers on her arm. "Personal bubble," she shouted as he walked past her and into the living room.

The conversation ceased when he entered the room. Everyone's gaze turned to him. "I know you still have no reason to trust me apart from Amy's word, but I know the Council's metal maze well. I've been there since its creation. There are only two possible places where I wouldn't have seen her. Opal's quarters or the magic deprivation chamber they use for interrogations." He ran a hand through his short midnight blue hair.

The shifters muttered amongst themselves. One of them broke from the crowd and walked up to Amy, his eyes a glowing amber, and he pressed a clawed finger to her chest. "How did you manage to escape? How do we know you aren't both working for Opal?"

Amy snatched the burly shifter's shirt and yanked him down to meet her eyes. "You shouldn't have said that," she whispered and shoved him back, making him stumble over his feet.

He curled a lip up in a snarl. "Why not? It's a fair question. You were being kept by Opal and got away unscathed? Then you show up with one of Opal's assassins claiming he's switched sides. I'm sure the lot of you are wondering too."

Dusk shielded his face. *This isn't going to be pretty.*

A young shifter that looked like Ayla curled his lip up and a fang poked out. "Why not, canary?"

Dusk smirked. "How about you let her tell you that, puppy?"

Amy put a hand to her chest and hysterical laughter escaped her throat. "If you think I would align myself with that bitch, you must know nothing about what happened after the War of the Twin Swords."

The wolf shifter blinked and turned to Iris. "What is she talking about?"

Iris grabbed the shifter's arm, holding them back. "Ze'ev, you picked the wrong person to accuse. Opal tried to kill Amy right after the war. She had to abandon her home and most of her family to survive as long as she has."

Ze'ev's jaw dropped. "This girl is the runaway mage Opal's been hunting for years? I know she has that god's object, but I just don't see it."

Amy clutched her pendant. "I don't understand why the object picked me either, and I haven't fully unlocked its powers yet. But I'd sooner die trying to dethrone Opal than allow her to continue wreaking havoc. I'm done running, and I won't run from your insults either."

Iris let out a sigh. "You're lucky Amy let you off with a warning, Ze'ev. Ayla, control your brother."

Ayla emerged from the crowd and yanked him back by the elbow.

Amy raised her eyes to the ceiling. "I don't know what you're talking about."

Iris gave Amy a playful nudge. "Please. I've seen what you can do on the rare occasion that someone upsets you."

Amy turned to Naru. "Am I really that scary when I'm angry?"

Naru rubbed the back of her neck. "Well. I've only seen

you angry once, but I wasn't the one the anger was directed at, so I just thought it was cute."

Ayla cleared her throat. "Do you plan on telling us how you found Freya's necklace?"

Amy glanced at Ayla. "Oh right. It caught my eye when I was at the craft festival downtown. A gentleman there sold it to me, and I didn't think anything of it until it protected me from Dusk over here. Although it was strange that I felt such a connection with it. It feels akin to the connection with my familiar."

Iris tapped their foot on the floor. "Interesting. Do you remember anything about the man that gave you the necklace?"

Amy picked at her chipped purple nail polish. "He said he was from Avia, and when I was walking away from the booth, I turned back to ask him something, and his booth had dissipated taking him with it."

The shifter's eyes widened as they stared at the necklace in her hand. "If *he* chose her, she must be one of the descendants."

Iris grabbed Amy's arm. "Let's not jump to any hasty conclusions. She had three sisters, so it seems unlikely that only one of them would be a god's descendant." Iris bit the inside of the cheek. "Although I've never heard you talk about your father. Do you remember him?"

Amy clutched the pendant to her chest. "My father died shortly before I was born. Thanks for reminding me."

"Amy. I'm not asking this for no reason. We need to know if you might have any direct connection to one of the Gods, especially Freya. Did people ever think you weren't related to your sisters?"

Amy wrung her hands. "I remember seeing pictures of my father, but he died shortly before I was born. I don't look much like my sisters or father. I'd always had questions about why when I was younger, but my mother had never given me any direct answers."

Iris tapped their fingers against their pants. "Then there's a possibility that you're a descendant. Especially with you carrying one of the gods' artifacts."

Amy swayed on her feet. As she fell back, an arm grabbed her, steadying her. "Thanks, Naru." Amy's eyes snapped to Iris. "What do you mean I'm a descendant of a god? Is this why I could levitate the pin, and why no one knew how to teach me magic?" Amy clutched at the hair on her head. "No, no. This can't be an artifact, can it? All I've seen it do is create light and turn something to gold."

Dusk walked over to Amy, placed a hand on her shoulder, and gave it a slight squeeze. Some of Amy's tension eased.

Iris rubbed at their jaw. "That's because you don't know how to unlock its potential yet. The artifacts are connected to the previous owner's abilities. Some of Freya's specialties were light, war, and love. That's why it helped you with light when you were attacked by Dusk. It sensed his malicious intent." Iris's steely gaze flashed to his golden one. *I still don't trust you.*

You don't have to, but trust that Amy is making the right decision. And trust that I know her well enough to help her handle this information. She doesn't like being responsible for the lives of others after what happened in the war, and you all want her to be the leader of your revolution.

Iris growled. *How else are we meant to take down Opal? Or are you hoping to make Amy give up on freedom and justice?*

He cut a glance at her. *I never said that.*

"Iris, stop. He's here to help." Amy warned.

Dusk's free hand came down to touch the pocket watch with the glowing cat's eye gem embedded within it. "Easy there. I'm going to help you get into Opal's hideout, remember?"

Iris glared at Dusk and took a few steps back. "Fine. Then

how do we get into that interrogation chamber you mentioned?"

Dusk shifted on his feet. "I can lead one person there, but it's right next to the Council room, so it's dangerous to sneak in. And being in there for too long can kill a mage or a human since the walls are made from a mixture of Rhodium and lead. The Council has a window in their chamber to view interrogations, so we should check to see if she's even there first."

Amy shuddered. "Do you know how to get me there?"

Dusk rubbed at his jaw. "Uh. I mean. I can, but that's going to be the most dangerous job. Are you sure you want to be on the front lines like that?"

Amy gave a curt nod. "Considering I'm the only other enchantment mage here and we'll likely have to disarm multiple enchantments to get there without getting caught, I'd be the best one for the job, correct?"

He pressed his lips into a thin line. "Yes, that part of the Council's base is heavily guarded and there are enchantments all over the vents and entrances. In order to stay under the radar, we'll have to be on high alert at all times. If I tell you to run, run and don't look back. Understand?"

Amy straightened her back. "I understand. How will everyone fit into this new plan?"

Eiji raised a finger. "Originally, we were going to have Nyoka sneak in through the vents, so they could search for potential weak spots in the Council's security and check for magic dampening metals. Since metal dampeners only affect enchantment and elemental mages, the shifters here can take down the guards anywhere that has magic dampeners. The glass mages and elemental mages would have found a way to get to Amy and her sister. If we ran into Opal, that team would abort their mission."

Dusk nodded. His gaze skimmed over the crowd. "Nyoka won't be able to search through the vents since they're covered in enchantments. They can go with the rest of the shifters. I like the idea of sending the shifter team to places with metal dampeners. They can create a diversion by knocking out guards in the prison ward. It could help draw attention away from us and increase our potential for success, but we should keep at least one shifter and a calligraphy stone on each team for communication purposes."

Amy nodded. "That sounds great. What about the elementals?"

Dusk walked up to Naru and sized her up. "What element do you control?"

Naru blinked. "Fire and air, but my magic first manifested as a combination of both, as a kind of heat lightning."

His lip tugged up at the corner in a half smile. "Good. I want to bring a small team with you to short out the security cameras wherever possible. You'll be in charge of our contingency plan, so you'll lead a few elementals to the living quarters." He massaged his temples. "As much as I don't want to do this, you'll be in charge of finding and capturing Raven."

Naru cocked her head to one side. "She has a pet Raven?"

Amy placed a hand on Dusk's shoulder. "Are you sure you want to do that?"

"We don't have a choice. Although I'm not thrilled with the idea of kidnapping a child."

Naru cleared her throat. "Hello. You didn't answer my question? Who or what is Raven?"

Dusk shoved his hands in his pocket, and Amy threw sidelong glances at him. "She's one of Opal's few weaknesses. A young girl that's related to someone Opal cared about."

Naru sneered. "I'm shocked that her blackened heart is still capable of giving a shit about others. Alright. Where can we find this girl?"

Dusk scuffed the toe of his shoe against the floor. "If she isn't with Opal, she'll be in her quarters just a few doors down from Opal's room. I'll draw it on the map."

A glass mage stepped forward. "And where do we fit into this plan?"

Dusk's gaze ran up and down the mages, appraising them. "What is your strength as a glass mage?"

The glass mage picked at his nails. "Support magic mostly. We work best with elementals, and can create powerful offensive magic, but only in short spurts."

"Hm. Then, you can create a diversion to help the elementals capture the girl. A few of you can try sneaking into the Council's room to see if it's possible to break the glass and get Garnet out through the viewing window but avoid getting too close to Opal. You don't want to deal with that sword of hers."

One of the elementals stepped forward, his hand ablaze. "And what is your plan for the rest of the elementals apart from the lightning mage over there? Or did you forget about us?"

Amy plastered on a smile, ignoring his snide remark. "The corridors looked like they were made of steel. If you have any elementals with a metal or fire affinity, they can warp the walls and trap guards. You'll work with the shifters and help release prisoners. Water elementals can work with Naru destroying security cameras from the outside. Wood elementals can stay outside and keep guards that are outside from going into the fortress since it's surrounded by trees. Understand?"

Ren blinked. "I think I see why Naru likes you now." He placed a hand over his forehead. "My hopeful fangirl."

"I'll end you for that," Naru said with a glare.

Ren crossed his arms behind his head. "No, you won't. You like me too much."

Dusk gave a hissing laugh. "That explains why she was so jealous earlier."

Naru bit her lip. "I wasn't jealous."

"Sure, you weren't," he said with a smirk, but his smile fell when he thought of Raven and how they were capturing her.

But maybe it will help her see Opal in a new light. She's tried to shield Raven from her destructive tendencies.

Amy gripped Dusk's arm. "Why did you choose to have us capture Raven? I thought you didn't want that."

Dusk placed a hand over Amy's. "We may need some leverage against Opal in case we can't retrieve Garnet. I don't think she'll do to her what she did to me. The girl is far too important, but maybe it can plant some seeds of doubt for her as well. She could make a good ally. Just...don't hurt her."

Amy squeezed his arm and nodded. "I'll tell them to be careful." Amy looked up to the group. "Now that we've got the formalities out of the way, is everyone clear on the plan?"

A chorus of "Yes." came from the crowd. Some of the shifters said it hesitantly, and Nyoka gave a thumbs up.

"In that case, we will leave tomorrow evening. Dusk will make the map for us tonight. Get plenty of rest, we'll need it for tomorrow."

CHAPTER 16

*N*aru yelled a loud "wake up."

Amy's eyes drooped like there were metal weights on them. She groaned and rolled over. "Five more minutes."

Naru ripped the covers off her. "You don't have five minutes,"

Amy shivered. With her eyes still shut, she threw a pillow in the direction Naru's voice had come from. "Naru come on, we don't leave until evening."

A small shock went through Amy's arm, and she opened her eyes, glaring up at Naru. "Was that necessary?"

Naru shoved an electric blue Crocorade bottle into Amy's hand. "Yes. Here. Drink this. I've been trying to get you up for hours and it's almost sunset."

Amy's jaw dropped. "I slept the whole day?"

Amy glanced out the window to see the sun was already lowering in the sky, drenching the room in a yellow-orange glow. "Sorry, I guess the injury and the magic must have drained me. Where is Dusk?"

Naru clenched and unclenched her hand at her side. "How are you doing, Naru? I'm fine. Thanks for asking."

Amy flushed. "Sorry, Naru. I didn't mean it like that. I just wanted to make sure he didn't run off. How is he doing?"

Naru huffed. "I hate to admit it, but the map Dusk made is extremely useful, and the plans are coming along nicely." Naru gave a short laugh. "Your new *friend* hasn't tried to kill anyone, yet."

Amy stood up from her bed and snatched her gem pouch from the nightstand. "Great. I'll go and get him. We should go ahead of the others, and I need to take a look at the map."

The strap on her tank top slid down and Naru adjusted it. Her gaze skimmed over Amy. "You may want to shower, use the bathroom, and I don't know, maybe change into something more *suitable* for a battle first. Somehow, I don't think pajamas will cut it."

Amy lifted a finger. "Fair point. But I don't exactly keep armor here."

Naru jerked a thumb at the door. "There's some light armor in the other rooms."

Amy blinked. "Armor?"

"Yes. The glass mages brought some equipment with them. No weapons unfortunately. They couldn't take that on the plane."

Amy grabbed a change of clothes and headed to the bathroom. As she swung open the door, the scent of wet dog hit her nostrils, and she plugged her nose. The lavender tiles were still slick with water and there were clumps of hair all over the floor.

The toilet seat had been left up and there were yellow spots on the porcelain. Amy sighed and lowered the seat to use the bathroom before putting her change of clothes on the only hanger that wasn't damp.

Once she'd taken her lukewarm shower and dried off with the only semi-clean towel, she changed into her v-necked black top and her black yoga pants.

Amy stepped around several discarded sleeping bags and

spare pillows to get to her door. She walked into the living room with Naru close behind.

Everyone was crouched over the map, reviewing plans with Dusk's guidance. When Amy and Naru entered the room, Iris raised an eyebrow at Amy. "I was starting to think you wouldn't wake up in time."

Amy rubbed at her arm. "Escaping from the Magic Council liar took more out of me than I thought." She placed a hand on Dusk's shoulder, and he turned to face her. "Dusk, we should leave ahead of the others since we have to get through the most defenses. Where is the part of the hideout that we're entering from?"

Dusk pointed to a map with detailed shading of prison cells and color-coded labels for each room. He pointed to spear and lens symbols that, according to the key he'd made at the bottom of the map, were cameras and guard stations.

Amy whistled. "You might have missed your calling as a mapmaker."

Dusk fidgeted with the edges of the light-yellow brown construction paper. "It's just a hobby. I like drawing things."

Amy ran a hand along the spot marked interrogation chamber. "Well, your map is great. I can see the place where she might be keeping Garnet over here and what looks like our point of entry there. Are these unmarked areas places that you're unfamiliar with?"

Dusk looked over at the blank space she was pointing to. "Yes. I'm assuming they're part of the prison ward, but I've never ventured to that part of the fortress, so I don't know for sure."

Amy looked up at the rest of the army. "Has everyone had a chance to review the map, so they know where to go?"

Eiji smiled. "Yes. We did all of that while you were sleeping. Here. You'll want this as well." He tossed her a leather chest plate studded with obsidian. One of the gems that could be used by glass mages and enchantresses.

"Thank you." She slid the armor over her shirt and tipped forward slightly from the extra weight. "Dusk, leave the map with them. We should go ahead of the others since we're the ones disarming the enchantments." Amy stood up and beckoned for Dusk to follow.

"All right. Here. We'll go ahead and signal once we've made it past the enchantments and into the vents." He pressed the map flat and stood up from the table. No one offered him armor.

"Shouldn't you grab something as well?" Amy asked.

Dusk shook his head. "I heal faster, and I need room for shifting. Let's go."

A teary eyed Naru grabbed Amy's wrist, stopping her progress to the door. "Please come back to me safely, okay?"

Amy took her hand. She placed a kiss on Naru's fingertips. "I'll do my best, but no promises. And you should be careful too. I don't know what I'd do if I lost you."

Naru's voice cracked. "You'd eat your weight in queso dip and binge your comfort shows all day for months on end."

Amy bit her lip. "And you'd probably live at the arcade and forget what a shower looks like."

Dusk sighed. "Touching as this is, we should go. It's best to arrive when the guards switch shifts. Thank you everyone for trusting me. I'll find a way to repay all of you. Especially you, Amy."

Amy shivered at her name on his lips. "And if we live through this, I'll owe you for saving me three times even if one of those times you were saving me from yourself."

Amy gave Naru's hand a last squeeze and then walked through the front door with Dusk at her side.

As they walked out to the car, she turned to Dusk. "Just in case something happens, I wanted to-"

Dusk held up his hand. "How about we both make it through this, and you can tell me whatever you want after?"

Amy shook her head. "I'm optimistic, but even I know we

might not survive this. So, I just wanted to say thank you. I missed having you in my life." She placed a hand over her chest.

Dusk rubbed at the dark tufts of hair on the back of his head. "I missed you too. It hurt thinking you'd betrayed me, but I should've known better."

Amy walked over to the car, obscuring her face. "I would've believed her too given the situation. I'm just glad to see you again as allies." Amy climbed into the driver's side and Dusk sat beside her.

"Me too." he said with a smile. Dusk glanced down at his pocket watch. "But we need to get going if we want to catch the shift change. It happens in about 45 minutes and the next change won't be for at least three or four hours."

"Got it." Amy put the car in reverse and crept out of the parking lot. Once she was on the main road, she slammed down on the gas pedal, knocking Dusk into the side door.

"Easy there. Let's not die on the highway getting there."

Amy unclenched her jaw. "Sorry." She eased up on the gas as she merged onto the highway and drove south towards the Everglades, giving an occasional glance out the window to check for cops. "I know the general direction, but when we get closer, you may need to remind me of how to get there," she said. Her hands shook on the gear shift, and Dusk steadied her hand with his own.

"Feeling a bit nervous?" he asked.

Amy gave a dry laugh. "That's the understatement of the year. I still struggle with basic spells unless Violet is helping. I must be out of my mind trying to face Opal as an incompetent mage who couldn't even keep her familiar in line."

Dusk shook his head. "That's not how I see you and clearly that's not how your allies and friends see you. You represent hope to them."

Amy dug her nails into the steering wheel. "Well, I don't understand why they'd trust me to be some beacon of hope.

Especially not Naru. If I cared about her and Garnet, I would have let them go. Their connection to me put them on Opal's murder radar. My stubbornness killed that man in the War of the Twin Swords and now my selfishness might kill two of the people I love."

Dusk's hand went stiff on hers. He didn't speak for a few moments, so when he responded, she jumped. "What happened in the battle that day wasn't your fault, and I don't think Naru would leave even if you put an enchantment on her and told her to never return. She's about as strong-willed as you."

Amy's stomach churned. "I'm still a killer. Opal was right about that as much as I hate to admit it."

Dusk shrugged. "That I can't argue with, but so am I. And what I did was intentional, yet you gave me a second chance. Why are you unable to give yourself that same level of compassion?"

Amy ran a thumb along the steering wheel. "Because I was supposed to be better, to do better. They all think I'm this savior. I don't think I can ever meet their expectations, and if I fail, they could all die. You could die." Her heart squeezed in her chest.

Dusk spoke through gritted teeth. "Their expectations aren't your responsibility. Maybe it's time to stop trying to live up to people's expectations and start living up to your own instead. Give yourself the same grace and kindness that you give others. That you gave me."

Tears burned Amy's eyes, and she wiped them away with the hand that had been on the automatic gear shift. "Ironic that I'm getting comforted by someone who wanted to kill me not that long ago."

Dusk snickered. "Believe me, the irony isn't lost on me. Didn't you have friends your age when you lived in our clan?"

"Not really. I was bumped up to the University classes shortly after my Choosing, so everyone was older than me. I was the weird gifted kid at school who preferred familiars over people. And during the war, you clung to Opal's side. Rosie wasn't exactly my biggest fan, and she and Crystal were inseparable. Coral was firmly in Joan's camp ally wise. You and Naru were my first close friends and that was after I left the magic world."

Dusk pursed his lips. "I had no clue. I suppose I looked up to Opal back then because she took the time to recognize me as useful rather than a nuisance, and she actually communicated with me using sign language. I didn't have to constantly lip read, so it was easier to talk to her."

Amy risked a quick glance at Dusk. He was looking directly at her with a fire in his golden eyes that sent a shiver through her body. "I never did ask about the details. What led Opal to lose control and cause that massive magic explosion?"

Dusk ground his teeth together. "When Opal had found Raven, she'd been so skinny her ribs showed. She'd been left alone in a cage with animals and people were screaming at her saying if she liked the animals so much, she could live like one. She had no shower, no water. Nothing. The animals looked starved too. It's a wonder they didn't eat her."

"I had no idea, but the explosion was so massive. She had to have been attacking something before she saw that, right? You normally have to already be channeling magic of a similar size for it to spin out of control."

Dusk said, "She hadn't intended to destroy as much as she did. Joan had told Opal about some members of the clan being mistreated, but when Opal saw the Raven's conditions and the half-eaten corpses of children in cages, she lost it."

Tears welled in Amy's eyes, blurring her vision and she wiped at them hastily. The words escaped her mouth before she could stop them. "Like me. She'd destroyed the village because she lost control like me."

Dusk shook his head. "No. This was more than a loss of

control. She kept muttering to herself that they all deserved to die for what they'd done. Her bloodlust overwhelmed her."

A shiver went down her spine. "The children didn't deserve that. She may have saved Raven, but what about the others?"

"When we'd gotten there, most were dead because of the torture. Some of them died in the explosion. She took over the Magic Council hoping to protect kids like Raven, but Opal is becoming the very thing she hated. She showed that she was willing to risk my life to call your bluff, and she wants to kill multi clan mages, her 'defective' members. That is why I'm siding with you."

Amy glanced at the sign that warned her they had another five miles before they'd hit the entrance for the Sawgrass.

Dusk gulped. "Can I be honest with you for a moment?"

She paused for a few seconds and then said. "Sure."

"Why did you insist on going with me instead of sending someone else? I figured you'd still feel nervous around me after what happened when you were captured."

Amy rubbed at her arm. "Honestly, I still feel uneasy around you, and I don't totally trust you yet, but the only other people I trust would most likely kill you if they were left alone with you. Our plans would be damned if they did that."

Dusk's eyes widened. "Remind me not to piss off Naru and Iris anytime soon. Any idea how to get on their good sides?" Amy opened her mouth, but Dusk held up a finger. "Actually, hold that thought. You're going to turn right up ahead. Just before the exit for the Everglades, you'll pull off the road and into the grass."

Amy put on her turn signal and started merging only to swerve out of the way as a large SUV zoomed past, his horn blaring a warning. "Asshole." she muttered and double-checked her blind spot before merging into the lane that would take her to the highway.

Amy's heart pounded faster, and her breathing came heavier. "Sorry. The drivers here are awful. Did I mention I hate driving?"

Dusk placed a hand on her shoulder. "Well, take some deep breaths. I don't want to die before I get the chance to repay Opal for the oh so lovely remark she made about me."

"Sorry." Amy relaxed her white knuckled grip on the steering wheel and let up on the gas as she got off the highway. "And as far as not pissing off Naru and Iris goes, good luck. I think Naru sees you as a rival for my affections. When it comes to Iris, you'd have to win over Luna first and she's the wolf shifter you heard screaming when you killed that Kitsune."

Dusk blanched. "Well. That would explain why Iris hates me. I would hate me too." Dusk tapped Amy's shoulder and pointed to the grass. "Go ahead and start slowing down. You'll want to drive off the road and onto the grass around here. Just double check your blind spot this time."

Amy nodded and guided the car into the grass, swerving to avoid an alligator relaxing on the side of the road. The car bumped through the grassy terrain and Dusk pointed at an outcropping of trees.

After they drove into a grouping of trees and got out of the car, Dusk reached his mental connection out to the shifters. "They'll be just a few minutes behind us, so we'll have to work quickly and quietly. Follow my lead so we can avoid the cameras near the doors and outer edges of the building. The guards patrolling the perimeters should be switching shifts in about two minutes which will give us a minute or so to do this."

Amy mimed zipping her lips and gave him a thumbs up. As he inched towards the edge of the tree line, she crept close behind him. His eyes turned the yellowed color of citrine and his pupils widened as his eyes enlarged. He held up two fingers to indicate two guards before putting a finger to his lips, and he held up a hand for her to stay.

She wished she'd paid more attention when they'd been taught sign language in school, so they could communicate better. Having him tell her what to do wasn't a good idea and any communication magic might alert the guards.

Dusk's hands curled into talons. After a couple minutes waiting in silence, he beckoned to her to follow him as the two guards left their posts. She stumbled along behind him as he zigzagged through the camera's blind spots. Once he was in range of the camera, he reached up and took out the lens with a swipe of his talons.

Her movements felt clunky as she tiptoed along with her gem pouch clicking at her side. Dusk motioned for her to hurry, so she sprinted forward. Too late, she saw a fallen branch as it crunched underfoot, and she pitched forward. She held her hands out to steady herself as the gems in her bag clinked against each other.

A guard's voice called. "Did you hear that?"

Dusk cursed. "Hurry."

Another guard shouted. "We should go check it out."

Amy clutched her pouch with one hand and sprinted forward. Dusk grabbed her hand and yanked her into the cover of the spot underneath the broken camera just as one of the guards emerged from the brush. "Stay here."

Dusk's head turned towards the first guard as he came into view.

One of the guards shouted. "There's an intruder. And Opal's assassin is helping her. Sound the alarm."

"Dusk. What are you going to do?" Amy reached out an arm for Dusk, but her blood chilled when she touched air instead. She glanced over to where Dusk had been and saw only empty space. *Shit. What's he going to do, kill them? I already blew our cover and left him to clean the mess. What's wrong with me?*

A gust of wind blew strands of hair into Amy's face, and she turned towards the approaching guards as Dusk ripped into the first one's neck with his taloned hands. The guard gurgled as blood gushed from the wound.

Dusk wrinkled his nose at the blood on his talons and turned to Amy who was staring at him with wide eyes. "Don't look at me like that. He was going to sound the alarm, and it might not kill him. That is if they find him in time."

The other guard's voice shouted. "Where are the intruders? Did you get them?"

Dusk pointed to another camera that faced what looked like a generator. "I'll take care of him. Take care of the camera over there. Now."

She blinked but didn't move, so he shouted. "Go!"

Amy shook out her hands. Her vision tunneled, focusing on the camera. Grass crunched under her feet and her breaths came in gasps as she raced towards it. The scenery blurred around her, and when she finally reached the camera, she panted next to it with her hands on her knees. *I should've trained harder during combat training with Iris.*

Amy looked up at the camera. Even if she stretched up on her toes, she couldn't quite reach it. *And I can't jump to save my life.* The wall next to it was smooth, so that meant she'd need something that could interfere with electronics even from a distance. She pulled out a smooth, shiny black hematite and ran her finger along it. She charged it with magic until it glowed a bright lavender and then threw it at the camera.

The camera fizzled and shorted out as the stone smacked into the lens. Her fingers felt clumsy from the lost magic, and she fumbled with the fallen stone and put it back in her bag before risking a glance at Dusk.

Amy gave him a thumbs up. Dusk dropped the now limp guard and wiped blood from his now human hands before giving her a thumbs up back. He put his finger to his temple to contact the other shifters.

He was in front of Amy in a few quick strides, glaring at

her." Next time be more careful. Our mission almost failed before it began."

Amy glanced up at him through hooded lids. "Sorry. I've never been much of a warrior, and I'm not stealthy."

He gritted his teeth. "In hindsight perhaps sending the two least stealthy members on a stealth mission wasn't the best plan, but it's too late now. Can you give me the calligraphy stone? I'll contact the elemental group next. We need to move fast. This place will be swarmed once those two guards' bodies are found."

Amy placed a calligraphy stone in his palm. Dusk traced a message on it with his finger. "Camera down. Go fast."

Dusk glanced at something in the distance and grabbed Amy's arm. "Let's keep moving before someone else comes by here. She still thinks I'm on her side. We can use that to our advantage, but not if someone sees us together." He pulled her towards one of the air vents, and his fingernails dug into her skin.

Amy pried him off her arm. "I can still walk. You don't need to drag me, you know." she said, but his back was turned, and he didn't respond.

She tapped him on the shoulder, and he swiveled back to face her. "Sorry. I can't always hear you even with this thing in. Was I gripping your arm too hard?"

She nodded. "It's okay, but maybe let me walk myself from here on out."

His gaze flickered to the vents. "Well, this is our in. How good are you at climbing?"

Amy's nails dug into her palm, and she let out a huff of air. "About as good as a fish is at climbing trees. Maybe you should go first."

"All right. Just do your best to follow after me. The whole thing is warded, so we'll have to disarm the enchantments as we go. Hopefully you still have enough magic left for that without your familiar."

He grabbed onto the pipe and shimmied up until he reached some slats. The grate was sealed shut with quartz studded bolts. It wouldn't pose too much trouble for her considering her gemstone was a quartz, but his was a beryl.

Amy pressed her lips together as his hands slid over the stone and a black glow encircled the gems as he undid the enchantments. After each spell, the shaking in his fingers worsened.

She eyed the metal pipe wearily but grabbed onto it with both hands and started clawing up it at a snail's pace. With every movement upward, her arms burned, and her feet scraped and slid against the sleek surface. The metal grate looked an eternity away, but she knew it couldn't be more than a few feet off the ground. She continued her slow progress upwards, afraid to risk a glance down.

A snorting laugh drew her eyes up to Dusk. He had already disarmed the enchantments and sat in the grate holding out a hand for her. "You weren't kidding when you said you were an awful climber. Maybe I should've towed you up on my back like a koala baby."

Amy eyed the outstretched hand but smacked it away. "No thanks, I can do it myself."

He shrugged. "All right. Suit yourself."

Amy grumbled and slid her hand up, but her palm was sweaty, and she slipped. Her injured leg gave way, and fell back from the metal pole. The ground rushed towards her and her stomach lurched.

A strong grip grabbed her arm, stopping her, and she looked up to see Dusk. "You don't always have to be so insistent on doing it all alone, you know." He lifted her the rest of the way up and into the grate.

Amy gave a slight laugh. "I want to be able to at least do some things without help from others."

"I don't think climbing should be one of those things. Now let's go before we get caught." Dusk crawled the rest of the way into the vent, and she scuttled after him and slid the grate shut behind her.

He pulled an opaque pink gem from his pouch, and a familiar pink glow filled the space between them. "It's Kunzite so I can see your lips. Since it glows naturally, we won't have to use up any magic."

Amy nodded. "Do you want me to hold it?"

"Yes, please." He held the gemstone out to her and then started crawling through the narrow tunnels. "These tunnels get too narrow to crawl through as you get further in, so we'll have to drop down right around the cell where Opal was holding you and make our way from there. I'll need you to monitor my noise and keep an ear out for guards since I can't."

Then how did you manage to work as an assassin? She thought. Her mind wandered back to his brutality in the face of those guards. *I suppose you don't need stealth when you can travel in the dead of night and rip out someone's throat like that.* The scene with the guards played over and over in her mind as she crept along behind him.

The journey through the dimly lit vents stretched on forever. Her lungs ached and her pacing slowed as the stiflingly hot air made her muscles burn. Yet, Dusk crawled ahead of her, unhindered. She tugged on his shirt, and his head swiveled around to face hers.

Dusk took in her shaking legs and gave a slight smile. "Just a little longer." he said and pointed to thin slats of light up ahead.

When she saw the shine of a gem come into the blue light, she pushed herself to keep up.

Dusk's gaze roamed over to the screws and he looked to Amy. He mouthed "Help." and Amy placed one hand on his thigh and kept another hovered over the enchanted gem.

Dusk signed out spells to disengage the enchantment. Since Amy knew few spoken spells, she closed her eyes and

231

focused on feeling around for the weaknesses in the magical lock.

By the time she'd disarmed one screw, Dusk had already managed to disarm the other three. He used his fingers to turn them until they were loose enough to remove them. Then he slid the grate aside and shoved his gem bag into her hand before dropping down as lithely as a cat.

He held out his arms and said jump in a too loud voice. Amy clutched the gem bag closer to her chest. After taking a deep breath to steady herself, she closed her eyes and dropped. The ground fell out underneath her, and the breath whooshed from her lungs when she smacked into Dusk's arms.

Amy blushed when her hand pressed into his chest as she tried to move from his grip. "Sorry." she muttered.

"I didn't realize you could be so handsy." Dusk said with a smile.

She jerked back, almost falling out of his arms. "It was an accident."

"Suuure it was."

She sputtered as he let her down. "Anyway. We should get going before they find us here."

His gaze searched the room. "Do you hear anything?"

She focused on the sounds in the building, but aside from the groan of metal and the sound of the air-conditioning, she didn't hear anything. "No. I think the coast is clear."

"Good. Let's get out of here before they find us." He grabbed her hand and ran towards the door on the left.

Amy's thoughts drifted off to her comrades. Will they be able to make it into the building? *We had a hard time getting in and that was with Dusk's knowledge of the place.*

The sound of footsteps on the tile floor jerked her back to reality. She tapped Dusk's shoulder, and he turned around. "A guard is heading this way. We have to hide." she whispered.

Dusk nodded in understanding and grabbed onto his cat's

eye gem. He held the gem out to her, and she touched it. When she looked down at her hands, she saw nothing.

A guard dressed in steel gray pants and a jacket with a dragon insignia of the Council emblazoned on it entered the room. Amy held her breath and gripped the stone tighter. Her back stiffened, and her lungs burned. Dusk traced the word "Breathe" on the top of her hand.

Afraid to alert the guard of their presence, she released her breath as quietly as possible. The guard came face to face with them, but he looked right through them before turning back to another guard. "There's no one here. I must have been hearing things." The guard turned and walked back out of the room. One the metal doors hissed shut, and the sound of the guards' footsteps faded, she let out a sigh.

Dusk slumped beside her and the spell shimmered out of existence. "I'm guessing they're out of earshot now?"

She turned to face him. "Yes, but they knew there were intruders. We'll have to be careful."

He muttered a "damnit." and glanced at the door. "Maybe, we could approach her as though I'm returning you to her. Although it will only work if Opal still believes I'm on her side and if no one saw me kill those two guards."

Amy shook her head. "No. I'm not letting her capture me again."

Dusk fiddled with the chain of his pocket watch. "Sorry, I know it's not the best idea. I just worry that it'll be difficult for us to make it through this with you not having your familiar."

Her hands flinched away from the cat's eye gemstone. "I'd rather take my chances. Opal will kill me once she figures out what I am, and I doubt she'd have much trouble torturing that answer from me now that I know what the pendant means."

"I suppose you're right..." He trailed off and his gaze moved to the floor.

Amy placed a hand on his shoulder and lifted his chin, so

they were gazing into each other's eyes. "Do you know why she's so desperate to learn about my magic?"

He fidgeted with the chain on his pocket watch again. "She wants to kill everyone else that has the same *defect* as you. According to her, 'half-breeds' or at least whatever clan's blood you have tainted your enchantment magic. Which according to her is why you can't control it."

Tears burned the back of her throat. "And you were okay with this? That's a massacre, a purposeful one."

Dusk held his hands out in front of him. "I didn't know that was what she wanted at first. I found out when Kuro overheard her talking to another Council member about it shortly after I'd captured you. Kuro warned me that Opal didn't care as deeply about me as I thought, but it took her gambling with my life and disregarding who I've become to realize just how little she truly cared."

Amy placed a hand on his arm. "Why didn't you tell me?"

Dusk bit his lip. "I was worried about what you'd think and afraid of the pitying look you're giving me now."

Amy smoothed the furrow in her brow and took a deep breath. "Dusk, if you want me to trust you, I need you to be honest about everything. Can you do that?"

His expression dropped into a frown. "Only if you answer me completely honestly one more time. Do you promise Garnet had nothing to do with Opal finding me that day in the hotel room?"

Amy squared her shoulders and took a deep breath. "I swear. She might be a little annoying at times, but she's not capable of something that selfish or cruel."

He gripped the cat's eye. "Okay. In that case, let's go get her. The chamber is just a little farther down. I might need your help to keep the illusion magic up. Are you any good with cat's eye gems?"

Amy shook her head. "It's not quartz, and it's not an air or water gem. I'll try, but my magic is extremely limited without

Violet. Undoing the screws drained me enough to make my fingertips numb, so I know I'm already running low on magical power."

"In that case we'll have to use this trick sparingly. If you hear anything, alert me so I can put up the illusion spell again." Amy nodded, and they continued through the door and walked down the endless metal corridors.

The next one they passed was shut with dented and sloppily welded metal. Fists thumped against the walls. Amy cringed thinking of how the trapped guards were bloodying their skin against the jagged metal.

Amy and Dusk skidded down the hall and ducked into another corridor that went north, towards the Council's chambers. Before they exited the corridor that fed into the main hallway, Amy listened for any noises that might signal the approach of a guard but heard nothing.

As they rounded one of the last corners, a long howl echoed through the metal maze. Amy tugged on Dusk's shirt and he whirled around "What is it?"

Amy nodded. "The shifters just signaled that they made their way in."

His gaze hardened, and he picked up the pace. "In that case we need to hurry. Her guard is going to be up now that she knows there are more than two intruders. We need to get there before she sends reinforcements to where Garnet is being kept."

CHAPTER 17

*T*he tension in Dusks' chest grew as they continued down the corridor. There were only two more hallways before they reached the Council's meeting room. *What if we get caught? Opal won't show any mercy if she catches us together.*

His gaze flickered to Amy, and his brow furrowed. *No, you can't turn back now. You owe her this much after what you put her through.*

The feeling of his shoes against the slick tile floors was the only thing grounding Dusk as they rounded the next corner. Amy tapped him on the shoulder, and he whirled to see her finger pointed to a guard coming around the bend.

Dusk froze, and Amy grabbed him by the chain on his waist, pressing him back into the wall of the corridor they'd just come from. She placed a cat's eye gem in his palm and mouthed. "Hurry."

He wrapped his fingers around the gem and light bent around them, making them invisible just as the two guards passed a few feet in front of them. The only words he could make out from the guards' whispers were "footsteps" and "intruders."

A shiver snaked its way down his spine, and his hand

instinctively traced the smooth surface of the cat's eye gem. His familiar perked up at the touch and said, *Opal's dragon is close. Be careful.*

Breath whooshed from his lungs, and the guards' postures stiffened. Amy placed a hand over his mouth, and a finger to her own lips as the guards searched for the source of the noise. Dusk's body tensed as they moved closer.

Now they were close enough that he could make out what they were saying. "Does this part of the wall look strange?"

The guard's finger reached towards Dusk's nose, and he jerked his neck back, slamming his skull into the metal wall behind him. The vibrations thrummed up the surface. *Well, if they didn't know we were here before, they do now. Better get them before they call for help.*

Dusk's talons slid out from beneath his fingertips, and he reached out for the guard's neck, but Amy grabbed his hand. She shook her head and held out a purple amethyst pulsing with magic.

That's right. Her affinity gem: It can put them to sleep. She slid the gem to the floor, letting it drop at their feet.

One of the guards shouted "Who's there?" when the gem clacked to the floor in front of them. The first guard's eye fluttered. As he slumped over, the other guard tried to kick the amethyst away, but his movements were clumsy as a drunkard's and he toppled over instead. Magic swirled around them as they both lay on the floor.

Dusk prodded the guard with his foot. When he didn't rise, Dusk tugged Amy towards the interrogation rooms.

The Council room was in sight at the end of the main corridor, but when he caught sight of silver hair, he skidded to a stop. Dusk nearly collided with Opal as she entered the hallway they were in. *We're dead. We're completely and totally dead.* Dusk froze in place as they came nearly nose to nose, but Opal looked right through him. He cocked his head to one side.

Why didn't she say anything? Dusk glanced down at his hands and saw...nothing. *The barrier is still up, how?*

Dusk lowered his hand to his watch and felt Amy's long, thin fingers pressed into his familiar's gem. *How had she managed to use his gemstone when it took all her effort to manage a spell with her familiar's gem?* He felt her whole hand shaking under his.

Dusk infused some magic into the watch, so the spell wouldn't flicker out, but as they crept past her, her hands went up and she signed. "Traitor."

Dusk pushed Amy back, breaking the spell as Opal grabbed the sword at her waist and swung it at him, stopping the blade mere inches from his neck. He stared at the shimmering silver sword as Opal held the blade there and lowered her face to his.

Opal moved close enough and spoke loud enough so that he heard her every word. "When I first saw you enter the fortress, I thought you were bringing the half breed to me, but now I can see that you've betrayed me. Give me one reason I shouldn't take your head as a trophy."

Dusk's fingers fumbled for the knife strapped to his back. Before he could reach his weapon, Amy snatched one of the blades and dove for Opal's legs. Her entire body weight crashed into Opal and the knife dug into Opal's ankle.

Opal wobbled on her feet, and Dusk winced when Opal's sword grazed his neck. He shoved Opal's chest, putting some distance between them. Then, he reached his hand into his gem pouch and grabbed a rough gem with ring shaped bumps. Without looking, he pulled it from the bag and was relieved to see a fire red stone with rings on it like a tree's trunk.

He channeled magic into the fire red agate, making it glow like a campfire. When his entire hand trembled, he tossed the stone towards Opal's feet and yelled. "Amy. Run!"

Amy's gaze caught on the fire red gem, and she jabbed at Opal's ribs with her elbow and bolted down the corridor. A few moments later, he released the gem's magic. Orange-red flames emerged and crawled up Opal's leg.

Opal's lips curled up in a snarl. "I trusted you, Cat."

He spat. "Liar. You didn't value me as Cat or Dusk. First you gambled with my life, and then you refused to accept who I am. I'm Dusk now. Cat is gone."

He caught a flash of hurt in her grey gaze, but the gold and silver crept back into her gaze, and when she spoke again, it was the thrumming voice of the dragon. "Those pesky emotions were making her inept again, so I'll be taking over from here."

The fire creeping up her leg stopped charring her skin, and she patted it down with her hands. The green veins of the Malachite curse crept up her forearm until it covered half of her sword wielding arm.

Opal lunged at Dusk, and he rolled to the side. He reached his mind out to Kuro. *Distract her for as long as you can. I need to help Amy.*

The pocket watch at his side glowed and reformed. Beside him stood a massive gemstone cat with smooth fur the color of night.

Kuro hissed and lunged at Opal. Dusk chased after Amy, trying to catch her before she ran into the lion's den. The Council's interrogation room.

CHAPTER 18

A gemstone clattered to the floor at Amy's feet just before Dusk signaled for her to run. *What is he thinking? She'll kill him if he faces her alone.* She glanced down to see a crimson stone with a pattern like the rings of a tree trunk. *A diversion. I won't waste it, Dusk.* Amy gave a swift jab into Opal's ribs with her elbow and ran down the hall.

Ahead there were two massive metal doors, but she couldn't remember which was supposed to be the Council room. *Why do they have to look the same? Here's hoping this is the right one.* Amy pulled open the first door and shut it behind her. She pressed her hand against the inside of the door to keep it shut and pain laced her hands like small needles punctured the skin. She felt along the wall where the door handle should be, but it was entirely smooth. *No. No. This would be my luck.*

A hoarse voice that sounded like Garnet's called out. "Amy. Why are you in the interrogation room? You got captured too?" Amy whirled to see her sister's violet gaze. One eye was swollen shut, and she had a split lip. Her throat was covered with red thumb prints and nail marks.

Amy's lips quivered. "Thank goddess you're alive, but what happened to you?"

Garnet licked her chapped lips. "She wanted information on what you are, but you can't torture information out of someone if they don't have it."

Amy put her arms around Garnet's neck, but she flinched at Amy's touch. "Sorry." Amy muttered and released her grip on Garnet. She glanced around the room which was covered in thick metal all around and saw a mirror that must be the one-way window. A chill went down her spine. "If you're here that means I walked…"

"Right into the magic deprivation chamber? Yes, yes you did. You're faring well so far, but maybe it's the shock. When she threw me in here, I screamed for the entire first hour. That's why it sounds like I'm a pack a day smoker."

"We came to…" Pain stabbed at Amy's throat like thousands of tiny needles. A cry tore its way out of her lips. Her veins felt like they'd been blocked up, and she raked her nails against her skin until they drew blood. *I want to peel my own skin off. How is Garnet so calm right now?*

Amy banged her fist against the door. *Dusk. Get me out of here. I hope you saw me run in here like an idiot. Opal will laugh and shove a sword through my heart if she catches me.*

Garnet said, "Banging on the door won't help unless you brought company. All you'll do is get Opal or one of the Council members running here."

Amy took in gulps of air that burned her throat like fire, but steadied her enough to speak. "I have an ally, but he can't hear me unless I'm extraordinarily loud."

"Wait. You found Night?" Garnet's back stiffened.

Amy bit her lip. "Yes. It's a long story, and he doesn't go by Night anymore. He's Dusk now." Amy pressed her lips into a thin line. *How can I contact Dusk in a way that doesn't involve gem magic or sound?*

Garnet's forehead beaded with sweat. The usual fire in her eyes had dimmed. "Wait, your friend became Opal's assassin. And you're working with him?"

"Yes. It's a long story, but he's helping us now." Amy banged on the door with a fist.

Garnet struggled against the chains binding her. "Are you out of your mind? He'll kill me when..." Garnet's voice trailed off as she bit down on her lip.

Amy thought back to Dusk's accusation about Garnet. *No, she couldn't have done that, could she?*

Garnet gulped. "Did Dusk tell you how he came to work for Opal?"

Amy's nails scraped the metal wall. "Yes."

Garnet lowered her head. "What did you say?"

Amy crossed the room and placed a hand on Garnet's shoulder. "I told him that you would never do something like that. You aren't the reason he was captured...right?"

Garnet bit her lip. "Unfortunately, he's right."

Amy's voice cracked. "But, why? He was my friend."

Garnet looked up at Amy with tears in her eyes. "Opal cornered me outside of the hotel. She'd heard there was a shifter in the area, and she wanted him for something, but she didn't say why. She said she'd allow me to escape if I turned you, the shifter, and the elemental girl over."

Nausea turned Amy's stomach. "But you didn't turn me in, and Naru wasn't captured, so why leave Dusk behind?"

Garnet tucked her head, making the chains rattle. "If I'd tried to take too many of you, it would've roused her suspicion, and she seemed most interested in getting a shifter. When I went up there to get my stuff, I snuck you out and stole Naru's phone hoping she'd go looking for it. It was sheer luck that she didn't cross paths with Opal."

Amy gripped the back of the chair and glowered at Garnet. "Coward! What if she'd killed Naru and Dusk? Could you have lived with yourself then?"

Garnet struggled against the chains. "I'm sorry for prioritizing my own safety. Is that what you want me to say?"

Amy slammed her foot against the metal. "You could at

least pretend to show remorse. Is that the reason why Opal took you instead of me?"

Garnet looked down at the floor. "She still holds a grudge against me for that deal going sour. When she saw me at the hotel, she captured me to get revenge. She used my magic fingerprint to disarm the shield in your house."

The amber necklace emitted a bright light that flooded the room. "So, you're the reason I got captured and tortured?"

"Yes. I'd say I'm sorry, but I know no apology will ever be enough to fix what I did." Garnet squinted at Amy's amber necklace. "How is that necklace glowing if your enchantment magic is blocked up?"

Amy gripped the glowing pendant around her neck. "It's a necklace that belonged to Freya, Brísingamen."

Garnet's face went pale.

Amy picked at her lower lip. "I'm guessing based on your reaction, that you know what that is. Which means you also know we aren't fully related."

Garnet nodded. "Mother told me just before you were enlisted in Opal's army, but she never gave me any details. She made me promise not to tell you."

Amy's chin trembled. "How much of my childhood was a lie?"

Garnet looked up at Amy. Her gaze softened. "Just the part about us all being related. Sardonyx still cared about you as much as the rest of us. I care about you too, even though I suck at showing it. Sorry to disappoint you."

Amy clutched her stomach as a wave of nausea went through her. "I'm not the one you need to apologize to. You should apologize to Dusk and Naru if we live that long."

Garnet glanced from Amy to the door. "Do you think you can use the magic in that pendant to open the door?"

Amy curled her fingers around the amber pendant. "I suppose I can try, but I have no clue how to control its magic."

Garnet leaned towards Amy, but the chains yanked her

back. "I'm sorry, Amy. I wanted to tell you about what I'd done the day l was kidnapped. That's why I'd invited Naru, so I could talk to you both over breakfast, but then you had to leave for work. I'd planned to go to the shop that day, but I got kidnapped."

Amy walked up to Garnet and tugged at her shackles, but they didn't budge. "When we get out of here, you can repay me by telling me where mom is. I want to speak to her myself."

Garnet shrank back into her chair. "I don't know her exact location, but once we get out of here, I can give you what you need to find her."

Amy crossed her arms over her chest. "How am I supposed to know you won't turn on me to save yourself again?"

Garnet fidgeted in her chains. "You came here to save me, and it would be a waste to turn back now. Can you honestly fault me for what I did? It was my life on the line."

Amy let go of Garnet's shackles. "I'd sooner die than betray my friends or family like that. I should leave you here, but I refuse to leave family behind even if what you did is despicable."

Garnet raised an eyebrow at Amy. "Pardon me for not having a martyr complex. Sorry, but I haven't quite reached that level of self-loathing."

"I-I don't. I'm not." The light in Amy's pendant dimmed as the anger clenching down on her chest ebbed. Amy shook the pendant "No. Don't go. I need your magic to get out of here." Amy went back to the door and banged her fists against the metal until her knuckles bled. "Dusk. Come on. I know you're too stubborn to get killed by Opal so where are you?"

Something slammed into the door and Amy jumped back in shock. "Dusk is that you?" Amy's voice wavered.

The door swung open to reveal Dusk's black hair matted with blood. A gash ran across his forehead. His right arm was red like he'd slid along the floor, and the pocket watch that held his familiar was gone. "I can't believe you ran right into the deprivation room. It shouldn't have been unlocked."

Amy rubbed at her arm. "That would be my luck, wouldn't it?"

"It seems like it, but let's hurry, we need to go. Kuro can't hold Opal off for long." Dusk grabbed Amy's wrist and his gaze caught on the bleeding scratch marks on her skin. "What happened to you?"

Amy gestured at the metal walls. "Side effects from having your magic trapped in your skin." She glanced over to Garnet. "I know we need to leave, but we have to get Garnet out first." Her voice came out flat.

Dusk looked from Amy to Garnet. "Did something happen?"

Amy shook her head. "Just scolding her for getting captured. Right, Garnet?"

A smile tugged at the corner of Garnet's mouth. "Right."

Dusk glanced at the false mirror that the Council used to observe during interrogations. "We need to break her chains first. Amy, hold this door open. I'll be right back. I think I have an idea."

Dusk handed the door off to Amy and started down the corridor. Amy glanced down the hallway. She heard a hiss that sounded like Violet's voice bouncing off the metal walls. *Dusk's familiar is a type of cat too, but that sounded like a Lynx.* Amy gripped the door in a vice. *It can't be.*

Violet's yowl clawed at Amy's mind through their mental connection. *How did she even get in here?* Amy reached out to Violet's mind. *Why are you fighting her alone? It's too dangerous.*

Violet's snarling voice pierced Amy's mind. *I'd rather die fighting Opal than live while she destroys more of my friends. Tell me why Kuro is on the front lines while Dusk is nowhere to be found.*

Amy balled her fist at her side. *Because they trust each other. They're a team and Kuro is helping so we can get Garnet.*

Violet screamed. *He's here fighting Opal, alone. The agreement is we lend you our magic so you can defend us, not to make us your sacrificial pawns.*

You're not our pawns, you're our, my, family. But you turned your back on me. Kuro and Dusk are helping me save my sister like you wouldn't. Amy shouted and cut the connection from Violet. *Even after everything we've been through, she doesn't trust me.*

Amy's heart squeezed as the thread of Violet's consciousness weakened. Violet's whimpers bounced off the metal walls. Amy's foot slid towards the exit. Her back stiffened. *No, I should wait for help. But he's taking so long. What if he's too late?*

Amy glanced between the hallway and Garnet with her forehead scrunched up. "What's wrong, Amy?" Garnet's voice rose to a squeak.

"Violet's in danger."

Garnet glanced at Amy's bare wrist. "Why is Violet not with you?"

Amy pursed her lips. "Violet didn't deal well with me teaming up with Dusk. She went after Opal on her own."

"I know you care about Violet, Amy. But even if you run after her now, there's a chance she'll refuse to come with you."

Amy slid a foot into the hallway. "I can't abandon her even if she hates me right now. I'll come back. I promise."

Amy slid off her shoes and used them to keep the door propped open. She ran towards the thrum of her remaining connection to Violet, but an arm jerked out from the Council chamber's entrance, stopping her from moving forward. Talons grabbed onto her shirt. She flailed against Dusk's grip. "Let me go, Dusk. I need to help Violet."

Golden eyes met hers. "So, you're going to leave the sister we broke into Council headquarters to do some death-defying stunt for a familiar that already made her choice? Because if you are, that's stupid even for you."

Amy grabbed onto his shirt. "I don't care if it's stupid. I can't leave her behind to die while we escape."

Dusk frowned at her. "I can feel Kuro's pain through the link too, but if either of us goes out there, we'll die and the whole operation to rescue your sister would be for nothing. You'd get captured again or maybe just killed. Is that what you want?"

Amy scraped her foot against the floor. "No, but I don't want Violet to die thinking I betrayed her."

Amy tried to walk around him, but Dusk blocked her path forward. "You can't change what Violet feels, but you can change your behavior. The sooner we leave, the better chance Kuro will survive. I doubt Opal will kill Violet. She knows you'll come back for her. I'm sure she's counting on it. We can try bargaining for her then, but we'll need leverage first."

I wonder if you'll leave me like Violet has when you realize I've tricked you into saving the person who damned you. Amy thought as she shuffled back to the interrogation room with Dusk at her side. Her gaze traveled down the lean muscles of Dusk's arm until it snagged on a saw with a rune for heat magic embedded in it. She tapped on his shoulder and pointed at the weapon. "Where did you get that?"

He gave a tight-lipped grin. "It was kept in my chambers for particularly difficult interrogations. I was supposed to use it on you before you escaped."

Amy gulped. "I'm afraid to ask, but how sharp is it?"

Dusk bit his lip. "It can cut through bone like butter, so it will be able to cut through the chains keeping your sister hostage without any trouble."

"Do I want to know how you know it cuts through bones like butter?"

His gaze went blank. "No."

Amy's heart squeezed as Dusk reached for the door back into the deprivation chamber "I'm sorry for trying to go after Violet alone."

Dusk glanced up at her through black bangs. "Don't worry

about it. Let's just get your sister before you try to do something else that'll get us killed."

Amy felt a sharp pang in her chest and her connection to Violet turned to static as Dusk opened the door to the deprivation chamber. *If I can't feel her then. Oh no.* Amy grabbed Dusk's shoulders, and yanked him into the chamber as a hollow laugh sounded behind Amy. Wind whistled past her ear. The blade swung down through the air right where Dusk had just stood.

Amy turned to face Opal and came face to face with her silver and golden gaze.

Opal placed a hand against the door, blocking their exit. "I can't believe you thought your pathetic familiars would be enough to stop me."

Amy grabbed onto her pendant, as Opal rushed her, but her magic couldn't grip onto the amber. She froze. Images of Violet lying bloodied and motionless flickered through her mind. *Perhaps I'll share your fate sooner than I thought.*

Amy shielded herself with her hands as the sword swung over her head. When the amber on her neck didn't glow, she squeezed her eyes shut, waiting for Opal's sword to slice her in two, but instead metal clanged against metal.

Amy opened her eyes and stared up at Dusk, blocking Opal's strike with the enchanted saw and pushing Opal back out of the interrogation chamber. Garnet had been released from her chains. Dusk shouted. "Run. Now. I'll be right behind you."

Tears stung her eyes, and a gemstone in her bag glowed. She fumbled around searching for its source and her fingers met a black teardrop shaped obsidian. They were supposed to be good for ridding people of curses and demons. "I'm not leaving you behind. Never again!" Amy ran past Dusk and Opal into the hallway. She reached out for her magic, but it felt thin and fragile like a fraying thread.

Amy poured all of her magic into the stone until her skin

felt...thin and cold. "Leave. Dusk. Alone." She shouted and threw the gem at Opal's head. Opal dodged it, and it landed at her feet, but wisps of black smoke rose from the stone wrapping around Opal's ankles.

As the magic took hold, her eyes flickered grey, and her voice softened. "Dusk. What's happening? Why are we fighting?"

Dusk clenched his jaw. "Opal, you called me by my name. Is that really you?"

Opal covered her face with her fingers. "I'm sorry. I." The hesitation was all that Amy needed. She dove for the sword, snatching it from Opal's grasp and threw it across the room.

The sword slid all the way to the opposite end of the corridor. "Dusk. Wait." Opal's face contorted, and she dug her nails into the arm covered in the Malachite curse. "Don't hurt him."

"Opal. It's not too late to stop this." Dusk said, his voice pained.

Amy latched onto Dusk's arm. "Come on Dusk. This is her battle. We need to fight ours."

Amy dragged Dusk away. Garnet stumbled over to Amy and took her by the hand. "You've rescued me. Now, let's go."

"Alright, but one thing first." Dusk pressed a finger to his temple.

Kuro limped out of the darkness and padded up to Dusk before turning into his pocket watch. Dusk gave one last glance back and then said, "Follow me" before running ahead, leading them towards the nearest exit.

Amy and Garnet stumbled behind him. Garnet leaned on Amy's shoulder for support. Amy kept glancing back, waiting for Opal to chase after them, but she didn't.

Amy's lungs burned and her limbs felt hollow as they pushed open the exit door and ran into the swamp. Pain shot through Amy's legs as they ran into the brush. When Dusk looked around and said, "I think we're safe. Let's contact the others," Pain ripped through Amy's entire body.

She heard a scream, and when Garnet shook her, she realized it was her own voice. Amy's knees buckled, and she fell to all fours retching into the grass. Her heart raced in her chest. Her throat burned, and her limbs shook. Her body felt hollow. The thread connecting her to the web of magic was severed, and her arms felt heavy as anchors.

Between gasps, she signed two of the few words she knew. "Contact. Friends"

Dusk nodded in understanding as he fished through his gem pouch for a calligraphy stone.

"Are you okay?" Garnet tried to reach out for her hand, but Amy smacked it away.

"I'm fine." she spat. Amy lowered her voice to a whisper. "You can repay me by telling me where I can find our mother."

Garnet tapped her pointer fingers together. "I can't use my magic to track her right now. I was in the chamber too long, but I have something I can give to you that will help you find her."

Amy rasped. "Fine. That will have to do. You can give that to me once we've gotten the rest of your rescue team out."

Amy turned to Dusk. "Are Naru and Iris's teams retreating?"

Dusk's face had gone pale, and he shook his head. "I think we have a problem."

Amy's heart dropped into her stomach. "What's wrong?"

Dusk kicked up dirt with the tip of his sneakers. "It's Iris."

Amy's entire body tensed. "No. What happened? Dusk. Please tell me Iris is okay."

Dusk shook his head. "Opal caught their group in the prison ward. They got captured trying to help Ayla and the others escape."

"We have to help Iris. We can't leave them behind. I have to go after them."

Dusk grabbed Amy's shoulder, stopping her. "You can't just rush into Opal's hands. That defeats the whole purpose. I'll contact Team B so they can head to the prison wing, but we should wait for the others before. We planned for something like this, remember? Trust me."

Those words made Amy flinch. *You trusted me, and I betrayed you.* She covered up her hesitance with a forced smile. "I trust you. You're right. We need to wait for backup. Especially since I can't feel my magic at all."

Dusk blinked. "You can't feel it at all. That's not good. You might need to go to a healer to fix that."

Amy stretched out her fingers, and they stung with pins and needles. "I know, but that will have to wait until later. We should bring the Eiji with us. He can impersonate me with an illusion and it won't drain his magic like it would for you."

Dusk nodded. "We can hang back in case he needs extra help or in case Opal figures out what he is."

Amy rubbed at her arm. "That's a good plan. Uh, Dusk. Thank you for helping with this plan."

Dusk placed a hand on Amy's shoulder. "Of course. What are friends for?"

He gave Amy a beaming smile that pricked at her conscience. "Right. What are friends for?"

CHAPTER 19

*O*pal's blood curdling laugh echoed through the prison ward sending chills down Iris's spine. *If she's here does that mean Amy failed?* Iris fumbled for the calligraphy stone Amy had given them, but it didn't glow with a message for their team. Iris glanced back at the team of mages and shifters behind them. "Run." Iris shouted as they stood in front of the other shifters.

Opal walked towards Iris with her sword drawn. "I'm guessing that Amy sent you. She'll be so disappointed when she finds out she was the cause of someone's death again," Opal said with a sickening smile. Her eyes swirled with amusement.

Iris held their hands out, blocking Opal from moving forward. Fangs pricked at their lower lip. "If you want to hurt them, you'll have to go through me."

"Great. Then I'll make sure to kill you first." Opal swung her sword at Iris's legs in a lightning quick motion.

Iris slid back as the swing whistled through the air. They winced and looked down to see a slice along their recently healed left leg. Iris's teeth sharpened into wolf teeth and their hands turned to claws. "You'll pay for that."

Iris lunged at Opal fangs first, but Opal pivoted to the side, and their teeth sank into Opal's arm instead. Iris's lips curled up at the copper taste of blood and malachite. *That must be the curse Amy warned us about.*

Opal dropped the sword and it clanged to the floor, revealing the green marbling that trailed up Opal's arm. "You have some nerve, mutt." Before Iris could react, Opal plowed into them with the force of a truck.

Iris gasped for air as they squirmed against Opal's grip. Iris lashed out with their teeth and caught Opal's fingers in their mouth, but Opal grabbed onto their jaw and pried it open with so much force that Iris's jaw cracked and they whimpered as Opal pinned their muzzle to the floor with their foot. "Not so tough now are you, puppy dog?"

Iris squirmed and struggled, but Opal wouldn't budge. *Beat me all you want, but you won't get them,* Iris thought as they chanced a look back. Iris's heart dropped into their stomach when the other shifters stood there stock still instead of retreating. Nyoka had shifted into their animal form and slithered toward Opal, but Opal paid them no mind.

Nyoka what are you doing? Iris thought.

Nyoka replied. *Making sure you don't die, hero complex.* Iris's blood chilled when Nyoka's fangs dug into Opal's exposed ankle.

Opal's boot loosened its grip on Iris's head when she reached around and snatched Nyoka up. She squeezed Nyoka tightly in her palm. "You insolent little bitch. Do you know who I am?"

"They don't care who you are." Ayla's voice echoed down the corridor.

Please tell me she isn't that stupid. Iris turned to see Ayla. *Yup, she's that stupid.*

What the hell are you doing, Ayla? You were supposed to run with the others. Iris hissed.

Ayla shook her head. *I can't leave you behind.*

253

Opal gave Iris's snout a last nudge with her boot and dropped Nyoka before striding towards Ayla. "A young shifter. She'll be perfect for testing the cure. I'll deal with you two later."

Iris scrambled towards the sword, but it slid along the floor towards Opal like it had a mind of its own. When Opal raised her arm and said, "Come Excalibur and Clarent," the sword flew into her hand. A bright swirl of silver and gold that was all too familiar wrapped around the blade. Iris mentally shouted at the others. *That's the magic she used to destroy Gemstone Forest. You all need to run. Now.*

Ayla's brows knit together, and her gaze went to Iris. "I'm not leaving you behind. Not even if you command me to."

Iris growled at her. *You always have to do it the hard way, don't you?* Iris dove for Opal's legs. Their teeth dug into Opal's ankle, and Opal turned around and swatted them away like a fly.

Ayla let out a howl and then slid across the floor fully transformed. Her teeth clamped around Opal's leg and she pulled Opal back, throwing her off balance.

What are you doing, Ayla? You and Ze'ev were supposed to stay away from Opal, remember? Get out of here!

Ayla growled. *And let you die? Our clan needs you whether they want to admit it or not and we have a plan.* She nodded her head towards a glass mage.

The mage held a glass orb in his hand while an ice mage froze the glass until it looked like snow. When it was infused with magic, he yelled "Glass in the hole."

Ayla released their grip on Opal and ran. Once they were all a safe distance from Opal, the glass mage threw the glowing orb. It landed at Opal's feet and shattered. Shards flew towards Opal like tiny bullets. The glass cut through her flesh and tore her skin open. Opal covered her face as bloody wounds pockmarked her skin.

The glass mage blinked. "Did we get her?"

Opal cleared her throat. "Unfortunately, for you I'm still alive, and I'm going to make you pay for that little stunt." Glass shards pinged to the floor as they dropped from Opal's skin. The green veins of the curse pulsed as her wounds closed.

When Opal lurched forward, Ayla jumped in front of the glass mage, pushing him out of the way with her snout. The mage skidded across the room just as Opal's hands wrapped around Ayla's throat. A growl turned to a whimper as Opal squeezed her neck.

The glass mage scrambled back. Ze'ev charged at Opal, but a silver and gold barrier threw him back, and he hit the wall with a sickening smack. "Don't you dare hurt her!" Ze'ev wheezed.

A growl forced its way out of Iris's throat. *You're not going to hurt either of them!* Iris threw their full weight at Opal's barrier. Magic crackled and singed their fur.

Ayla's lower lip quivered. "Iris, please stop. We did this to help you."

Iris attacked the barrier even as their entire body burned from the magic trying to force them back.

Opal turned at the sizzling and whimpering noises and grinned at Iris. "Ah, the Amethyst Killer's friend. It looks like you value this pup so much you're willing to risk your life to save her." She yanked Ayla up into the air by the throat and threw her out of the barrier. She landed with a thud beside Ze'ev. "There you can have her back. I'm much more interested in you, my little experiment."

Iris froze as Opal's hand reached for them. Iris sent their thoughts out to all the shifters in the area. *Leave me behind. Retreat and take the twins. Now!*

Iris took one last look at Ayla and thought, *I'm sorry.* As Opal grabbed Iris by the throat and slammed them into the wall.

"Once I use you to lure in and kill Amy, I'm bringing you

back to the lab. You'd make an excellent candidate for the new version of the cure," Opal said to Iris.

Through bleary eyes, Iris saw Abir haul Ayla away. The glass mages grabbed Ze'ev and dragged his limp form out of the Council hideout.

Iris's breaths came in gasps as they headbutted Opal with the last of their strength, trying to keep her busy until everyone was out of sight. That was when they got a message from Dusk. *Amy and Garnet are out, retreat.*

Iris sent out the message. *Team C is heading your way without me.* Before Opal's fist slammed into Iris's jaw.

CHAPTER 20

*A*my ran towards Iris's team with tears streaking her cheeks. *You were supposed to be there no matter what, Iris. You were the strong one, not me. I'll fix this somehow, I promise.*

As Amy rushed up to Eiji, her heart pounded double time in her chest. She approached the group of shifters, panting. Amy placed a hand on Eiji's shoulder. "I need you to go back in there with me."

Eiji's jaw dropped. "Iris just risked their life to get us out. Opal is in there. Why would we go back?"

Amy raised her chin. "Because we can't leave Iris behind. They've protected me, helped me control my magic. It's my turn to help them. I know they're important to you too."

Eiji cocked his head to one side. "And how do you plan to get Iris back without getting captured or killed?"

Amy lifted her chin. "We're going to use our bargaining chip."

Nyoka bit down on their lip, "You mean kidnapping the girl."

Amy nodded. "Yes, Naru's team is going to meet us at the prison wing, but we need to hurry. Iris likely won't last long against Opal."

Amy jumped when she felt a hand on her shoulder. Dusk held up his hands. "Sorry, I didn't mean to startle you. But I overheard your conversation. You aren't going back in there without me. I already lost you once to Opal. I won't lose you again."

Amy rubbed at her jaw. "Okay. What are you planning to do?"

He nodded. "I'll stay out of sight and jump in if you need help."

Nyoka raised their hand. "And I'll join you as well. In case you need additional muscle." They flexed their arm.

Amy gave a sheepish smile. "Thank you."

Nyoka shook their head. "No need. I'm doing this for Iris's sake. I was mistaken when I thought they were an inadequate pack leader. I owe them one. They are pack after all."

Amy nodded. "Thank you. Now, let's go." Amy ran along the side of the building clutching the knife she'd swiped from Dusk earlier. Nyoka, Eiji, and Dusk followed closely behind.

Amy brushed her hand against an amethyst in her pouch, but the stone felt lifeless under her fingers. Her magic sizzled and popped like a broken lightbulb. *Let's hope my luck doesn't run out here.*

Her three comrades trailed behind her as she opened the door near the prison wing and listened for Iris. A long whimper echoed through the hallway, and she followed the pained noise.

It didn't take long for the glint of Opal's sword to come into view. Before they came into Opal's sight, Amy held up a hand. "Are the others close?"

Nyoka nodded. "They should be here in a couple of minutes. Only a few of the group members are coming here. The rest evacuated."

Amy bit her lip as Opal raised her sword to Iris and held it to their throat. "We won't have a few moments if we don't do something now. How does your transformation magic work?"

Eiji held out a hand, for Amy. "Just give me something with your DNA on it."

Amy placed one of her amethyst's into his hand. "Will this work?"

"Maybe put some of your blood on it just in case."

Amy slit her hand with her stolen bloody knife and poured a few drops onto the stone, then she pressed the hilt of the weapon into his palm. "Take this too. You'll need a weapon."

He turned the weapon over in his hand and wrinkled his nose. "Thank you, I guess."

Amy pushed him towards Opal. "You're welcome. Now, please help Iris."

Eiji nodded and a blue flame briefly flickered before her eyes. When he snapped his fingers, a mirror image of herself appeared, purple hair and all.

Nyoka placed a hand on Eiji's shoulder. "Be careful. Remember we're just buying time."

Eiji flicked back purple hair from his face. "Of course."

When Opal pressed the knife further into Iris's neck, Eiji sprinted over to Opal's. He hit Amy's knife into Excalibur and a clang rang through the corridor. Eiji winced as his knife was pushed back towards his face and Opal's head whipped to the side as she turned her attention to him.

Opal grinned. "Your recklessness never ceases to amaze me. Does this shifter matter that much to you?"

Eiji didn't answer as his feet slid back. Opal shoved against Amy's knife before raising her weapon again. "What's wrong, cat got your tongue?"

Opal swung out, and Eiji lifted the knife to block. A scream tore from his throat as Opal's sword glanced off his knife and the blade cut into his right shoulder.

Out of the corner of her eye, Amy glimpsed a small group of mages with Naru and Ren at their head, dragging a sulking Raven to Opal. "Retreat!" Amy yelled, but Eiji didn't budge.

Opal raised her sword again.

"Retreat. Now! They're here." Amy repeated, her voice rising to a shout.

Opal smiled at Eiji like a lion ready to sink its teeth into an antelope. "Ah, an imposter. Maybe I didn't give you enough credit."

Eiji smiled, his ears showing. "Bingo." and held up a hand glowing with fox fire. He shoved the fire into her face, making her scream and snarl as he ran back over to Amy.

Opal grabbed Iris from the ground and shook them "I think you forgot something, Amethyst killer."

Amy stepped out from her hiding spot and pointed at the approaching group. "Not quite."

Opal frowned. "What did you do?"

Naru stepped into Opal's view with Raven in tow. "Why don't you take a look?"

Opal turned towards Amy. "You wretched bitch. Killing wasn't enough, so now you stoop to kidnapping?" Her hand gripped the sword with white knuckles. "You wouldn't dare hurt her. You're bluffing."

Amy lifted her chin. "I would because you took my mentor and my familiar." Amy's gaze flickered to the dented amethyst bracelet on Opal's wrist. "Now it's time to return both of them unless you want to lose someone important to you. Bring her forward, Naru."

Naru yanked the metal chain attached to the handcuffs on the girl's wrists. The girl jerked forward, eyes downcast.

Opal growled. "You must have a death wish. I'll kill you for daring to put your hands on her." Magic swirled around the Twin Swords and Opal gritted her teeth.

Naru wagged her finger. "Nah ah ah." Electricity sparked in her free hand. "If you do that, I'll have to send electricity into the cuffs and I don't think she'll like being electrocuted."

Opal glared daggers at Amy. "This is low even for you. You'll regret using Raven to get to me." The gold and silver threading through her gaze disappeared. Only the grey showed. She lowered the sword.

Amy glanced at her weapon. "If you want Raven back, we'll need Iris and Violet first. Drop your sword and step away from Iris. And take Violet off your wrist."

Opal spat out, "Fine." and threw the sword down. It clinked against the floor. Opal signed something to Raven who gave a small nod in response.

Amy glanced down at the sword. "I know you can call it, so I'll need it further from you before we make the exchange."

Opal huffed. "I will, but only because she appears unharmed." She kicked the sword across the room.

Amy stepped on the sword so it wouldn't get called back to Opal.

Opal slipped the bracelet off her wrist and threw it at Amy. It smacked her in the nose before falling to the floor. Amy glared at Opal as she picked up the bracelet and slid it on her wrist.

Opal held up her empty hands. "There I have no weapon, so let the girl go. Now. Or I will kill every last one of you."

Amy nodded to Naru. "Go ahead, you can let her go."

Naru hesitated, moving towards Opal on wobbly legs. Her face flushed. "Are you sure?"

Amy gave a dry laugh. "No, but we have to give her back eventually."

Amy's legs felt like jello and her skin like air.

Naru and Amy shared a tense look, the same thought likely running through their heads. *She might still turn on us the second she gets what she wants.* Amy was prepared to run, but the question was, could they all outrun Opal?

Naru's back stiffened as she came within striking range of Opal. *Why did you come here, Naru? You should have retreated with the others.*

Amy bit her lower lip as Naru removed the handcuffs from Raven and released her into Opal's care.

Opal examined Raven from head to toe. She crouched down to the girl's level and patted her head before signing something to her. Raven shook her head and signed something to Opal who let out a long, "I see. In that case, I'll respect your wishes even if I don't like them."

Naru flinched when Opal held out her hand. "Luckily for you, Raven is far kinder than I and demanded I not hurt you because you were gentle with her. If she weren't here, I'd slice you from head to toe. You have about ten seconds to remove yourself from my sight. Go. Now. Before I change my mind."

Naru's gaze darted to Amy's. Amy raised her voice. "Everyone. Go. Quickly."

Amy backed up with Opal's sword still underfoot. As Naru passed her, she whispered "If you die here after everything we went through, I'm bringing you back just to kill you again."

Amy rolled her eyes. "I'm right behind you. Go."

Dusk eyed Amy and Opal and mouthed. "Are you sure?"

Amy nodded, and Dusk snuck out of the fortress just behind the elemental team.

As Dusk retreated, Opal added. "You may leave too, Amethyst, but know that I will show you no mercy the next time we meet."

Amy gave her a wry smile. "I wouldn't expect anything less." Amy glanced down at the sword once more. *If Excalibur and Clarent wouldn't kill me for it, I would take this damned thing from her now.*

Amy backed up until she reached the exit, afraid that if she turned her back Opal would stick a sword through her. But the sword stayed on the floor, and Opal made no attempt to attack. Opal just hugged Raven and muttered. "You're safe now. You'll be okay."

Amy felt a knot forming in her chest as she fled the scene. *She hasn't reverted to her cursed state yet. Maybe this girl is the key to breaking her bond with Excalibur and Clarent.*

Amy ran out of the Council's hideout. Her heart was

pounding until she reached their meeting spot. When she returned, Naru was curled up on the grass rubbing Ren's back as he vomited in the grass. Dusk loomed over Garnet whose face paled at Dusk's scrutiny. "When we get back, I want proof that you didn't betray me."

Amy bit the inside of her cheek and approached Dusk. She waved her hand in his peripheral vision, and his shoulders sagged. "You're okay."

Amy frowned. "I am. Thank you for being there for me even if I didn't deserve it."

Dusk cocked his head to one side. "What do you mean?"

Amy placed a hand on his shoulder. "Let's talk about this over there, okay?" She pointed to a spot further into the tree-line and away from Garnet and Naru's prying gazes.

Dusk eyed her wearily. "Is something wrong?"

Amy's heart dropped into her stomach as they stepped into the isolated outcropping of trees. "I'm sorry Dusk."

Dusk cocked his head to one side. "About what?"

Amy rubbed at her arm. "About Garnet. I was wrong about her. She did turn you in."

Dusk's entire body tense. "How long have you known?"

"Not until we were already rescuing her. She accidentally told me when I said we were working together. I should have told you right away. I'm sorry."

She reached her hand towards his, but he yanked his hand away like he'd just been bitten. "You told me she had nothing to do with this. That there was no way she'd turn me in. You had me help her even though she told you she was guilty? How could you?" His voice raised to a shout and talons grew from his fingertips.

"I'm sorry Dusk. I didn't know how to tell you after everything we'd gone through to help, and I was worried you would have abandoned her if I told you. Truthfully, I wanted to leave her behind when I found out too, but she's my sister and she has information about my mother's location. I need to find my mother to know what I am."

He scoffed. "I can't believe this. In the end, you used me just like Opal."

A lump formed in Amy's throat. "Dusk, I'm sorry. I wanted to tell you sooner, but I was afraid."

Dusk blinked at tears. "And I was afraid to help you because I thought you'd turn on me. I should have trusted my instincts. Violet was right to abandon you. You only care when you think it will benefit you."

Amy reached out for him. "That's not true. Please stay, Dusk. I'll make this up to you somehow."

He smacked her hand away. "Stay back. I can't look at you right now."

Amy's lower lip quivered, "Dusk, I still care about you, but I had to save Garnet. Please. Let's talk this over."

"No. I'm tired of love with buts. How about you put half the effort you put into people's perception of you into actual self-improvement," He screamed as wings burst from his back. His talons grew, but this time his transformation didn't stop there. His nose changed into a beak and limbs shrank. His pupils enlarged and his legs disappeared. Within a few moments Dusk had fully transformed...into a hawk. He gave a last screech and then swooped upwards into the air, leaving them behind.

As he soared up into the sky, she reached out her hand. "I'm sorry, Dusk. I'm so sorry." She whispered at the shrinking speck of his retreating form. "I'll find you again and fix everything. Somehow."

When she returned to the clearing of mages with her head hung low, Garnet was gone and all that was left was a piece of paper wedged underneath a red stone.

"She lied about not being able to move. Why am I not surprised?" Amy snatched the note from under the rock and read it aloud. "After seeing what rescuing me did to your friendship with Dusk, I think it's best if I fade into the background for now. As promised, here are your instructions to find our mother: you must seek out the forgotten portal that leads to the land of the gemstone creatures, the motherland for our familiars."

Amy groaned. "As cryptic as ever, I see."

Amy turned to the group of shifters and mages. Many of them were covered in scratches or had open gashes on their arms and legs. A glass mage was curled up in the fetal position on the floor and Ren stared blankly at a tree. The knot in Amy's chest tightened, and she clutched the letter in her hand. "Everyone. I know today doesn't feel like a victory, but many of us still live. We will grieve, but we will not give up or give in. We will win this war, but first we need to regroup. I'm going to go searching for my mother to get answers about my powers, and I want you all to continue gathering allies both here and in the magic world. We're going to destroy Opal and her Council for what happened here today."

To Be continued...

AUTHOR'S NOTES

If you liked this story and would like to know what else I'm working on, you can sign up for my newsletter by going to https://sendfox.com/wanderingteacherbooks. I send weekly updates, new releases, sneak peaks of new stories, book give-aways, and author events.

Thank you so much for reading this story. If you'd like more stories like this don't forget to leave a review. You can review *Amy's Rebellion* on Goodreads, Amazon, and Bookbub.

You can also connect with me on the following social media sites to find out about fun competitions, giveaways, and writing and self-publishing tips:

Twitter- https://twitter.com/ButterflysDust

Facebook-https://facebook.com/wanderingteacherbooks

Tiktok-   https://www.tiktok.com/@wanderingteacherbooks?lang=en

Happy reading!

OPAL'S VILLAIN ORIGIN STORY

Want to see how Opal became evil? Then check out her villain origin story in "War of the Twin Swords." There are sorceresses, gemstone familiars, a Choosing ceremony, and a magic war.

Only 99 cents!

Amazon ASIN: B084KHX7SV

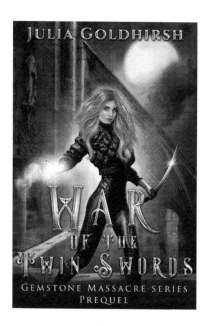

RAPUNZEL RETELLING WITH EVIL NYMPHS

Rose has been bound to a glass prison by a curse since she was a child, but on her birthday she meets a mysterious Courier named Gabriel who agrees to help her find a way out, permanently.

Check out "Rose is Spellbound"

Amazon ASIN: B07TSYFPC6

ACKNOWLEDGMENTS

This book ended up being one of my toughest and most time-consuming edits yet, and it's one of my first novels where I really got to delve into my LGBTQIA+ background. I want thank all the amazing people who helped with beta edits especially Val and Sam. They were both amazing at catching my silly mistakes and character inconsistencies, and my mother spent a ton of hours looking over my final draft to catch anything missed in the editing phases. Thank you Vicki for being my biggest cheerleader, and I also want to thank my amazing sensitivity reader and my awesome proofreader who got that last round of edits done quickly for me. And finally, thank you to my fantastic artist that did the illustrations. Anyone who reads this book is amazing, and I hope you enjoyed the first of many to come in the Gemstone Massacre series. Finally, I want to say thank you to my cover artist. You can check out their services below.

Cover Artist- Vicki Adrian/ Creative Cover Book Designs
Content editor- Erin/ The Word Faery
Editor- Megan/ Dragon Eye editing
Proofreader - Geetha/faireditions.wordpress.com

Printed in Great Britain
by Amazon